Juic

*Also by Bob Judd*

Formula One

Indy

Monza

Phoenix

Silverstone

Bob Judd

# JUICE

M
MACMILLAN
LONDON

First published 1994 by Macmillan London Limited

a division of Pan Macmillan Publishers Limited
Cavaye Place London SW10 9PG
and Basingstoke

Associated companies throughout the world

ISBN 0-333-62289-8 (Hardback)
0-333-63133-1 (Paperback)



1 3 5 7 9 8 6 4 2

A CIP catalogue record for this book is available from the British Library

Phototypeset by Intype, London
Printed by Mackays of Chatham PLC, Chatham, Kent

‘After *The Wizard of Oz* I was typecast as a lion, and there aren’t all that many parts for lions.’

Bert Lahr

# chapter one

The telephone stuck an electric finger in my ear.

Three more rings and my machine went, 'I'm sorry Forrest is not in right now. If you BLEEEEP' and the machine broadcast her famous voice in the dark.

'Forrest. Pick up, you asshole. Come on, you gotta be there. Whattareyou, in the bathroom? You should get a phone in the bathroom, Forrest. Saves time.'

Reluctantly I rolled over and picked up the phone. 'Who is this?' I said. My old joke.

'This is your star, dummo. Calling a future star. What's it like in London?'

'Heavy darkness. Raining. Cold.' I stretched to look at the clock glowing on the nightstand. 'The way it usually is in January at two in the morning.'

'How soon can you be here?'

'We've been through all that.'

'We haven't been through anything. Anyway, I'm not calling for me. I'm calling for a friend, Mel Tietjens. You heard of Mel Tietjens?'

'Not *the* Mel Tietjens.'

'Don't jerk me around, Forrest. Mel's a very big producer and he's doing a film called *Juice*. I told him you'd be perfect. How soon can you be in LA?'

'I can't come to LA, Virgin. I have commitments here.' Which was true. In two weeks I was due to be the guest speaker for the South London Hozuki Dealers' January Marketing Lunch. That loomed large on my calendar.

'Not for me, dummo. For you. Listen to me. I got you a part.'

'A part what?' I said. I am not at my best in the small hours. And conversation with the world's richest over-the-hill pop star is like tossing a grenade back and forth. You never knew if she had pulled the pin.

'WAKE UP, Forrest. I mean it's all set, but you gotta meet Mel and you gotta meet my agent. Have you met David? You'd know if you did. Anyway the film's called *Juice*, staring Sam Miles. PLUS she directing. Can you believe it, Samantha Miles is directing? PLUS she's starring with Sean Finlay. Sean is hotter than Tom Cruise now. Listen, the screening's Sunday.'

'Sunday is tomorrow.'

'Right tomorrow. No big deal just the first dailies but it's the only time there's a chance to meet Mel and Sam maybe before they start shooting again. Sean, I don't know if Sean is going to be there, but David definitely. David talked to your agent, what's his name, Ed Victor. Victor is all for it. Isn't that great? Aren't you really glad to hear from me?'

'It's a treat to hear from you, Virgin.' I turned on the light. 'How are you?'

'You have somebody there, in bed? I AM THE GREATEST FUCK OF ALL TIME. ASK FORREST. HE KNOWS! There, did she hear that?'

'She's in Paris, Virgin.' Or Rome. Or the Seychelles. Susan's cards had stopped coming. It wasn't working. Susan said she needed time. Space. A place of her own. Well, a racing driver in winter is a lousy room-mate. Almost as bad as a racing driver in summer. 'Are you in it?'

'Nah, not me. Just my money. David Allen, don't tell me you haven't heard of David Allen.' There was a pause. 'You *must* have heard of him. David put that whole buyout deal for like four billion with Hozuki and Olympic Films. So this is his first package with the new Olympic Studios. I'll tell you about it when you get here. Anyway, David is my agent and as a favour he let me in for a piece of the gross on *Juice* so I have a little pull. And when they lost their driver, there's a lot of driving, Sweetie, I suggested you because you're comfortable driving two hundred miles an hour and they want to meet you which is as good as OK.'

'I'm not comfortable at two hundred miles an hour unless I'm on an airplane, Virgin. What do you mean, "a part"? I can't do it, but as long as you woke me up you might as well tell me about it.'

'Hey, wait a minute here. Don't give me this shit. I checked it out. It is off season, it is cold, miserable, wet, and dark in London. London sucks now, and the sun is shining a zillion watts here. We're talking a single light source eighty million miles away shining down on you in Southern California giving you a deep tan as a background for your white teeth, as in big wide smile. You are in a rut, Forrest, and you are too stubborn to recognize it. Tell me this? You want to drive those funny little cars around in circles all your life? Where else can you re-invent yourself overnight except in the movies?'

'I don't want to re-invent myself, Virgin.' No doubt I have flaws like canyons and one day soon I must go rafting down them on a voyage of personal discovery, as they say in Hollywood. But in the mean time I had to raise several million dollars if I was going to get my seat back in Formula One. OK, I was going around in circles. I had been around this find-the-money-get-a-seat track before. I've won five Grand Prix races and I could win again, given the chance, but that's not nearly enough any more. The woods are full of drivers with enough talent to win. The teams that win races don't hire drivers to win races any more. They hire drivers to bring them enough money to buy the technology that wins races. The South London Hozuki Dealers were good for £25,000. I needed at least two million to be sure and the days were slipping by.

'Hey, you don't want to re-invent yourself, you don't have to. There's people here who can do it for you. Come on. A couple of weeks, Forrest. Billing. OK, not top, but there, on the sheet. A lot of money. But forget the money. This could be a breakthrough for you.'

'Virgin . . .' I said, trying to get a word in. Trying to get a word in with Virgin when she is wound up is like trying to stop the wind with your hands.

'Listen to me. Will you just listen? I mean I know I told you, but I *know* you could be a star. Like a tiger I fought for you. You could be major, Forrest; a major, major star. Yes. OK, it's not a featured part, but it is a part. You'll be great.'

'I appreciate your confidence, Virg, but I don't think they could afford me. I'm looking for two million.'

'Well good luck. I don't think they are gonna go two million. You buying a house?'

'I'm looking for sponsorship for Formula One and it is a full-time, boring, tedious, and repetitious job.' My voice shifted down into the serious business side of Forrest Evers. 'Do you want to be featured on the side of a Formula One car? VIRGIN cruising past four billion viewers at a hundred and fifty miles an hour. We could do your face or your hooters, Virg. Hooters would be extra but maybe we could work them on to the sides of the front wings. We'll give it some thought. Let me make a presentation. Sixteen countries on five continents and an audience of four billion.' I plug my Please Sponsor Famous Racing Driver Forrest Evers cassette into the back of my head and off I go.

'Anyway, I appreciate the offer, Virgin, but I can't afford the time.'

'Hey, Forrest, wait a minute. Slow down. This is a fifty-five million dollar production. Plus the promotion is budgeted thirty-five million. Guaranteed distribution in a hundred twenty-seven countries. Plus video sales AND rentals. And a tie-in with a major international automotive introduction from Hozuki with the world's first practical electric car. Hey, maybe we could work a deal, something like you appear in the movie and they put *Juice* on the side of your car for the international distributors. How's that sound? You get your sponsorship, they get international exposure. Let me do this, Forrest. Let me have David call your agent, what's his name, Ed Victor.'

# chapter two

The sky is black and so is the earth and the dawn is a thin blue line on the low horizon. There is no sound.

In the middle of the horizon a dot of light vibrates. The light grows and separates into two lights coming closer.

Two young California Highway Patrolmen, their faces green from the glow of the dashboard, are talking and do not notice the lights. The two lights grow larger and brighter through the window, lighting the side of the face of the blond highway patrolman and a pump-action shotgun mounted on the scratched plastic and steel mesh partition between the front and the rear seats. The two men are silent, staring straight ahead, drinking coffee out of Big Boy refillable take-out cups, while the lights continue to grow larger in the side window.

The cop in the passenger seat notices the lights, puts his coffee in a holder, picks up a laser radar-gun and, taking his time, points it at the blazing headlights, panning with the car as it goes by in silence. The red tail-lights of the car grow smaller in the dark as they head towards the red glow of a city over the dark horizon.

The readout on the radar gun is 223 mph.

In the distance the small red tail-lights rise up and disappear. A small balloon of red at the bottom of the black screen rises and grows, turns orange in the middle, grows larger, fills the screen, and the orange turns white hot in the middle, dirty red at the edge. The balloon pales and fades. Then the screen is black again except for the red glow of the city in the distance.

The cop holding the radar-gun, looking into the dark where the fireball has just disappeared, mouths the word 'FUCK.'

The lights in the screening-room came up to a comfortable golden glow. We were seated, as you are always seated in

Hollywood, according to rank. Top rank in the back row, secretaries, gophers and assistant production assistants down in the front.

Virgin and I had been the last to arrive and as soon as we walked in the door the lights began to dim. David Allen from his seat in the middle of the back row nodded slightly to Virgin and a well-groomed hand indicated the empty seat next to him. Also the empty seat next to Virgin's for today's plaything. Which I took.

I had come straight from the airport and was buzzing with an eight-time-zone jet-lag. Any seat was fine with me.

'Thank you, Charles,' David said, a trace of London posh in his voice. As in 'thenk yew'. 'Is that all the footage you have of the car?' David was handsome in a soft and pampered way. Tanned, fresh from a shower and the hairdressers. Just a touch of silver at the temples. Crisp new white Oxford shirt and that rarest of appendages in Hollywood these days, a necktie. Which featured watery red, white, and blue stripes hand painted slightly off-centre so you would know they were hand painted and not just another necktie.

'It was the first take.' Mel Tietjens, the 'big' producer, in the next row, turned to face David. 'Shot before sunrise on the first day. One of the shots we wanted to get in the can before the principals showed up. Actually it was four shots, one inside the cop car . . .'

'The question is, can you use the shots? I don't want to blow the production schedule before we get started just because we've had an accident.'

'Sure,' Mel said. 'A little video edit on Paintbox and we can lose the explosion and have those red lights going off into the distance for as long . . .'

David had turned away from Mel and Mel's voice trailed off. Mel was thin, in his thirties, with curly blond hair going bald on top. He smiled and shrugged. What it was like, working with David.

David turned to his left, to the slender man in a chrome-yellow linen shirt with an oversized collar and freshly pressed blue jeans sitting next to him. 'Is there any way it could have been the car's fault? Like a loose nut, say? I'm thinking of our liability exposure. If one of us has to carry the can we might want to put a few more handles on it.'

'Well, nothing is perfect and anything is possible, David,' the man said, showing a lot of teeth in what I assumed was a grin. He looked about twenty-one but he must have been older. 'We did wind-tunnel tests up to a hundred and fifty which is about twenty-five miles an hour faster than the car was going and the car was solid as a rock. Our factory guys went all over the wreckage and they couldn't find anything. And the insurance investigators looked at it this morning and they couldn't find anything either. So I have to think there maybe isn't anything to find. Maybe a sudden cross-wind. Hi, Forrest.'

'I didn't realize you two have met,' David said.

'We haven't,' the man with the grinning teeth said. 'Dad said,' he dropped his voice in mock solemnity, 'convey my good wishes to Forrest. He holds you in high esteem, as we say in the old country, Mr Evers.'

'Tell your father I'm honoured to meet his son,' I said.

'Forrest, this is Akiri Hozuki, director of public affairs for Hozuki, North America. You all know Forrest Evers,' David said raising his voice half a notch to include the room. Virgin squeezed my thigh and blank faces turned around to look at my route-mapped face. And then moved their gaze over to Virgin who was wearing a white silk drape that was transparent if the light was right. In the soft light of the screening room, her gauzy white top looked innocent compared to her purple lipstick and today's solid silver hair, cut short with long bangs in front. Or was it a wig?

'Good,' David said. 'Why don't you share your thoughts, Forrest, since you have been kind enough to come all this way?'

'Thoughts?' I said. 'I thought the car was going two hundred and twenty-three miles an hour.'

Mel turned his head halfway around, not quite looking at me but making the gesture. 'We shot an insert with the readout at two hundred and twenty-three. The car was going maybe a hundred and twenty-five. We're making movies, Forrest, not documentaries.'

'A hundred and twenty-five then. Thirty miles an hour is fast enough to tear your leg off. How is the driver?'

'He's still in intensive but doctors are saying that's short term and they expect a full recovery with the possibility of some motor loss,' a young woman three rows down said, turning around to look earnestly at David. 'We have a signed release from prior to the shoot so we're covered on liability.'

'What are his "thoughts", then?' I said. 'He was the one who was there.'

'He's not conscious yet, Mr Evers.'

'And the car just lifted up into the air and turned over?'

'That's what's so weird,' a small cloud of blonde hair in the seat in front of me said, twisting around in her seat and resting her chin on the back the way an eager child would, giving me all of her attention. She certainly had mine.

She said, 'He wasn't going any faster than he'd driven before. We did a couple of run-throughs on Friday, the day before, when we were setting up. He said he wanted to get the feel of the car and he said the car was OK. I mean it was really just a pass-by. Hi, Forrest,' she said, extending her hand, 'I'm Sam.'

You expect to see beautiful women in Hollywood. The most stunning teenagers you have ever seen still drive their daddies' cast-off cars from Des Moines and St Louis to Hollywood. They live four and five to a rented apartment, take acting classes and work in dry-cleaning stores, insurance offices, escort services, and soda fountains until the big break or the first baby comes along. Living on hope while their dreams die like flies. I had been to Hollywood often enough to know that physical beauty in Movieland is about as common as corn in Kansas. But Sam was breathtaking, a lily in a field of cornflowers.

The Evers Law of Feminine Beauty holds that what we usually see as beauty in a woman's face is a combination of average features and plenty of blank space. Take any young woman's face, make the nose, the chin, the forehead, and the eyes more or less average, and she will be very attractive. We might even see enough of our ourselves in her to call her beautiful.

Sam knocked the Evers Law of Beauty on its head and out of the ballpark. Her nose was too big and one large eye was closer to the middle of her face than the other, giving her a quizzical look as if she was thinking about something you said. She had an exaggerated figure, long delicate hands holding her chin as she waited for me, a mouth that was just a little too full for her face with a delicious curl to her upper lip, and a cloud of unruly blonde hair in the casual stirred-by-the-wind way that probably took a hair stylist hours to get right strand by strand. She wore no make-up that I could see, just that clean and fresh out of the shower look. Something about the deep set of her eyes hinted at a sadness, as if there was something she didn't want to think about, something that made her glad to be talking to you to take her mind off the ghosts. As if she needed you. But of course I have always been a fool for a pretty face.

'I'm Sam Miles,' she said, repeating herself to fill in the gap, and a quizzical smile to bring the stunned, jet-lagged mullet back to life. 'And I will be your star today. You know, like heavenly? It's a trick of the light. We only shine in the dark.' She threw her head back, camping it up for the man with the blurred mind.

'And take off before dawn,' I said witlessly.

Sam let the amused look hang on for a beat then let it go. 'So, Mr Evers, did you see anything in the footage?'

You are staring, Evers, answer the woman. 'I wasn't there. I'm not even sure I'm here. But without seeing the car, I don't see how it could be the driver's fault unless he fell asleep.'

'You mean like he must have been stoned or drunk.'

'I have no idea. Anybody in this room can drive a car at a hundred and twenty-five miles an hour down a straight road with one hand on the wheel.'

'That'll be your job, Evers. Think you can handle it?' she said, raising an eyebrow over a smile.

Mel said, 'Sort out the cars, if there is any sorting out to do. Drive the stunts.'

'David,' Virgin said, her voice rising, 'you said . . .'

'I said we might arrange a small cameo for Forrest, once we had a chance to take a look at him and hear what he sounds like. I think he looks all right and he sounds OK. And he should boost our distribution in Europe, South America and the Far East. Places where they've actually heard of Grand Prix racing. Akiri likes him. What do you think, Sam?'

'We'll have to be careful how we light him or he's going to read ten years older. And he's certainly not going to upstage Sean in the pretty department. I can live with him if he's just a walk-on, David. And maybe he could add something. But not a lot. I don't want to be negative but whenever I see some celebrity in a film they look like they came from another planet.

I mean did you see Karen Wilson in *House Paint*? Jesus. Just because she has a talk-show. But OK. I can always cut his little bit out if he doesn't work.'

'Forrest doesn't have any little bits,' Virgin said.

'I'm happy to take a shot at it,' I said. 'And if it doesn't work, fine.' As long as I got paid, I thought. But I didn't want to look too hungry. Wolves are never asked to sit down at the dinner table.

'Every minute of finished film,' Mel said, 'will cost us around a quarter of a million dollars. So we like to know if it is going to work before we start shooting.'

'Only trouble is,' Sam said, smiling, despite that sadness in her off-set green eyes, 'you never know, do you?'

'Maybe it would help if I knew what the film is about,' I said.

'Now that is an intelligent question,' David said to all of us. 'One we ought to ask more often. We have two objectives here, Forrest, and they are linked. Hozuki, as you know, has developed a new electric car that will challenge the performance and the price of the fossil-fuelled devices we all now drive today. The car will be called EVIA . . .

'EVIA has a number of associations from flight,' Akiri said with the relaxed confidence of a marketing man, 'which is why we pronounce it Avia. We were looking for something that suggested performance and was also felt ecological. Officially it means Environmentally Viable Integrated Automobile. Translated that means you can plug it in to the existing infrastructure because it runs on gasoline but it doesn't pollute. The power unit is a fuel cell, developed by Hozuki from the high-tech fuel cells NASA has used on board their spacecraft since Apollo One. It is close to one hundred per cent efficient and its exhaust is drinking water with zero pollution.' He smiled as broadly as a magician pulling a rabbit out of a hat.

David continued, 'EVIA is scheduled for a world-wide launch eighteen months from now next year in June. As you no doubt also know, Hozuki now owns Olympic Studios' – David nodded to Akiri – 'and it is our job to add some juice to the public's perception of an electric car.

'That's one objective.' All the faces were turned, facing him. As if they hadn't heard this before.

'The other objective, without which we won't achieve the

first, is to produce a superb major-box-office motion picture. Nobody is going to spend their money to see a movie about an electric car. The cinema is not a slice of life, it is a piece of cake. People will pay to see a fresh, exciting and very human story. A story of courage, and like all great Westerns, a story of redemption. About a man being reborn. Just as Hozuki is giving new life to America's idea of the automobile.'

David closed his eyes and put his soft manicured hands behind his head, the dreamer, and the seer, pausing for a moment, enjoying his vision. 'Sam,' he said, 'why don't you take us all through *Juice*. I'm sure Forrest would like to hear the story-line and I'd like to keep it fresh in all of our minds.

'Movies, Mr Evers . . .' he said, as Sam got up and stole my attention. Sam was sidestepping out to the aisle, tight, faded, and torn blue jeans. Short little swishy cream silk T-shirt. Just your everyday multi-millionaire working woman. She stood at the front of the screening-room like a star pupil called on by the teacher. I tried to keep my mind on what David was saying.

He was saying, 'Movies are only dreams. Very expensive dreams, but only dreams. And not necessarily good ones. You would be amazed how often people spend millions making a bad dream. They don't think they are making a nightmare. They think they are making a miracle. And it's not that they are asleep. It's because the dream they have in their head is nowhere near the dream everybody else on the project has in their head. Which is why I believe in retelling the story-line from time to time just to make sure we are all in the same movie.

'*Juice*,' David said, leaning back, his hands behind his head, 'is *Tender Mercies* meets *Northern Exposure*.'

David turned to me for the first time, looking unblinking into my eyes. 'The way to sell a movie in this town, Forrest, is to tell somebody else how to sell it. When somebody tells us about an idea for a movie we like to be able to see what the advertising is going to look like,' he said in his quiet, even, touch-of-English-gentleman way. '*Juice* is Samantha Miles makes Sean Finlay into a man. And *Juice* is Sean Finlay makes Samantha Miles into a woman.' He smiled at his super-seller phrase, the idea and the package rolled into one, and gestured for Sam to begin.

Sam leaned back against the railing at the front of the room, making eye contact around the room. No bra under that swishy little cream silk T-shirt, I thought with my usual penetrating intellectual insight. Pay attention, Forrest.

'*Juice* is about an American hero; a racing driver, played by Sean Finlay, who has' – Sam dropped her voice down an octave to mock serious – ' "that combination of street-wise toughness and raw sensitivity to change from one generation to another". As they say in the PR department. Anyway Sean is sexy and a pro and one of the reasons I wanted to do this project was he's in it. He's hot, right now. Very hot.'

'He's a hot pain in the ass,' Virgin whispered loudly in my ear.

'Anyway,' Sam went on, 'Sean's character is Macklin, a racing driver who almost made it to the top, and failed. And in his failure, Macklin comes West, to hide and to start over. He comes to a small western town where he knows no one and no one knows him, OK? Only instead of riding into town on a horse, he's coming in on a Greyhound bus. *Juice* will open with the terrible crash through the titles, the crash at Indy that ended Macklin's career. So we know what haunts him, why he is afraid to race and why he walks with a limp when he gets off the bus.

'Macklin sets up a car repair shop, and meets Jill Clemente, who will be played by me.'

David spoke up from the back of the room. 'Samantha Miles,' he said, 'I will earn my daily bread by saying, is not only the loveliest star in Hollywood, she is the only woman with enough power at the box office to open a film on her own. With,' he added quickly, 'the singular exception of Virgin, who is also a client of mine and is, as we all know, a force of nature.' A fatherly nod of his perfectly groomed head to Virgin. 'Sorry for the interruption, Sam. But I like to see the credits at the beginning of the movie.'

'Jill,' Sam said, pacing at the front of the room as if she were improvising the story, 'is a teacher at the local elementary school. The school is under-funded, stressed with racial conflict and drugs, and Jill is badly paid and trying to keep an old car on the road. Left to her by an old boyfriend. She thinks Macklin is cheating her when he tells her what it will cost to fix her old car. They fight, she drives away and later has an accident.

Exactly what Macklin said would happen. Which makes her like him even less.

'Macklin not only fixes her car, he converts her car to uh, let me get this right, an Evironmentally Viable Integrated Automobile, which as Akiri told you, means the car is powered by a fuel cell.'

'Just like NASA,' Akiri Hozuki chimed in from the back row.

'Which he scrounges from his local friendly neighbourhood Hozuki dealer. Naturally at first Jill resists this "gift" from Macklin just as she resists Macklin. OK. So naturally they fall in love and move in together. Which is tough at first. Jill has a twelve-year-old girl named Candy. Candy is not really her daughter, she's the daughter of her ex-boyfriend. But because Jill is an all-round neat lady and a soft touch and just out of adolescence herself she is bringing up Candy. So Candy hates Macklin because Macklin is not her father. Hates Macklin because Macklin is not married to her mother. Hates Macklin because Macklin is her rival for her mother's love. And she hates Macklin because her mother is her rival for Macklin's love.

'So, one night Macklin and Jill have a bottle of wine with dinner to celebrate Macklin's paying off his bank loan and they say, "Hey, Candy's in bed, let's go over to the Buzzard's Nest, have another couple of drinks. Celebrate."

Candy hears them leave and sneaks into Macklin's workshop to set fire to it and she is trapped in the fire. Macklin and Jill see the fire from the bar, and Macklin saves Candy even though the memory of the fire in his crash makes this terribly difficult for him. The child is badly burned and suffering. Because the town is so isolated, there is no ambulance, the state police won't take the child and the only helicopter rescue available wants $2,500 to take Candy to the hospital over the mountains a hundred and sixty miles away. They don't have the money. The doctors at the hospital estimate the child has two hours to live if they don't get her to intensive care. Macklin has to face up to his fear of racing, Jill to her terror of speed. They take Jill's car, the electric car that Macklin has built, and the only car capable of making the trip in time.'

'That car's performance,' Akiri said, 'except for top speed which will be governed on the production cars, is virtually identical to the performance of EVIA. EVIA,' he beamed at Sam, 'will be announced the same week in June next near when we introduce *Juice*. And it will look a lot like a 1965 Mustang, although it'll be smaller and more rounded.'

'OK,' Sam said, as if that were enough interruptions. 'So they take off out of Velma, to save Candy's life. It is a hellish trip through the mountains. It's night, raining and foggy. And it looks as if the child will die. There are rock slides. The road is narrow, twisting, dangerous. The cops get their messages crossed and chase them and try to stop the car in the mother of all chase scenes. But they make it. Macklin realizes he can race again, Jill realizes she doesn't have to stay stuck in Velma for the rest of her life and Candy thinks maybe Macklin isn't such a monster after all.'

Sam opened her arms to the theatre with a small mock bow; there was a scatter of applause.

David said, 'So that's our story and I think we could script in a part for you, Forrest, without disrupting our production schedule. Could even, as I say, give us a little extra vigour on international distribution. I was thinking something like a drinking buddy for Sean.' David's hands were behind his head, eyes closed. 'Or, just a moment, I have a better idea . . .' he said, coming back to life. 'You could play yourself, Forrest Evers. A world-famous driver, name of Forrest Evers, shows up and recognizes Macklin and Macklin is too embarrassed to say hello to Forrest. Something along those lines. So all you'll have to do, Evers, is play yourself, something I expect you do very well indeed.'

David stirred in his seat, his hands holding a big block of air, as if it had weight. 'This is better. Maybe Evers is embarrassed too, to see his old buddy brought down low. On one level they are just old friends with not much to say to each other. On another level, Forrest can represent everything that Macklin has lost. Evers could represent the outside world they are both afraid of. Can you do that, Arnold, have it on my desk in the morning? Just the one scene. We're on a tight schedule.'

A small man in the second row with a bald spot on the back of his head turned around and said, 'No problem, Mr Allen.'

'OK, you have that on my desk first thing in the morning and I'll fax it out to the location to you, Sam. You do with it what you like. Although, Forrest,' David Allen said, looking at me for the first time, 'Ed tells me you only have three weeks' availability. Which, correct me if I'm wrong, Mel, should be enough to get all the driving sequences in the can with a day for Forrest's scene with Sean.'

Mel turned in his seat. 'We've got a couple of pickup days in the schedule so yeah, we can. We'll keep you busy, Forrest, all day every day for three weeks. You are going to have to teach Sean how to drive. The damn kid has so identified with the role he thinks he's a natural born racing driver.'

On the way out of the screening-room into the hot sun of the parking lot, Virgin tugged on my hand like a happy child. 'See, you're gonna be bright and beautiful, Forrest. You are going to be a star with a whole new life. Working with Samantha Miles. What do you think of her?'

'I don't think her pictures do her justice,' I said, ignoring Virgin's look. 'But she seems too nice to be a director.'

'I knew you'd fall in love with her,' Virgin said, getting into the Mercedes coupé she drove around LA to avoid being recognized. 'Everybody does.'

Sam was waving at me across the lot.

'You're on your own,' Virgin said. 'You know what they say: if you get the part, play it.'

The mirror window of her Mercedes slid up, reflecting, behind my jet-lagged face, Sam moving across the studio parking lot, cream silk T-shirt swishing in the sun, a big happy smile. Just for me, I thought. I looked around and, behind me, across the roof of Virgin's car, David was in the doorway, talking quietly on a pocket phone, taking in Sam's beautiful smile as if she were just another ranch-hand on his ranch.

# chapter three

'Goddammit, Billy, I don't know when we can fit it in. It's got to be in the first three weeks of shooting.' There was a pause. 'Christ, I don't know. David has Arnold sending him the script before I even see it. I know, but once we get rolling he'll lose interest and stop breathing down my neck. You know how David is. Probably just one setup. Yeah, at the goddamn gas pumps. Sean and him.' Another pause. 'Just goddamn do it. He isn't my idea, he's David's little whim. So there isn't any alternative and if it helps, I like it less than you do,' Sam said into her little flip-lid cell-net phone.

We were in the back of a big yellow Hozuki limo. I didn't know Hozuki made limousines but this one said Hozuki in raised chrome letters on the front grille and in tall chrome letters on its bulbous trunk. Probably built for the Japanese diplomats in Bolivia. It looked twenty-five years out of date except everything in it was brand new. A rolling time warp.

'Yeah, he's here, sitting next to me,' Sam said giving me a quickee imitation of a smile. 'Looking like shit. We'll probably have to go soft on close-ups so he doesn't look like an old fart. Yeah, silks. What's the weather report?'

I took the little fliptop phone from her surprised hand. 'Old Fart here, Billy, but you can call me Forrest. This wasn't my idea either. On the other hand, I'll be gone in three weeks, so let's keep it simple, and do it right the first time. Just remember my left side is my best side.' I flipped the phone shut and handed it back to Sam.

She held it clenched in her long perfectly manicured fingers and swivelled to face me on the vast blue velvet seat. 'Look, you silly FUCK of a stunt driver or whatever you are, I am the director of this film, you are not my idea, you are David's idea.

Or maybe you are Virgin's little toy and David is playing this trick on me because he owes the old broad a favour. So I am supposed to put up with you. But let me tell you, if you do anything, anything remotely like that little meaningless stunt you just did with my phone, you are out on your ass. Can you understand that?'

Outside we had crested the peak of the Angeles mountains, cool breezes stirred the tall evergreen trees, and the freeway headed down towards the flat hot desert floor twenty miles away.

'What happened to the sweet and smiling angel back in the screening room?' I said. 'I liked her.' I still liked her, but then I am a sucker for cheap physical attraction. The way Sam's upper lip curled up made her look like a soft and cushy kisser. And the intensity of those green eyes wasn't a threat, it was a challenge. No real rose comes without real thorns, I told myself.

'Samantha Miles is alive and well and America's Screen Sweetie of the Week,' she said, giving herself a quick check in the vanity mirror. 'And while that fragile little dream lasts she gets eleven point seven five of the gross of whatever project she is in. Plus whatever bank robbery David can arrange on her behalf for expenses and I wouldn't touch a hair on her head,' she said, pronouncing the word 'hay-ed'.

'But don't let Samantha Sweetheart fool you. This is the first film I've ever directed and it has got to be right. I can't afford to fuck around.'

'Or be polite,' I said.

'Look, I've got to take some calls. Do you mind?'

I should have let it go. Even if she was a spoiled brat, it was only three weeks, and the sun was shining. And God knows the money was my boarding pass to Formula One. So I had every reason to keep my mouth shut. But I was unbalanced by jet lag and I respond badly to rudeness. Maybe I am still angling for my mother's attention. Or I wanted those shifty points beneath that little cream silk T-shirt to wobble at me. Whatever, something childish made me say, 'Fuck you.'

'You should be so lucky,' she said, punching numbers on the flat black little handset. Then she stopped, looking back up at me. 'Maybe we don't need a new scene from Arnold. With dialogue like that you could write all your own lines.'

I laughed. 'Now I know how you got where you are. Charm.'

'That's right,' she said, doing a little camp siren-hiding-her-face behind her arm, 'all of my charms. Look, I'm sorry I'm such a shit,' she said, straightening up. 'We haven't started shooting yet and we are already three days behind schedule.'

'What made you want to be a director?'

She let out a long breath, shifting down. 'Greed. Power. Control. Screw a lot of stars. The usual reasons.' She made a face. 'Seriously. The life expectancy of a pretty face is about two hours and ten minutes on the screen. Men can go on for ever, like Clint Eastwood and Paul Newman. I mean, you see Clint in *In the Line of Fire* with a twenty-five-year-old woman, nobody says boo. And he's over sixty. But if you did a sixty-year-old woman with a guy in his twenties the story would have to be about that. And it's not just age. If a guy is difficult on the set he's got "an artistic temperament". If a woman has an opinion she's "difficult". One way or another, whether it's a rotten script or bad lighting or you don't look twenty-two any more, they get you. Just when you get used to the money, you're finished. Your friend Virgin must know something about that. My daddy was a producer and the bastard died when I was twelve, before I had a chance to do anything. So maybe I am just proving something to him. The magazines always love that story. Anyway I want to direct because I want to. I screw up this picture and that's it. No second chance in Follywood.'

'Don't let me hold you back.'

'You couldn't if you tried.'

She made her calls. One after the other. To her assistant director to make sure they had weather insurance for the mountain driving scenes, her script supervisor to alert her to the change in the script to include this racing driver they dug up, to her hairdresser to tell her that she, Sam, would want her stand-in for blocking to have the same hair do because the cinematographer was going to preview the lighting, to her cinematographer to ask him to preview the lighting of the second setup in the afternoon. Some of the calls were to other limos heading out into the desert and I thought of those black and white World War II movies where the pilots in the bomber squadron over the English Channel talk to each other on the radio with the big earphones saying, 'Here comes Charlie, twelve o'clock high.'

I fiddled with the walnut picnic tables that folded out of the chauffeur's partition, admired the cut-crystal decanter and the champagne flutes and brandy snifter mounted in red velvet behind the picnic tables, dialled the air conditioning up and down and watched the scenery change from green to brown, from mountains to hills to flat as we drove out into the desert floor at a steady sixty-five. From time to time Sam would look up from her phone calls and give me a five-hundred watt absolutely dazzling smile along with the helpless shrug of the truly occupied. As if she was sorry, but this would have to come first and really she would really rather be talking or whatever with me. I was learning the power of an actress's gestures and the absolute zero of their meaning in real life. In the hot blue sky, Air Force bombers flew lazily overhead, and heat rose off the flat desert in waves. 'Fifty miles,' the driver said, answering Sam's question, 'to Velma.'

Edwardes Air Force Base where the Space Shuttle touches down, twenty miles to the right.

# chapter four

The phone ringing in the dark brought back an old feeling from years ago; from those mornings before corporate sponsors turned Formula One into a multinational marketing tool. Before motorhomes, pretty PR women, fancy hotels, and phones in your pocket. Reaching out to shut the phone the hell up I thought I was in nowhere Spain, getting up in the freezing dark and driving out to some track where my racing car wouldn't start and there would be plenty of time to stand around and wonder why I'd gotten up at five, why there was no coffee, why I had forgotten my jacket when I knew it was freezing and why I did this for a living. A phone waking me up before I remember what country I'm in always reminds me of those hard and simple days and the longing I had to be on the track, screaming into a corner.

The phone said, 'Six fifteen, Mr Evers. Your car is here.' Through the curtains a big yellow Hozuki limo waited with its lights on.

America.

Showtime.

We drove into Velma and after a minute of dead storefronts came out the other side.

A half-mile beyond beautiful downtown Velma, a day's worth of Interstate traffic had strayed off the road and parked. Tractor trailers, motorhomes, generator trucks, cars, limos, and vans lined both sides of the road. Up ahead, there was a bright glow of lights.

Under the lights was 'the location': an old-fashioned gas station with two old-fashioned gas pumps out front and a mechanic inside. No SELF SERVE signs, no rows of factory-food machines for those folks doomed to eat and drive. A big round metal sign swung from a pole with a faded red winged horse. GAS, LUBE, OIL it said in blue letters at the bottom of the sign. We drove past a crowd in front of the garage, standing as still as if they were posing for a portrait.

Fifty yards down the road the driver stopped the limo. He turned around in his seat, a small face, beefy and mottled as a double whopper. 'You get out here,' he said. 'Breakfast.'

'What's your name?' I said.

'What's it to ya?'

'Just wanted to say thanks for the ride. Is there some reason everybody has to be rude to everybody out here?'

'Hey. Your contract says you get a ride to the set and a ride back to the motel. It don't include psychiatric analysis.'

'Don't go to any extra effort for me,' I said, getting out of the car.

'Hey, wait a minute.'

I waited, the door open, letting in the cool desert air.

'I'm a Teamster,' he said as if that explained everything. 'I work to the rules, that's all.'

'That's what the Nazis said.'

'Don't give me that shit,' he said. 'You heard all the Teamster jokes, right?'

'What's a Teamster joke?'

'A Teamster joke goes like: "How many Teamsters does it take to change a light bulb?" '

'And the answer is?'

' "Seventeen. Wanna make something of it?" ' He stuck out a small, soft and hairy hand, smiling now that the joke was over. 'See, that's the kinda premisconception we gotta put up with every day. My name's Frank, Mr Evers.'

'Call me Forrest, Frank.'

'Whattareyou, born in the woods?'

'That's what my father used to say. My mother thought it sounded English. Where's breakfast?'

'Other side of that truck,' he said, pointing. 'Just tell them what you want. Then you go over to make-up, that's about six down to where they're shooting, just past the wardrobe truck. So you're not an actor, right?'

'I didn't know it showed,' I said, still holding the door open, one leg out, one leg inside the warm limo.

'Actors,' he said. 'They meet somebody, they're on. Know what I mean?'

'Not really.'

'Like they gotta have an audience and if you are in front, you are it. What do you do for your day job, Forrest, in real life?'

'I'm a racing driver.'

Frank gave me a shrug like no big deal. 'You gonna replace Pierson, huh?'

'You mean the driver that crashed.'

'And died. Yeah him. Pierson Waddell. He was, you know, just a regular stunt driver. He didn't get no big-time limo treatment like you got. What Waddell got was fucked.'

The desert air was still and cool and my jet-lagged brain was thinking coffee. I slid back inside the car and closed the door. Back inside the corporate warmth of Hozuki. 'I didn't know he died.'

'Last night around eleven, I heard.'

'That was the first time I heard his name. I never heard it before.'

'Yeah, well, in this business if you aren't here, you're history. Know what I mean?' Frank had turned around to face me, elbows draped over the divider, with large patches of yellow leather upholstery peeking through his small forearms. Strings of black hair were combed carefully over his scalp.

'Like racing drivers,' I said.

Frank shrugged.

I leaned forward, driver to driver. 'What happened, Frank?'

'Like I said, he was fucked.'

'Like stoned? Drunk?'

'Not fucked *up*. Fucked. Waddell is a pro. 'Scuse me. Was a pro. Been doing stunts since he was seventeen. He was very professional, very careful. He had to be. Like the first film he did was rolling the '49 Ford in *Thunder Road* with Bob Mitchum in what was it, '57, '58, something like that, where the car rolls, lands on its feet and zooms down the road in the opposite direction. Most of these asshole drivers you got these days couldn't do it, ten tries. What I mean is, you don't do stunts like that as long as Waddell did and still be walking around unless you know what you're doin'. You should see that *Thun-*

*der Road*, you get a chance. Film opens with these Treasury guys inna '57 Chevy come up behind Mitchum who's running moonshine in a '49 Ford. And the Treasury guys got this big bumper snatcher on the front of their '57 Chevy they glomb on to the back of Mitchum's car. Mitchum pulls a lever—'

'What happened to Waddell?'

'I don't know what happened to him, except what I hear is he'd got a cracked skull and a broken back and he was burned black all over. It wasn't even a stunt. It was a drive-by, for Christ's sake. My mother coulda done it. He was fucked. Poor bastard took four days to die. If you are gonna take his place you better watch your ass.'

'It's going to be tough watching my ass and driving at the same time, Frank.'

'You'll get used to it,' he said. 'I do it every day.'

Catering was a large aluminium truck with one side raised like an awning and a bunch of people standing around in front of the counter holding foam cups of coffee and picking off paper plates. A lanky woman with a narrow face and eyebrows like black caterpillars over blue eyes leaned on the Formica and said, 'What can I get you?' A carved wooden sign on the counter said THE GOOD SEED.

'Black coffee would be fine.'

'We've got Kenyan Mountain Arabica, that's a nice full-bodied coffee if you like a kinda winey one. And we got Chocolate Macadamia Nut and Raspberry Mocha coffee for the special flavours. If you'd rather go espresso I can give you mocha, latta, regular caf, and decaf and double decaf although you look like the wake-up call went right over your head.'

'Double espresso,' I said. 'Maximum wake-up jolt and . . .'

'And,' she said, 'I just baked some nice nine-grain, cold-rolled whole oat-bran organic Capuchin monk's bread. I could toast that for you if you like. And there's Irish organic oatmeal, organic Granola, organic muesli, turkey sausage, herbal tea.'

'Just a piece of plain toast,' I said. 'No butter.'

'You doing penance?'

'I'm a racing driver.'

'We get all kinds,' she said.

As she poured out a cup of coffee a voice behind me said, 'So she married her childhood sweetheart. Then she left him for his father who still takes every drug that has ever been prescribed for him in his life.' The voice behind me was around forty in a grey sweatshirt. She had a large round forehead and her cheekbones held up her face as she smiled amiably at me and kept talking to the two slim men sipping coffee. 'But that's the way it is in this country with prescriptions. No prescription ever does you any good. You'd be better off if you went and stood in a wooded area.'

'You an extra or crew,' she said to me, 'I'm Robin Leckonby. We're all extras.'

The two men stuck their hands out. Tom. Bill.

'Forrest Evans. I'm not sure if I qualify as an extra. I'm a racing driver.'

'If it's just a walk on, don't let them get a good look at your face or you'll never get another job. Worst thing an extra can do is get recognized. Although looking at you,' she squinted her eyes, 'I'd guess you have a camera face.'

'They said they might give me a couple of lines,' I said.

'Well say them and get your hands on your pay cheque. I've been in film for, well never mind how long, and I'm, I dunno . . . I got weird vibes about this one. That driver getting all mashed up and burned to death before we even get started and everybody pretending like it didn't happen. You can't repress things like that, you know. You have to let them out or they just get worse.'

Make-up saw me sitting in a deck-chair in a motorhome with two blazing photo lights pointed at me and a bib around my neck. A woman with hair that looked like a rusty Brillo pad dabbed a powder puff on my nose and said 'next'. So much for filling in the crags.

Out on the set, the sun was rising behind mountains, giving them a jagged outline and throwing a long shadow behind me as I stood on the edge of the gas station. An actor took the nozzle off the faded red gas pump, flipped up the lever to turn the pump on and light up the frosted globe with the winged red horse on top of the pump. He popped the gas flap, unscrewed the gas cap and squeezed the grip on the nozzle.

'The light's changing fast,' a short woman in a candy-stripe shirt with a clipboard said, looking into a light meter.

'Good,' Sam said. 'Let's do it again with another car.' Sam was wearing blue jeans, cowboy boots and an old leather jacket that looked big enough to have belonged to John Wayne. She saw me and looked back at her scene. One camera was low to the ground, on the end of a long arm that came from the back of the truck. Another camera was mounted on a short and sturdy platform, a huge glassy frog eye inches from the gas cap on the car.

'Hi, Forrest,' a voice said quietly into my ear. 'I'm afraid we're running a little late.' His face looked pleasant, relaxed, but his hand running over his bald scalp gave him away.

'Morning, Mel,' I said, feeling at home on the movie range. 'What's she up to?'

'Sam wants to show a year's time passing, to show how Macklin's trapped. So we're shooting exactly the same action, with different cars and lighting. And you see the desert and the mountains reflected in the cars, the passing of the seasons which we'll do in the lab, and later we might shoot an insert for the sequence in Sean's sunglasses. The whole thing will take maybe twenty seconds on the screen depending on the cut, but I think you'll have a sense of the seasons and the beauty of a small desert town along with the boredom of a year of doing the same thing. She's going to be a fabulous director.'

'Sean wears sunglasses at night?' Another voice. Akiri in a baseball cap and sharply creased faded jeans, and new blue Air Pumps on his feet.

'No, no, just in the daylight shots,' Mel said quickly. 'Part of the symbolism of hiding. And looking hip at the same time.' He turned to me and put a hand on my shoulder. Man to man. 'I know you're scheduled for a run-through, you know, a rehearsal, now, Forrest, before we shoot you. But you can relax for a while. We're going to be another five, fifteen minutes here.'

'He means maybe they'll get to you before lunch.' Akiri had a way of talking softly so you had to strain to hear. 'Fabulous directors,' he said, 'don't start off their first day of shooting behind schedule. You should tell Sam she can always pick up this artsy shit at the end of the shoot if we've still got the extra time. You want to look at the car, Forrest?'

Akiri was wearing purple reflector sunglasses that wrapped around his head and he was bundled in a bulbous pink, lime and purple down Parka. A sure sign of living in Beverly Hills, where they reach for the goosedown when the temperature plummets below 60° F.

'You mean the wrecked one?'

'No, the wreck is in our shop in San Diego. You'd have to pry a couple dozen technicians off it just to look at it. Take them two, three days to rebuild it. I mean while Sam is farting around we might as well get you acquainted with the real stars of our show. They're in a trailer down the road.'

Akiri started to turn away and Mel put a hand on his shoulder. 'I don't know how many shoots you've been on, Akiri,' Mel said.

'Sixteen TV commercials including two Golden Palm winners at Cannes.'

'But this is your first feature. We have a hundred and twenty day shooting schedule. And on every day, all day, Sam is the director and I am the line producer. Do you understand what I am saying?'

'What you are telling me is you don't understand I control the money.'

'David controls the money,' Mel said quietly with that touch of Southern California friendliness they apply to all occasions. 'You just work for your daddy. We'll do our job, you do yours.'

'Just do it on time,' Akiri said, smiling with a lot of teeth showing, 'and I won't pull your plug.' Behind him Sam was looking over a prop man's shoulder as he spritzed spray-dull on a 1979 Buick to keep the flares out of the lens.

Walking over to the trailer with the cars I told Akiri, 'The first day of shooting seems a little soon to come down on Sam and Mel.'

'They know they can't bullshit me because I went to film school at USC.'

'I see what you mean,' I said.

'Hey, look, Spielberg did some of his best stuff when he first got out of film school. Don't knock it. I'll bet you're just like everybody else; like you want to be a director.'

'I never thought of it.'

'The other thing is, Dad told me to ride herd on them, you know? Like Hozuki has over six billion dollars in EVIA so we're not exactly relaxed. We've built plants in Brazil, in Spain, Malaysia, as well as the one you probably read about in Arkansas. If EVIA takes off we've got options on plants in Indonesia.'

'And this movie is that critical to them.'

'Hey, listen, this is a revolution. If we could change all of the cars in the world to fuel cells, we could end pollution from cars. Really. The regular gasoline engine is around ten to twenty per cent efficient, electricity from big central power plants runs around forty to fifty, and our fuel cell is over ninety-seven per cent. And the thing poops water, man. We're using gasoline for the fuel 'cause the infrastructure is there, but a fuel cell can use all kinds of stuff if you set it up right; methane, alcohol, hydrogen. Hydrogen is the ideal fuel, Forrest. Just pull it out of the air. Most plentiful element in nature. No more oil spills because we wouldn't need oil. Costs around three cents a mile to run. Plus they're not like these lead-sled battery cars. The suckers really move, man.'

'I don't understand. What's a fuel cell?'

'Hey, where have you been? They kind of look like batteries, big boxes with two poles. But they don't store electricity, they make it from fuel. It's a chemical process that converts fuel into electric energy and water. The trick has been cost because they had to use like platinum or gold and some incredibly expensive plastics, so the old fuel cells cost like $50,000. But we've gotten around that with graphite and a new plastic. Believe it, EVIA is going to be the first, a fucking major global event whatever the hell happens to this movie. But yeah, it's critical, Forrest. In the automobile business, everything is critical.'

Two Teamsters in bulging T-shirts pulled open the doors of a large, unmarked semi-tractor trailer and we walked up a ramp and into the brightly lit interior.

The two bright yellow convertibles looked like Ford Mustangs, only smaller, with black plastic upholstery and a dent in the right front fender.

'The 1965 Mustang is America's sweetheart. Aren't they great?' Akiri said.

'Yeah, great,' I said without enthusiasm. 'I don't understand the reverence some people have for old mass-market stuff.'

'You don't have to understand it, Forrest. You just groove on it.'

I looked at the two cars and I thought scrap heap. I said, 'You must have been around minus twelve when the Mustang came out. Like the old gas station you're shooting. I don't understand that either.'

'What don't you understand?'

'Why you are introducing a new technology as if it was still the 1960s.'

'Hey, if you want people to accept high-tech, set it in Retro. Makes people feel relaxed and at home. Like, OK, it's new but it feels familiar. See, what we're doing is giving EVIA a heritage. Like it was always there. Like it's part of the American past. And hey, everybody loves the Mustang. In California they collect 'em like baseball cards.'

'Retro,' I said, 'was your idea.'

'Well, no. Not my idea exactly. But the instant they mentioned Retro I understood what they were talking about and I approved it.'

'So you approved the ideas for the movies.'

'No, no, not the movie ideas. I just make sure what they do dovetails with our promotional strategy for EVIA. Anyway,' he said, picking up speed again, 'I picked up on Retro because I thought it would make a better movie. When you were a kid they were always making movies about the future. Like *ET* and *Star Wars*. People used to look forward to the future. But that's all changed now. Now the future scares people shitless. The past isn't so scary. *Star Trek* happened and hey, we lived through it.'

I decided he really was twenty-one.

He kept on talking. 'See, we were looking for a property to introduce EVIA to America. And this script was written to take place in the 1970s. And I thought, great, let's bring it up to date. I mean the time of the film is now, but the town is so remote, it's like in everybody's past. Get them feeling really comfortable with the idea of an electric car, like there has always been a Hozuki electric car out there. The other thing was, we couldn't use a real gas station because of the oil companies. So a generic one saves us a lot of hassle.'

'The oil companies don't want your movie?'

'Are you serious? How would you feel if you were Mobil or Exxon and somebody announces a car that runs on ninety per cent less gas? And if we run 'em on hydrogen they won't need any gas at all. The big oil companies are going to like our new car about as much as General Motors will. Want to take it for a ride?'

'Not before I look it over,' I said.

'Hey, Forrest. My man. Good to meet you.' The famous crooked grin behind the sunglasses. Faded torn greasy jeans, torn T-shirt to show off the tan, leather jacket and a heavy fuzz of three-day-old whiskers. Sean Finlay. The Kid. The new hot property. Looking hip.

Don't let anybody fool you, real stars have real power and you can feel it. Especially when it is aimed in your direction with the assumed good-buddy friendship that stars grant to other stars and to the very rich.

'Good to meet you, Sean. I thought you were pumping gas.'

'That's my stand-in. They save me for the good stuff. What say we take one of these suckers out and kick ass?'

'Yeah, right,' I said. 'Maybe we'll find out what made Waddell's car take off like a big-ass bird.'

Sean jerked his head back. He took his sunglasses off and his deep-set blue eyes looked hurt. It was his trade mark. More sinned against than. James Dean is alive and suffering in a thousand Hollywood hopefuls. 'Whattaya mean?' Sean said.

'I mean before you pull the trigger, you ought to know if the gun is loaded.' I gave him a grin to let him know it wasn't all that serious.

'Oh yeah, right. Sure. Hey, I'm a big fan of yours, Forrest. I saw you win that Formula One race at Monaco.'

'I'm glad you did. But that was four years ago.'

'Yeah, right, the year you almost won at Indy. Christ, that was a shame.'

'Big shame,' I said. Ten steps behind Sean, one of the grips, a man with hollow cheeks, a Fu Manchu moustache, a salt-stained red bandanna, and a pony-tail, was watching. Even among the world-weary grips the big stars had their followers.

'Hey, Forrest Evers?' A slender young woman with a pixie

haircut, satin shorts and a down hunting jacket was outside the truck. 'They want you over on the set. Here,' she said, handing me a sheaf of papers, 'is your script.'

'Catch you later,' Sean said.

'Get it right the first time,' Akiri said. 'And be careful.'

# chapter five

'Hold it right there. What I want you to do, Evers, is sit there looking in the mirror without moving while Billy lights you.' Sam was crouched next to the car, peering through her fingers held like a miniature movie screen. She stood up and walked away with Billy. William Howard Mayberry: cinematographer, director of photography, winner of five Academy Awards, and the great surly bear behind the camera. There was plenty of light so lighting meant positioning big reflector boards to fill in shadows and erecting silk screens overhead to soften the harsh sunlight. Sam was saying, as they walked away, 'What do you think, Billy? Can we get Sean in Evers' door mirror so we can see what Sean looks like from Evers' point of view? And can we pick it up quickly when we shoot the scene tomorrow? I don't want to get stuck on it.' They moved off towards the garage office where the script supervisor kept their shooting schedule and shooting script.

I sat in the car, the desert sun coming down.

I had driven Mel's silver Mercedes 560 S into the gas station seventeen times. The first dozen had been for lighting and setting up the camera angles and getting the timing right. To give the car the illusion of speed they were shooting the establishing shot of the car in wide angle. Since I was playing the part of a racing driver they wanted me to come in fast, sliding a little to kick up dust and look exciting on the screen. They also wanted me to stop on an exact mark alongside the pumps about six inches from a camera mounted on a heavy steel dolly. It was an easy move, starting at around seventy-five; tap the brakes and twitch the wheel, get on the accelerator to bring the back end around, and then get on the brakes hard and come sliding to a stop on the mark. The Mercedes had ABS brakes which made sliding difficult, but they didn't want anything flashy, just a man in control and in a hurry.

When the sun had risen up to full glare, and Sam had put on a big wide-brimmed cowboy hat, they shot the move five times and they said they were happy. Now, before they set up for the shot where Sean comes out of the garage with the car in the foreground, they were talking about doing another extra shot. I could feel my pale face which had been in the dark of British winter until yesterday begin to lose its English mushroom grey and glow pretty pink.

The repetition and the waiting didn't surprise me. Years ago I had done a film called *The Last Race* with Arthur Warren. I'd been technical advisor and driven the racing scenes until Arthur threw a tantrum halfway through the movie and insisted on doing the rest of the driving scenes himself. (If you see *The Last Race* on late-night TV, the driving scenes where the driver does not wear driving gloves are mine.) The picture bombed and I wasn't about to remind anybody of it. But it had taught me that unless you are the director, what you mostly do in feature film production is sit and wait. Sit and wait for the cloud or the plane or the truck to pass by. Sit and wait while the director and the cinematographer discuss lenses, angles, and cranes vs. tracking shots. Of course everything is meticulously worked out on story-boards and charts and a shooting script before shooting begins. But making a movie is like war. Once the shooting begins, all the plans are off.

I got out of the car.

'Hey,' Sam said from the garage door, 'where the hell do you think you are going?'

'Sit in the shade, read my script.'

'For God's sake, Evers, you only have five lines. You are playing yourself. I know it's a dumb part but I think you can handle it. You know how to play yourself, don't you, Forrest? Goddamn it,' she said to the desert, 'I hate working with amateurs. You get back in the car,' she added, 'and sit there.'

'I'll be happy to sit on a spike if you're shooting, Sam. But while you're talking about it, I'm sitting in the shade.' I walked over to the shady side of the garage.

She followed me. I sat down in one of the camp chairs the grips had set up alongside the garage for the cast and she stuck her face in mine. Sam said, 'If you were a real actor instead of an asshole, you wouldn't work again.'

'Never said I was an actor,' I said, opening my script.

'Jerry,' Sam called out to one of the grips, 'bring me a spike.'

Sam walked back to the garage office and I opened my script to my one on-camera appearance.

**14. EXTERIOR OF MACKLIN'S GARAGE. NOON.**
**From a distance, an expensive foreign sports car drives down the empty highway and pulls up in front of the gas pumps. The driver, FORREST EVERS, honks the horn. MACKLIN comes out of the garage, sweating, dirty shirt and dirty jeans. FORREST EVERS wears a dark green silk shirt. He takes off his sunglasses.**

**EVERS**
**Mac. My man. How the hell are you? It's good to see you. I haven't seen you since you qualified alongside me at Indy, what, two, three years ago. Christ, what are you doing in this Godforsaken place?**

**MACKLIN**
**I'm on vacation. What can I do for you?**

**EVERS considers the question. He wants to help, to say something, but there is nothing he can do. He shrugs.**

**EVERS**
**Fill it up.**

'You shouldn't talk to her that way, you know.'

I put my script down. A girl with long thin blonde hair, T-shirt and baggy pants and basketball sneakers was standing in front of me. Large, slightly slanted green eyes and a small pointy face with a long nose gave her a pretty but slightly rodent look. 'Talk to who?' I said.

'Mom. She's really starving for affection, you know. That's

why she's an actress. If you keep being a shit to her she'll think it's her fault. Then she'll really get pissed off.'

'You think I should just sit in the sun and shut up.'

'You don't have to make a big scene about it.'

'OK, I was childish.' The kid was right. I could get some sunblock and sit there. It would certainly be easier than trying to squeeze several hundred thousand pounds out of some Yorkshire chocolate company to sponsor my Formula One car. 'How old are you?'

'People always ask you your age so they can put you down. I'm fifteen, almost. Next thing is you'll say I'm grown-up for fifteen.'

'You talk pretty grown-up.'

'You ever hear of virtual reality?'

'Sure.'

'Well, I'm a virtual adult.'

'I see what you mean.' She had her mother's green eyes, I thought. But longer legs and a larger mouth in a smaller, pointier face. And something else. The way she stood and held her head, chin up, sure of herself, as if she was challenging you. Although just to look at her she was definitely a kid. 'What's your name?'

'Delilah. Which is dumb so everybody calls me Di-Di. But I'm getting a little old for that. I'm thinking of shrinking it down to Di, like the old princess in England. You think Di sounds OK?'

'I think Delilah's delightful.'

'Everybody says that. Look, I didn't mean to go all rude on you. But you should cut Mom a little slack. Like, you know, everything is easier for men in films. Way easier. I mean everybody expects guys to look like old saddlebags. Mom has to get up at five in the morning and soak her face in lemon peels and cucumber tea so she looks fresh.'

'You think she was being fair back there?'

'Fair? Wow. That's Jurassic. I mean it's been for ever since I heard that word. Mom has to make a movie and she has to star in it and she has a hundred and twenty days to do it. And this is really it, her whole career. You have to say five lines in three weeks, and then you can take your money and go home. What does fair have to do with anything? The other thing is I think Sean is being shitty to her.'

'Sean hasn't had a chance to be shitty to her. He hasn't even been on camera yet.' I knew this because there had been a lot of to-ing and fro-ing with stand-ins for Sean's appearance in the scene. It wouldn't be the first time he would be on the screen in the finished movie. Getting off the Greyhound bus would be his entrance. But coming out of the garage would be the first time he would be on camera in the shooting schedule so they were treating it like an entrance. Major consultations about how dirty, tired, and sweaty he could get and still be heart-throbbingly handsome for the thirteen-to-fifteen-year-olds who made up the majority of his audience base.

'It's nothing to do with the movie,' Delilah said. 'I think she's all over worried it won't be "a lasting relationship". Can you believe she really said that? She's just bonking him, for Christ's sake.'

'Bonking Sean,' I repeated witlessly. The idea took some getting used to.

'Sure. One way or another, Mom says, the director always fucks the star.'

'I think your mother was probably speaking in metaphors,' I said. I had to get out of England. I was sounding as stuffy as an old sofa.

'You don't know anything about it.'

'No, I don't. But I do know your mother is a fine actress and Mel says she is going to be a great director. Anyway you're right, she does have her hands full.' Jesus, I thought, change the subject. 'Are you going to be an actress?'

'I *am* an actress. But that's mostly because Sam had me written into her contract. But I don't see it as a lifetime career. What I really want to do is direct.' She looked over her shoulder, bored with me. 'I gotta go. See you around, Spike.'

I went back to my script, thinking it didn't sound right, when I heard, 'Forrest'. I looked up towards the sun. Julie, an assistant producer with long black hair, purple lipstick and a face even whiter than mine, was standing over me, looking like she was in mourning for the dead of some other generation. Until she smiled. She stood there, smiling. Patiently. 'They want you back in the car.'

'Sure,' I said.

Sam was standing by the car waiting. Before I got back in I said, 'I'm sorry, I didn't mean to be difficult. I was worried about looking pasty face in one scene and sunburned the next.'

'You're only on camera in one scene. But sure, let's get some sunblock on you and make sure make-up keeps you on an even tan.' I opened the door to slip behind the wheel and her hand was on my shoulder. 'I'm sorry too,' she said. 'I'll have to learn to be better with actors.' She gave me one of her quick all-purpose smiles. 'Especially when they're not actors. Look, we're going to break for lunch in twenty minutes,' she said. 'Come over to Sean's motorhome, have lunch with Sean and me. Oh, and Irving Shulman will be there. You'll love Irv. Just don't piss him off.'

# chapter six

'I always liked shooting in the desert,' Irving Shulman said, looking out towards the mountains. 'Everything is so damn still it intensifies the action. Perfect backdrop. You see, the lens knows this. You look through the lens and even the smallest details have a dangerous clarity in the desert air.' He sat back, enjoying the sound of his words. Closed his eyes. 'So what do you want to achieve with this film, Sam?'

Sam made a face. 'If you really want to know, Irv, I want to show a woman can make a better film than a man.'

Shulman leaned towards her. 'For God's sake, my dear little Samantha, don't aim so low. If you don't try at least to make the best movie that has ever been made, you won't do anything.' His face came around to me, looking for approval.

Close up, Irving Shulman looked like a frog. A short stumpy body, no neck and a wide and lumpy frog face and a wart on his cheek. I suppose he didn't get what he was looking for from me because he snorted and took a long sip of chilled white wine, then his face changed, his smile spread back to his ears, and he leaned back and said in a light tenor voice, 'Perfect. Absolutely perfect, my dear Miss Miles.'

We were seated around a glass-topped table in an enclosed, air-conditioned glass veranda outside Sean's motorhome, having lunch. The desert spread away from us in still life; dirty sand, rocky scrub, small cactus, and sage brush. Heat waves made the mountains wave like curtains in a breeze. We were in a cool oasis of potted green shrubbery and a burbling waterfall while outside the glass panels the world fried.

'It's a treat to be at the début of a talented new director,' Shulman said, holding up his glass to Sam. 'The salmon is delicious, and you know I'm a sucker for Far Niente chardonnay. But you really shouldn't be here, Sam. You ought to be out there, with the crew, having lunch with them. They can tell you a hell of a lot more than I can. You pay attention to what your crew tells you and they'll do anything for you. You go all high and mighty with them and they not only won't give a shit what you say, they'll screw you up and you'll never know how they did it.'

'Irv, I know, but I wanted this little bit of peace and quiet and wisdom from Uncle Irving before I jump out of my skin.' She gave him a girlish smile and batted her eyelashes, a camp come-on look.

'What wisdom? You want wisdom, ask Sean here, maybe he knows something. Like where can I find a housemaid as pretty as your young Di-Di.' He lifted his gaze to Delilah across the table. In baggy shorts and NO FEAR T-shirt she had been silently staring out at the desert looking seriously bored while Shulman was talking. At the mention of her name she gave Shulman a look and put her hand on the back of Sean's neck, and left it there. She looked back at me and then, taking her time, across the table to Sam, returning Sam's glare with the heavy teenage disdain.

Irving went on, sipping his wine and swirling it in his lightly frosted glass. 'It doesn't get any easier. You stand next to the camera watching the take and you think maybe the lead actor's line is little awkward, maybe you should rewrite it. So while you are watching the scene play you think of other ways the actor could say the line but you are not sure. Maybe it is the way the actor is saying the line that makes it sound flat. Then a plane passes over and the sound man turns towards you with a puzzled look like maybe he hears it on the track, and out of the corner of your eye you see the tracking camera hesitate for a moment and you think maybe the camera operator is going to call cut, while your actor takes a half step towards the camera instead of back like he is supposed to and you wonder if the assistant cameraman kept him in focus or if you can cut around it with another shot when the camera assistant holds up a finger to say there's just one minute of film left. And at the end of the take everybody looks at you and wants to know how it was. And you really can't say because you don't know any more than anybody else.'

'You must have had some idea,' I said. 'They don't give the Academy Award away and you've won, what, five?'

'Six. *On the River*, that one I knew was right, right from the first shot. Malewkovich just wrote a hell of an elegant script with the emotional impact of a roof falling on your head. But the rest . . .' He sighed, dismissing his life's work with a wave of his hand. 'Get a good crew, treat them well, keep them happy, close your eyes and trust them. A director is supposed to be God, Evers,' he said to me, 'see everything, know everything, do everything. But we're not God. If we were God we'd make better movies.'

He took another sip of wine, easily commanding the table, his soft brown eyes remembering some other afternoon. Then he put his empty glass down, sliding it towards Delilah half an inch without looking at her, and turned to me. 'Although one thing I can tell you, Mr Evers,' he said pleasantly, 'if *Juice* were my film, you wouldn't be sitting at my table having lunch. You'd be on your way home.'

'It's hard to get good help these days,' I said, thinking I'd pass it off as a joke.

'No, it's not. There are at least five hundred men in Los Angeles who could do your role on this film better than you are doing it. They are professional actors. There are seventy-eight thousand members of the Actors' Guild and eighty-five per cent don't get one single job in a year. You have taken their place, their role. You are taking their money and maybe their one chance in a lifetime to break into feature films and to treat it as casually as you do is an insult to them and to your director. By the way,' he said mildly, watching Delilah fill his glass, 'never question your director. If you have a question, talk to the AD. Stars talk to the director, you talk to the assistant director.'

'Irv,' Sam said, leaning forward, taking hold of his hand on the table, 'that was my fault.'

'You're damn right it was your fault, Pussycat,' he said, bringing her hand up for a courtly bullfrog kiss. 'If you didn't give me this delicious lunch I would probably spank you like I should have spanked you when you were playing Sascha in *Envelope*. You played that sensitive girl like a cheerleader and I never should have let you get away with it. Anyway, you're an actress, Sam. You know how wobbly you get before a scene.

Talk to your actors before their scenes. Hold their hands,' he said, squeezing hers for emphasis. 'Give them a piece of professional advice or a joke. Something that makes them think you care about them. Gives them the illusion that you are in control. You can cover all the angles and light any way you want but if an actor doesn't at least *try* to give you his soul you can forget being a director. You walk away from an actor on the set and leave him standing there like you did to Evers while you go have a think, as if the actor doesn't exist, that actor is going to take revenge on you. Treat actors like cattle and you'll end up with cow shit on screen. Count on it.'

'And directors take revenge on actors,' Sean said, to me, 'by hogging the conversation and the wine.' Sean's face had those deep-set blue eyes and that sensitive, angry squint the schoolgirls love. He smirked at Sam. 'They talk about that depth-of-field shit, axis, motivational conflict, and all that film-school crap. My glass is empty, kid.'

Delilah gave him a teenage version of a sultry look, sticking her lower lip out and trudged up the steps and into the motor-home for another bottle.

'So when are we going to check these cars out, Forrest? Burn up a little pavement?'

'You got a helmet?' I said.

'Helmet,' Sean said, getting red in the face. 'Shee-it. We're making a damn movie. Macklin doesn't wear a damn helmet. He doesn't even own one. What the hell would it look like if my character wore a damn pussy helmet every damn time I got in a car? Sam, that does it. I don't give a shit what kind of release you want me to sign, I'll sign it. I'm driving my own stunts. Christ, Steve McQueen drove his own stunts and the fans loved it. A helmet, for Christ's sake!'

Sam looked at me, eyebrows raised.

I said, 'Far as I'm concerned you can drive all the stunts you want. Personally I am superstitious about cars that jump off the road for no reason.'

'Forget a release,' Sam said. 'David would never allow it.'

'He's your agent, not mine,' Sean said, standing up. 'I'm calling my agent now, telling him I do my own driving in this movie or I am outta here.' He pushed his chair back and went up the steps of his motorhome, grabbing the bottle of cold wine from the hand of Sam's daughter as he pushed past her.

'Sean,' Sam called after him.

'Let him go, Pussycat,' Shulman said. 'Let him have his little tantrum. And let him do a few drive-bys and slide around on the dirt if he wants to. The stunt-performers' union will kick up a fuss while your lawyers find the clause that says the dangerous stuff will be done by our friend Mr Evers here. Sean's just in a twit because he hasn't been on camera yet.'

'It's not that simple,' Sam said.

'Then make it simple. Di-Di,' he said to the teenager, 'be a good girl and bring us another bottle of that divine liquid, if you would be so kind.' She went.

'You're not shooting any driving scenes this afternoon, are you?' I asked Sam.

Sam looked off into the desert, her long fingers rubbing the bridge of her nose. Her face was flushed from the sun in the morning, and her hair was spiralling out in all directions. She looked fragile, as if this movie might be too much for her, although I knew she was tough. Counting the scenes on her fingers, she said, 'We're shooting Sean's entrance coming out of the garage, Sean in your mirror, your dialogue, you and Sean, and you driving off. So you driving off is the only driving scene and that's in Mel's Mercedes.

'That reminds me. You know what that shit did, Irv?' Sam said, suddenly turning to Shulman. 'Mel's charging five grand a day to Production to use his personal car. For the whole damn shoot. Slipped it right past me. I hope you roll Mel's precious little Mercedes into a ball of tinfoil, Evers. Anyway, we're shooting another pass-by and your first stunt tomorrow afternoon before sunset.'

'While you are shooting Sean, I'll check out the cars. Can you close off a section of the road for me? A mile would be plenty.'

'Just let my AD know when you need some open road and where you'll be and she'll tell our rentacops.'

'Sounds just like a Western,' Shulman said, beaming his wide thin-lipped grin as Sam's daughter came bounding out of Sean's camper with another bottle, letting the door slam behind her. 'Evers here is in charge of the horses.'

'How many screen writers does it take to change a light bulb?' Delilah said to Sam, Irv and me as she put the bottle on the table.

We shrugged.

Sam said, relaxing for the first time, and smiling happily at her daughter, 'And the answer is . . .?'

' "What do you want to change it for?" ' Delilah said.

# chapter seven

'The fuck you doin' in there?'

I pushed my creepy-crawly out from under the car, an upside-down crab. Frank's gloomy face loomed over me.

'Hey, you don't got a card you don't look under the car. Some of these union hardasses, they get the wrong idea, they don't look to see who's under the car, they see the legs sticking out they kick your nuts off. I brought you a cuppa coffee. It's cold out here.'

I sat up and a soft hairy hand held out a Styrofoam cup. 'Not as cold as London,' I said. Which was true. California, seen from under a car in the cold morning desert, was warmer and friendlier than dripping London at high noon in January. California doesn't have cold, dark months. On the other hand, rural California has yet to learn about coffee.

'Tastes like shit, huh?' Frank said, seeing my involuntary grimace.

'It's perfect, Frank. Thank you.'

'My cousin Dino has one a these old Mustangs,' he said, nodding towards the car. 'Calls it Wendy. Whatcha looking for?'

I stood up. 'I don't know. Something. Whoever built this thing did a hell of a good job. Under the skin this car is a NASCAR stocker.'

'What's that supposed to mean?'

'They took an old NASCAR racer, which are about as strong as a car can get this side of a tank, freshened up the bushings and the suspension, dropped a high-performance Chevy V–8 in it, and covered it with a Mustang skin. Doesn't it seem strange to you it doesn't have an electric engine?'

'Not really. Akiri said they didn't want to give any secrets away and they didn't want anybody getting a look at their, whataya call 'em, fuel cells before they launched the car. So they went with a conventional motor. Prop cars are a mess anyway. Most of 'em don't have an engine.'

'It looks solid as a rock to me. Want to take it for a ride?'

'I wouldn't touch it with a stick. Whattareyou, testing it out?'

'Right. Give it a run, see how it runs.'

'You know what Waddell called these things?'

I shrugged no.

'La Puerca Encantada. The Enchanted pig. They was built in Mexico, three of them. That Jap kid, whatsis name, Akiri, was in charge of the deal. Waddell called them Puerca One, Puerca Two, Puerca Three. Said they handled like pigs on ice. So that's it? That's all you gotta do? Check out these cars?'

'That and some lines on camera this afternoon. I'm supposed to be playing Forrest Evers, racing driver, but the lines don't sound right.'

'So don't worry about it.'

'That's easy for you to say. It's me up on the screen saying something stupid.'

'You don't have to. Happens all the time. The actor goes to the director and he says, "What's my motivation here?" And the director tells him some shit like, "Your mother died when you was six and you never had enough to eat when you was a baby so you have this hunger, this sexual hunger." And the actor goes, "I understand that, but I would never say these lines." And the director goes, "Sure you would." And you, the actor says, "It's not in character." And they go back and forth for a while. "Yes, you would," "No, I wouldn't." And the director goes, "So tell me what the character would say." And you tell the director. If you got pull the director says, "OK, let's shoot it that way." Happens all the time, don't worry about it.'

'Watch me again, Sean.'

It had been a long day. I am not a good teacher. What seems as easy to me as picking up a spoon can be as difficult as balancing a dime on a balloon to somebody else. Sean was sitting next to me looking resentful. I said, 'To do a three-sixty turn at a hundred miles an hour, you have to start at the beginning.'

He said, 'Skip the beginning, Forrest. Get to the point.'

Puerca One handled like a Puerca on ice. It wallowed, it bottomed out, it bump-steered. It was slow to turn in and when it did it had terminal understeer, the front end wanting to plough along, straight ahead. But you could allow for all that. With its skinny little 1960s-style tyres it was easy to slide. Sean sat in the passenger seat, arm on the door sill, head thrown way back like James Dean, elaborately relaxed. As if this had nothing to do with him.

I thought he had a picture of himself, arm out the window, one hand on the wheel, spinning the car and carrying on down the road. Which, as his character Macklin was supposed to be an Indy driver, was fine. But first you have to learn how to do all those separate movements while the car is bounding out of control, the tyres screaming, and the mountains whirling around you like an MTV video. 'Just show me, Evers, OK?' he said. 'I can handle it.'

Delighted, I thought, and yanked the wheel down, pushed in the clutch, and pulled up the handbrake. We were doing about 105 and the world whirled around us like the snap on a fairground ride, accompanied by the howl and smoke of four tyres scraping their treads off. Just before halfway around, when the road came sweeping into my vision like a spinning black pointer on a giant sundial, I popped the clutch, let off the handbrake, and as the road swept off the dial stood on the gas, and we were rocketing down the road again, same direction as we had been heading before the spin, a figure-eight of whirling black tyre marks in our wake. I yanked the wheel down again, glancing over to Sean as I pushed in the clutch and yanked up the handbrake.

He was heads up now, a lot of white showing in his deep-set blue eyes. His hands gripping the seat back and the door sill. I brought the car out of its second spin, accelerated hard, and did another snap spin to keep his attention. When I stopped the car there were three evenly spaced black spin marks on the black top over the last mile. Clouds of blue tyre smoke floated harmlessly across the surface of the desert.

'First,' I said, 'you have to learn to control a twenty mile an hour spin. Because if you can't do that, you won't be a driver in a hundred mile an hour spin, you'll be a passenger.' He looked at me and nodded. OK.

*

'Ow,' he said, 'be careful, Forrest.'

'I am being careful,' I said, cinching up the safety belts another notch. They were changing the tyres again and I was out of the car, pulling up the slack in his safety harness. 'You can't do a stunt like this if you're busy trying to sit down. And I don't want you falling out of the car. What happened out there, Sean? I thought you were hungry to learn all this racing car stuff.'

He said, 'Yeah, right. I know. I'm sorry.'

'Sorry about what?'

Sean turned to me, squinting, not from the sun but from thinking. 'She's got me all messed up,' he said. 'We had a really good thing going. I am talking passion, man. I mean OK, she's a little older, but that's fine by me. I liked that. I like her. And I thought it was my idea, making a movie together. Although as soon as I said OK and signed the contract, she says it was her idea. What I was thinking was it would be great, you know? We were serious, spent a lot of time together over the last what, two, three months. Sam had just about moved into my ranch up in the hills, she had a lot of her clothes and stuff there. And Delilah would come up for the weekends from her school. And I thought instead of the way couples usually go in Hollywood, you know one of them goes off on location like London or Africa for six months while the other one stays at home reading scripts and then they hardly know each other any more. Instead of that I thought maybe if we worked together we could get really close. You know like Tom Cruise and his wife, Nicole, you know, Kidman, did *Far and Away* together. I even said, "Hey, let's bring Delilah, she'd be good and it'd be good for her to be with us for more than a weekend for a change." It was the dumbest idea I ever had. 'Cause I'll tell you, the more Sam got into making this movie, the more it's like she doesn't want to know. You know what I'm sayin'?'

'Delilah told me you were giving Sam a hard time.'

'Yeah, well. She was never all that big on me and Sam together. And she kinda likes to twist things around.'

'You weren't exactly helping your cause at lunch with Delilah.'

'Yeah, that was dumb, I guess. I was trying to make Sam jealous, but I think she just doesn't give a shit, whatever I do. You got any idea how I could reach her? Sam, I mean? I'm really all over hurtin', man.'

'You could talk to her.'
'Like how?'

**19. DESERT HIGHWAY. SUNSET.**
**(MUSIC: MACKLIN'S THEME) In the golden late afternoon light, a long shadow runs down the highway in front of the car. MACKLIN is driving JILL's car for the first time with the new electronic engine he has installed and it works. IT WORKS.**

**CU MACKLIN behind the wheel, hair blowing in the wind, radio on (MUSIC UP) exhilarated because he has done it, fixed JILL's Mustang. Made the electronic engine work. Celebrating breaking out of the hell-hole of his garage/welding shop. Celebrating Saturday night coming up and a good chance of a date with JILL. There is no engine sound. The electric engine is nearly silent. We hear the wind and the music. MACKLIN's hand pulls down sharply on the steering-wheel.**

**The car does a 360-degree spin in the road. Continues. Then brakes to a stop. MACKLIN turns the car around and heads towards the sun, towards Velma. The car is outlined against the golden light as if it is sunrise now and JILL and the town of Velma, where Macklin is headed now, is full of promise.**

The wind had picked up and it was fluffing Sam's hair. She was wearing a World War II bomber jacket with the collar up, standing on the mound of earth they had piled up to hide the No. 1 camera from the 'copter, talking to the helicopter in her headset, and looking down the road towards the sun setting behind the western mountains through a little telescope meter. 'We haven't got enough light for a run-through,' she said, brushing a long strand of hair out of her face. 'We've got time for one take and if we're lucky we'll get another one but I doubt it. The light's fading fast.

'Forrest, are you're sure he's OK to do this?' she said. 'You know he's just a kid.'

'We went through six sets of tyres,' I said. 'As long as he keeps it below fifty he'll be fine.'

'Let's go for it,' she said into her headset. 'Soon as you're ready, Sean.'

There was a pause and in the distance we heard the wail of a NASCAR V–8. And I wondered for the umpteenth time why, if this film was supposed to be about electric engines, we were still using the old American V–8s. We saw the chopper first, a hundred feet off the ground, nose down, Billy's legs hanging out the open door, the camera on a mount on the side of the chopper pointing down towards the road.

Sean came by us at, I would guess, around 85–90 mph. The camera swung by to follow him as he headed towards the second unit fifty yards down the road with their two set-ups. He was going too fast, but I thought he might get away with it.

Sean had quick reflexes and once he'd realized he had a lot to learn he learned quickly. By the end of our session, he had worked his way up to two fifty mile an hour spins. The spins weren't as smooth as I would have liked, but they were good enough for a movie stunt. And the difference between a fifty and a ninety mile an hour spin, I told myself, is one of degree. Anyway, I thought, as the car began to spin, he was just a kid showing off, trying to get her attention the way kids do, and he'd probably be fine.

But the car didn't spin. The old yellow Mustang convertible seemed to falter for a moment, then kneel down as the front wheel folded under and the car levered itself up into the air, rolling.

It came down hard on the passenger side, bouncing the car up into the air again, turning in the air and crashing down on the road, with the crash and scrape of metal on pavement and breaking glass. The car bounced up in the air and began to roll over and over, flinging shattered fibreglass from its replica body, banging into the pavement and bouncing up again. There was nothing to stop the car as it smashed itself into a cigar shape rolling down the black top, over and over and for a while it didn't appear to slow down, flinging its doors open, smashing them flat. At one horrifying peak, Sean's arm was flung up high and it looked like he was waving like a bronco buster. Waving goodbye.

# chapter eight

The dot on the road grew into a silver Mercedes convertible, top down, going fast, suddenly braking hard, smoke from the tyres, turning fast right into a faded country gas station and sliding to a stop in front of the pumps in a cloud of dust. The cloud of dust floated away and Sean walked out of his garage. The Mercedes driver, green silk shirt, expensive round dark sunglasses, looked in his door mirror and Sean loomed larger than life, dirty and tired.

I looked from the mirror and turned in my seat to look at Sean, and a smile spread across my craggy face. I said, 'You look a hell of a lot like a race driver I used to know called Macklin.' I stretched my hand out to Sean's character, Macklin.

Macklin wiped his hands on a dirty rag and said, 'I don't want to be rude, Forrest, but you don't want to get your hands dirty.'

I take my sunglasses off with my outstretched hand to smooth over the awkwardness of a refused handshake and look at Macklin. 'The last time I saw you, Mac, the Indy rescue crew were wheeling you into an ambulance on Turn Two. I heard you were six months in the hospital. Are you OK?'

'Can't you tell? I'm on top of the fuckin' world. What can I do for you?'

I look away down the highway, then back at Sean. I put my sunglasses back on and say, 'Fill it up.'

The TV screen went blank. David Allen was leaning back in his black leather chair behind his desk, holding his chin. In the old days, the lions of Hollywood decorated their vast offices as if they were baronial dens. Acres of carpet, stained-glass gothic windows, desks the size of swimming pools, that kind of thing. David's was the office of a businessman. Small computer monitors told him their stories in numbers. Three telephones waited for him to speak. Behind him were the trophies of his trade, photographs of David with the Japanese Prime Minister, laughing with the President, with his arm around Virgin on the sound stage of *Second Coming*, and a picture of Sam that looked as if it had been taken last week. There was an original Monet, two Oscars and a Giacometti bronze sculpture. So it was richer than the office of your average corporate Titan, but it wasn't that different either. The overall colour was beige.

David was at home here, in his pin-stripe suit. His face was sleek, smooth, well fed. Only a vein at his left temple just under the careful casual haircut, blue and pulsing, showed that the agent called the most powerful man in Hollywood might be under any stress. 'That's not the way it was written, is it, Forrest?' he said quietly.

'I didn't change it much,' I said, 'But the way it was written wasn't what I would have said.'

'The bit with the sunglasses your idea too?'

'They were in the script,' Sam said, 'but we thought having Evers put them back on emphasized the distance between Sean and Forrest.'

'I like it,' David said. 'It's got a nice feel to it. I have to admit you look good, Evers. Just right. You never really know, do you, till you see the footage. Like Zanuck killed his career trying to put his bimbos on the screen. The screen just doesn't give a shit who your rabbi is. I still can't tell who she is going to put her silver arms around and who she is going to kick in the ass. But you'll be all right, Evers. You'll be just fine,' he said, a little secret smile putting a dimple in his cheeks. 'Have any of you spoken to Sean?'

'I called the hospital and they said he came out of the operation OK, but that he really wouldn't be awake until this afternoon.' Sam said, 'I was up most of the night with the video transfer and editing the bit you've just seen.' Sam was standing behind the couch where I was sitting with Akiri, her long white hands with the perfect manicured nails on the black leather. She looked fresh as a daisy, her blonde hair tied back with a green neckerchief.

'Well GET TO HIM, GODDAMMIT. Shower him with candy and kisses and let him know we all love him. Do whatever the hell it takes. I took a call at home this morning from Jo Don Morton to tell me his client has twenty-seven stitches in his face and Jo Don as his manager is advising him to sue us for several hundred million in lost earnings because his face is going to look like a baseball. No hard feelings.'

'He signed a release,' Akiri said.

'I've seen it. If he can prove your car was at fault, you could find yourself exposed to negligence.'

'Shit,' Akiri said. 'This is not exactly the publicity we were looking for.'

'You looked at the car, Forrest,' David said.

'Before and after the crash. It looked good to me. Solid as a rock. I think Sean was going about ninety when the car rolled. Which is as fast as I was going when I did the same spin. Watching it happen, it looked like something broke, a wheel, the suspension, the right front tyre losing air, it could have been any number of things. After the crash everything was broken and I couldn't tell you what went first. The wheels were old.'

'They were authentic,' Akiri said, 'the kind of mag wheels put on their cars in the seventies.'

'And aluminum gets brittle,' I said. 'But I don't think anybody is going to be able to say for sure whether something broke before or during that crash.'

'Well thank God for small favours,' David said, getting up and walking slowly, black tassel loafers on the wide expanse of his pale blue carpet, crossing the room to stare out at the city, the crooked blue vein at his temple pulsing. In the smog, the distant buildings of downtown Los Angeles looked faint, brown ghosts of the old glitter town. As if the real world was inside David Allen's office and the city outside was make-believe. 'The question is, how do we replace Sean? Is that all the footage you have of him, Sam?'

'Just what you saw. There's about eight takes. And of course, Sean's crash. We've got all that on film but I didn't transfer it.'

'What would it cost to wind up production now?' David said.

'Don't even think about it,' Akiri said. 'I don't care what it costs, we have to make this film work.'

The door flew open and Virgin was saying, '. . . or Big Daddy will have your ass, won't he, Sweetie? Hi everybody.' Virgin was wearing a chrome-yellow halter top, tight, elaborately ripped blue jeans, and yellow platform shoes with bananas and cherries piled on the toes. She looked like a tropical bird come to nest with the sparrows. I stood up and we hugged for a while. Virgin puts a lot into a hug. Along with heavy perfume she smelled of the cigarettes and weed of the recording studio. 'So what are you going to do with my money? I had breakfast with Sean this morning.'

She flopped down on the sofa where I'd been.

There was a pause. 'And . . .' Sam said.

'And he had a syringe full of Darvon and I had a disgusting cup of coffee.'

'So he wasn't conscious,' David said.

'You are all fucking heart, David. You know I hope he sues you so I can see if you ever change expression. Who are you getting to replace him?'

'We were just coming to that,' Sam said, sitting on David's desk, crossing her long legs. The star taking centre stage. 'I'll bet you have a list, don't you, David.'

'I have a list of who we can't get,' he said, going over to his desk and reaching around Sam to pick up a sheet of paper. 'Gere is committed until fall next year, so's Dillon. Tom Cruise is only doing his own projects now.'

'Gibson, he's got that battered look,' Sam said.

'He's filming in Africa,' David said. 'And Nolte's put on too much weight.'

'The buttered look,' Virgin said. 'What about that guy, what's his name, does the DJ in *Northern Exposure*?'

'He's doing commercials for Chrysler,' Akiri said. 'We can't have him in a Hozuki film. We really got a break with Sean because he was willing to forgo script approval. Any of these guys, they are not only going to cost a bunch of the gross, they're going to want control of the project, take it away from us.'

'I don't think you are going to find a lot of actors eager to leap in that car now that it's crashed twice. Almost killed two guys,' Virgin said. 'How about you, Sweetie? Are you eager to drive that thing?'

'Compared to driving a Formula One car on a race track,' I said, 'it's a bank vault. I've always said I'm happy to drive the stunts.' Which was true, I'd said that. Happiness for me was getting the sponsorship. I wasn't relaxed about driving the Puercas but no pain no gain, as they say in California.

'I think we might go beyond that,' David said. He walked over to his desk and sat down in the big black leather chair. Command position. 'I liked what I saw this morning. Virgin was right about our friend here. Forrest has a real presence on the screen. Would you consider Forrest?'

'Consider him what?' Sam said. 'This is my first film, David. Don't lumber me with a goddamn amateur. Besides, who the hell ever heard of Forrest Evers?'

'Oh, Jesus,' Akiri said. 'Outside of Hollywood, everybody. In Japan, Europe, Australia, and South America, according to our market surveys, more people have heard of Forrest than heard of Sean. We could do a promotion: "A new car and a new star." I like it.'

'You just like him because he's cheap,' Sam said to David.

'And worth every penny,' I said, getting no reaction.

'Look, David,' Sam said, getting red in the face, 'you liked him in that footage you saw this morning because he's playing himself, driving up in a flash car and driving off again. Well, you know as well as I do it's one thing to play yourself and another to play another character. Ask Virgin.'

'Sure, ask me. I'm always happy to give lessons. You got a little point there, Sam. But it's not the big point. The big point is, once you and Evers are on the screen together how is that gonna work? If it looks like there's something going on between you, then it works. If it doesn't, it doesn't and we go beat the bushes for some fresh talent. Although I got to tell you, David, if Evers can't strike a few sparks off little Miss Trisket here, I'd like to meet the man who can.'

'Thanks for the endorsement, Virg,' I said, 'but Sam's right. I don't know about playing a role or whatever you call it. On the other hand, Macklin isn't that far from me. I've driven at Indy and I crashed there, maybe not as bad as Macklin but it was a hit. And I was out of racing for over a year. So I know what it's like to be on the outside, looking in.'

'Oh, Christ, now he wants to be a movie star. It would change everything,' Sam said. 'Sean has this fantastic appeal to teenagers, fan clubs, the works. I mean you can talk all you want about Forrest being big in Japan and Timbuktu, but if we don't make it with the kids here, we don't make it. You'd have to rewrite the whole role for him.'

'So rewrite it,' Akiri said. 'Teenagers don't buy new cars. I like the idea of making a more adult movie. We're budgeted $38 million advertising and promotion for *Juice*. That's enough to make anybody famous.'

Sam was red in the face, taking deep breaths. I went over to her, inches away and said quietly, 'From what I've seen, acting in movies is boring, repetitious, tedious work. And movie stars, from what I have seen, are some of the most miserable, selfish, paranoic people on earth.' I gave her a nice crooked Evers grin. 'So no, Sam, I don't want to be a movie star. But I do think that if I had been doing my job, Sean never would have been driving that stunt in the first place. And if I had taught him better (*a*) he wouldn't have gone that fast and (*b*) if he had gone that fast he would have known how to handle it. So I feel some responsibility. And if I can help I will. Just don't make it any harder than it is.'

'Don't take your seat belt off, Evers. There's more to acting in a movie than you will ever know. And if it is such nasty work, what the hell do you want to do it for?'

'For you,' I said.

'Right,' said David. 'Let's see a test. What about the first love scene in the script, Sam? The time when Jill's little girl, Candy, sees them making love in the schoolroom?' He consulted a paper on his desk. 'The set is built, isn't it? If you shot that on tape tomorrow morning we could look at it in the afternoon. If it works, we'll start telling the world we have a new star. If it doesn't . . .'

'It'll work,' I said.

'It has to,' Akiri said, 'it just has to.'

'Nothing *has* to work,' Sam said. 'The only reason *anything* ever works in film is the script is brilliant, the director's brilliant, the actors are brilliant, everybody works their asses off, and a trainload of good luck falls out of the sky. I'll do it on one condition, Evers.'

I was standing inches away from her. Could feel Sam's breath on my face. And the heat of her anger. She was trapped in a corner, and furious. 'Which is?' I said.

'You do *exactly* what I say.'

# chapter nine

The next morning, as alarms and clock radios were dragging Angelinos out of their sleep, Sam and I were at the bottom of a cavern big enough to park a 747. Stage 6 was empty except for the schoolroom set where we slouched in canvas chairs, a floor-lamp making a pool of light between us. There were rows of desks, a blackboard, lights, cables, camera dollies, and the two of us reading through our lines. Sam was helping me to get a feel for my character and rehearsing before the crew showed up to set up for shooting.

Sam looked as sweet as strawberry ice-cream in her Jill outfit, a red clingy Rayon dress with yellow and green birds and white running shoes with white cotton socks. Hollywood's version of what a star would wear if she was an off-beat schoolteacher in the south-west. The dress was loose on Sam, and under her wispy blonde hair Sam's eyes had that sadness I'd noticed on the first day. Some memory or maybe just the way her green eyes were set.

'You've got to put a little more heart into it, Forrest,' she said. 'Flip through the script, read some random lines.'

I turned pages and read, 'If you'd take a look outside this goddamn little town just once, you'd see what a piss-ass dead-end town Velma is.'

Sam put down her script. 'Forrest, you are not reading a weather report, this is supposed to be a person, talking. With feeling. Look, don't try to *act* in front of the camera because you don't know how. OK? Just relax and be yourself and you might get away with it. Try another line.'

I tried another line and Sam said, 'Is something bothering you?'

Lots of things were bothering me. I picked the top of the list. 'Sean asked about you,' I said.

'Oh, how is he?' she said, looking away, sounding guilty.

'He said he misses you.'

'That's not what I asked.'

Why, I asked myself not for the first time, was I attracted to this woman? Why did I care what she thought? I have been in too many hospitals, walked down too many wide shining linoleum corridors with their doors gaping open to the still and the dying on display, and I have seen too many friends twisted and bleeding to have much sympathy for excuses about not having enough time. If you care there is always plenty of time. 'It's what he asked,' I said. 'He wanted to know how you are.'

Sam looked annoyed, waving him away with her hand.

'I told him you are just dandy,' I said.

'Forrest, look. I'm sorry, I really am. I thought I was in love with Sean and maybe I was. Maybe I'll see him tomorrow. I just don't think I could face seeing him today when he's so badly hurt. I'd probably say something dumb like it's my fault. He was trying to impress me, wasn't he?' She looked at me as if she was the bright girl in the class who had come up with the right answer. She said, 'We have this screen test of yours to do for David. Do you mind if we just read the lines?'

'Something's wrong with this script,' I said. 'It doesn't sound right to me.'

'Your first screen test and you're acting like you're Dustin Hoffman.' She laughed and stretched in her canvas-back chair. 'Don't worry about the script. This is just a test, dummy. Just try doing it the way it's written. You are a racing driver out of water, if you know what I mean. And you are in love with Jill. Try to put a little longing, maybe a touch of frustration, in your voice, give it an edge. Can you do that?'

'Let me have another look at it,' I said, stalling for time. Agreeing to act in *Juice* had been easy. Nothing to it. It even seemed like the gallant thing to do. Big, strong Forrest Evers steps on stage and fills the frame with charm or action if that's what they wanted. Any idiot could do it, I thought. Look at Schwarzenegger. Now I realized that Sam was right. It was one thing being myself, driving into a gas station. Playing somebody else was something else. I hadn't any idea of what to do. I looked down at the script.

**34. EXTERIOR SCHOOL. EARLY EVENING.**

**The parking lot is almost empty as MACKLIN drives in and parks JILL'S car. He hesitates for a moment, then bolts out of the car, slamming the door behind him, and runs across the grass to the side door of the one-story brick building.**

**35. JILL'S CLASSROOM**

**The light from the afternoon sun floods through the windows onto the empty desks and aisles. JILL sits at her desk in the front of the room, grading papers. The clock on the wall says 5:39 and the room is still.**

**MACKLIN opens the door and it bangs against the wall. JILL looks up, gives him a half smile, and goes back to her work.**

**JILL**

**You're early.**

**MACKLIN**

**Walking into the room slowly, on strange turf. His hair is combed and he is spruced up. The short sleeves on his fresh white shirt are turned up like cuffs.**

**I didn't think you'd mind.**

**He stands behind her, looks over her shoulder.**

**Why don't you take this stuff home? It's nice out now.**

**JILL**

**Not looking up.**

**I like to keep my schoolwork in the school. So I never lose anything and I know right where it is. And there are no distractions.**

**MACKLIN**

**Putting his hand on her shoulder, bending down.**

**I have a surprise for you.**

JILL

Annoyed at his touch.

Are you going to let me finish this?

MACKLIN

Your car is outside.

JILL

You fixed it? It works?

MACKLIN

Better than ever. Fixed it so that old heap of yours will blow the doors off of Porsches.

She smiles at him, keeps on working.

That's it? That's all you're gonna do?

She stops. Looks up at him.

JILL

What did you expect? You know I can't possibly pay you.

MACKLIN

Oh, I thought you'd probably throw your body at me in gratitude.

JILL gives him a look. She's heard this before. She goes back to her papers. MACKLIN, in frustration, lifts her out of her chair, and kisses her. He puts a hand on her breast. She breaks free, and slaps him hard across the mouth. He lets her go and she slumps back against the desk, scattering the neatly piled stacks of papers. He fakes a slap across her cheek and it turns into a caress. There are tears in her eyes.

I'm sorry, Jill. I thought you'd be glad to see me.

JILL

I was. I am. But not here. Not now. I have things to do.

**MACKLIN**
**Everything in its place. Where's Candy?**

**JILL starts gathering up the papers that have been knocked off the desk. MACKLIN bends down to help her.**

**JILL**
**She went home with Rudy Huber. I've got to pick her up in an hour.**
**She reaches out a hand to touch his cheek.**
**I'm sorry I hit you, Macklin. You scared me.**

**Their faces are close. He touches her cheek and they kiss. JILL pulls back and goes back to picking up the scattered papers. Then she looks at MACKLIN again and lets her papers drop and they kiss again. They stand up embracing each other, still kissing. They pull back as JILL puts her hands on MACKLIN's chest, half come on, half pushing away.**

**MACKLIN**
**What's that?**

**JILL**
**You'll see.**

**MACKLIN**
**No, I mean I thought I saw something in the window.**

**The camera follows MACKLIN's line of sight out the school window to track into the tree just outside the window. Behind the leaves, CANDY is watching.**

**JILL (Voice over)**
**Pay attention to the teacher.**

I put the script down and Sam said, 'So what's your problem, Evers?'

'Macklin seems like kind of an oaf.'

'He is an oaf.'

'Then why does Jill find him attractive?'

'Because he has a good heart and he needs her. She wants to be needed. Let's run through it, see how it goes.'

'Just the interior scene?'

'There are moments, Evers, when I think you have the perfect lack of intelligence for the part.'

We went through it, my coming in the door, Jill at her desk. Under that dark red Rayon dress she moved with an easy grace. I had Macklin's cowboy boots on and I clumped around, bumping into the desk, into Jill and forgot my lines. A goose out of water.

'Put yourself into it, Forrest,' Sam said. 'You are lonely and you are hopelessly in love with a beautiful woman. You have been working for weeks on this car for her. You have been thinking of almost nothing else but her for weeks and now you are alone with her in an empty building and she has slapped you hard and now she has just told you she is glad to see you. You can't act the part, you have to be Macklin. Have to be. 'Cause, in the close-ups the way your eyes move give you away. You can't fake it. If you are somebody you won't have to think about it. Let's take it from where I've just said I'm sorry I slapped you.'

We got down on the floor, squatting awkwardly, picking up scattered papers. And we kissed. I was Macklin and I reached out for Jill, touching her cheek, bringing her to me.

Kissing Jill brought a sea-change to that large open chilly space. Her mouth was soft and warm, I was in a small haze of perfume, and when we stood up I held her tight against me, her green eyes wide with surprise, kissing her, kissing that lovely deft curl of her upper lip again and bending her back and I gently held the soft wobble of her breast and she slapped me. Hard enough on the mouth to draw blood.

There was a pause.

'What's the matter, Evers.'

'Slapping me isn't in the script.'

'Right. You had your tongue halfway down my throat and you grabbed me and that wasn't in the script either.'

'I thought it was.'

'It was in the scene we just did before this one. Or did you forget? Anyway I thought you were improvising so I improvised what Jill would have done. If you are going to change the script you'll have to learn to take what comes. Play it the way it happens, Evers. You are an actor. ACT TOR.'

'Sometimes it's hard to tell the difference.'

'Well, work on it.'

'Hard to tell the difference, I mean, between the actress and the woman.'

'Forget the woman, Forrest. She'll be right back after this film is finished. What's that?' In the background there was a scuffling noise and Delilah came out from a distant wall, walking towards us. 'Come on, Di-Di, honey,' Sam said, her voice going down an octave, 'I just have time to get you to school before we have to do this damn scene.'

Later that morning, after we had shot the second kiss scene for the third time Sam held on to me for an extra beat, her breath warm on my neck, her hand on the middle of my back. 'I'll give you another reason why Jill is attracted to the oaf,' she said. 'It's physical. She's physically attracted to him.' She pulled back, started to walk away to look at the scene on the monitor. Then she stopped and said quietly to me, 'Are all racing drivers built like you?'

We finished shooting just before noon. Sam went into an Olympic editing studio and I went back to see Sean. His hospital room was a small forest of flowers, plants and get well cards. Which I thought was especially impressive since his accident hadn't appeared in the papers yet. Sean was sitting up, drinking some brown drool through a plastic straw for lunch.

'Sure you won't have some, Forrest?' he said, a blot of the stuff soaking into his white hospital frock. 'It's good for your bowels.'

'It looks like it already made the trip.'

He weakly flipped his straw at me, giving me plenty of time to duck. A small shower of brown goo pellets arced across the room and went splat on the wall. 'Virgin was a bunch of laughs this morning. At least that's what the nurse said. I didn't wake up for her performance. But it's great to hear you insult my lunch, you dumb fuck.'

'How are you feeling?'

'Like I was chewed on by a pack of dogs. Did you see her? What'd she say?'

'She said she used to think she was in love with you, now she doesn't think she is any more. She said maybe she'll come tomorrow.'

He closed his eyes for a moment. 'If she can work it into her schedule. What else did she say?'

'She says she doesn't think I'm a good enough actor to take your place.'

'What the fuck is that? You can't take my place, I got a contract.'

'I wanted to tell you before you heard it from somebody else. What they say is because the movie is tied to the launch of the car, they don't want to hold up production while your face heals.'

'So write it into the script. It's only six stitches.'

'David thinks you're stitched up like a baseball.'

'Yeah, well, you can see for yourself. A lump on the back of my head and three stitches on my forehead and three on my chin. It's just a concussion, a lump on the head. You have to realize everybody exaggerates around here. Discount everything everybody says by a hundred and ten per cent. But listen, this is not a big deal. The doctors say a few days' rest and I'll be OK. A couple of stitches could make me look macho. They can write it in the script. Say I'm still recovering from the Indy crash. It could work. Christ, I can do it. I'll sue their fucking asses off.' He sank back on the bed, exhausted. 'Are you gonna do it?'

'Depends on the screen test. Do you remember anything about your crash? What happened? I thought you were doing around ninety.'

'Something like that. It felt like something broke. I didn't think that sonofabitch was ever going to stop rolling. How do I look?' he said, obviously worried. There was a hand mirror on the nightstand alongside his water glass.

'You look like you've been in a car wreck.'

'No shit. So you're gonna do it?'

'What do you think about it?'

'Jesus, she is a ballbreaker.'

'I don't think it's Sam's choice.'

'Tell you the truth, Evers, it's been a while since making a movie with little miss Frosty Freeze sounded like a good idea. My agent was in here this morning with three fucking lawyers and they are all going that release I signed holds me responsible if production is held up. So what they are saying is I could be out around two hundred thousand a day. I'll threaten to sue their asses off for ruining my face, they'll buy out my contract, I'll hang on to a piece of the gross and wish you good luck. I thought I was gonna make it.'

'Not at ninety miles an hour,' I said. 'You have to work up to it.'

'I was working up to it. Tell you what, you teach me how to drive, Evers, I'll teach you how to be an actor. Everybody thinks they know how to act, but you have to work up to it.'

'After this morning's screen test, I don't think I'm going to have to worry about acting.'

'It didn't go good?'

'It didn't go at all. Sam said I had the emotional range of a piano leg.'

'Yeah, well, you never know until you see the footage. You can go a long way underplaying. Did you ever watch Robert Stack in those old Eliot Ness things on TV? All he ever did was look left and right, never changed expression in sixty-five shows. Don't let it bother you.'

'Does it bother you that nobody seems to care that these damn cars are crashing?'

'Yeah, it bothers me, but it doesn't surprise me. Nobody else gives a shit. A movie is a machine for making money, Evers. And if they get that part of it to work they don't give a fuck about the rest. Sure you wouldn't like some shit for lunch?' he said, offering me the container. 'It's the first step towards being a real actor.'

# chapter ten

Anyplace else in America and it would have been a bumpy back road. But this little two-lane black top was bouncing up into the hills of Bel Air, a pathway to the stars, twisting back and forth, speed limit twenty-five. Not that the stars live in Bel Air any more. Stars live in Utah, Hampstead, Rimini; stars live wherever they damn well please. But the real power still lives in the castles in Bel Air.

As I drove higher, the houses grew wings, columns, and more stories. Single tennis courts gave way to two- and three-court compounds and swimming-pools grew to Olympic size. Gardeners multiplied into small armies of men and women in brown uniforms, cutting, pruning, watering, and mowing. Above the mere millionaire line, miniature deer peered out suspiciously from behind chain-link fences decorated with video cameras and DANGER HIGH VOLTAGE signs.

At the top of the hill high over the Los Angeles basin, with a stunning view of the smog, David's sprawling mock-Tudor brick compound was announced by 2123 on the mailbox. I stopped at the gate, the voice in the little squawk box said, 'Good evening, Mr Evers,' the heavy wooden gates slid open on rollers, and I drove down into the brick-paved courtyard just as Sam was getting out of her little burgundy Porsche cabriolet. The courtyard looked like it had been designed for coaches, carriages, and fox hunters. A daffodil Rolls-Royce convertible, two Ferraris, and a Porsche Speedster looked right at home. I didn't give the cars a second glance. Sam, legs swinging out of the Porsche, was in her power suit, the modern businesswoman version of the modern business suit; no shoulder-pads, softly cut, dark grey pinstripe CEO jacket, making her look small, frail, and wealthy beyond words, with a short tight grey pinstripe skirt showing shapely business-woman leg. And a soft ivory strictly business silk blouse unbuttoned to the third button. If businessmen had to wear what women wear, I thought, there wouldn't be any businessmen. On Sam, the power suit was a weapon. You suspected that whatever businessman she was talking business with didn't have a chance. Her soft, innocent face and those deep-set green eyes could destroy your concentration with a single glance.

'Lunch,' she explained, 'with a producer. Did you talk to David?'

'No, only to God.'

'There's hope for you, Evers,' she said, taking my arm. 'Did you know this was Michael Landon's house?' No, I didn't know.

The front door opened as we went up the front steps and a maid who looked like she lifted weightlifters led us through a vast library lined to the ceiling with leather-bound books and furnished in a Hollywood decorator's version of an English gentleman's club. Unlike the real English gentleman's club, there were no holes in the carpet and the brightly lit room was unlittered with cigarette ash, dirty tea cups, smudged whisky glasses, or balding English gents in rumpled suits. None of the green leather sofas and chairs looked as if they had ever suffered the indignity of being sat on. The coffee tables and the end tables had photos of Virgin, of Sam, Dennis Quaid, Julia Roberts, and Richard Gere, all smiling truly sincere smiles, all with truly sincere inscriptions to David. The maid waved us through the open french doors and we stepped out on to the veranda and walked across the lawn to the pool. At 6 p.m. the sun was setting somewhere behind the smog, but there was still enough heat in the air to make me glad I wasn't in freezing England. The pool was deep blue and sparkling. Akiri waved from the chrome ladder, climbing out of the water and grabbing a towel. David sat in his tennis shorts at a table talking to another tennis player who was doing the listening.

'There they are,' David said, standing up. 'Sam, you know Ron Radnor, Executive Vice-Chairman and Director of Production at Olympic Studios.' Radnor nodded glumly. He was about thirty-eight, I guessed, his face pockmarked from teenage eruptions, his thin nose dripping sweat from the middle of his long thin face. Bushy eyebrows over red-rimmed brown eyes. Five o'clock shadow like Richard Nixon. In his yellow tennis shirt and blue tennis shorts he looked like a financial officer from General Motors on a ten-minute holiday. 'And this is Forrest Evers,' David continued, 'whom I've just been bragging about.'

Radnor gave me a quickee imitation smile and said, 'If you are so famous, how come I never heard of you?'

'Maybe you lead a sheltered life.'

'Christ, maybe I do. Where was I when the agents started winning tennis? Couple of years ago, the only person an agent ever beat in tennis was another agent.'

David looked cool and relaxed, a flip of the hand indicating empty chairs. 'It's what makes power worth having, Ron. You never have to lose.'

'Maybe you don't have to,' Radnor said, wiping the sweat from his face with a small white towel, 'but Jesus Christ, David, we are one day into production and you are four days behind schedule and you got a star in the hospital with his face cut up and his lawyers screaming negligence. I am looking at what could be a potential total loss here. I got a lot of concerns on this project, David.' Radnor's voice was soft and confidential and if he hadn't kept dabbing at his face with the towel you might have thought he was relaxed.

'Comes with your territory, doesn't it, Ron? If you weren't worried you wouldn't have anything to do. Would anybody like a drink?' A young Eurasian woman in a T-shirt and jeans stood quietly behind David. The T-shirt said JUST ASK in small letters above her left breast. There was a pause and David said 'Just some ice and water, Marie, if you would, please. Unless our friend Mr Evers would like a gin and tonic, say?'

'Water's fine,' I lied. I would have liked a gin and tonic, but I don't drink. Not at all. I considered a long tall frosty gin and tonic and the clean taste rinsing away the grit and salt of the day and said nothing. I would be driving in two and a half weeks and the first drink would be delicious, followed by the second because what the hell, one more wasn't going to do anybody any harm. And three wouldn't be nearly enough. In the year after my accident at Monza, when I had nothing better to do, I damn near drowned in gin and tonics. Until one morning after a jolly night I saw my bloated face in the mirror. Not waving, drowning. Bite thy lip, Evers, enjoy the French industrial well water.

'I'll have a large gin and tonic,' Akiri said sitting down, his hair glistening from his swim. 'Put it on my bill.'

Nobody paid him any attention.

Ron twisted the towel in his hands. 'OK, we knew going into this we were gonna get some flak. But this is hard and the fuckers are just warming up. The automobile and oil guys in Washington are already going around Congress making presentations about this Hozuki putting a million out of work. They own enough of the press to give us a rough ride when *Juice* gets reviewed.'

'As you say, we knew that going in,' David said. 'And you know how we counter that. Every time they say Jap invasion, we say, "Think global. Think of the world we live in. A new technology that will provide millions of new jobs worldwide. Cleaner air for all of us. Save our oil for heat and defence. Eighty per cent of content of EVIA is sourced from North America. EVIA is a non-polluting alternative to burning our precious oil." If you have trouble connecting the sentences, Ron, ask Akiri. He's got the script. We knew they'd come after us.'

'Yeah, we knew it and they are doing it. And maybe they could screw us up in production with the Teamsters, some hired guys, you never know. But fuck, David, we haven't even gotten started and we are in shit up to our ears.' Radnor was saying this quietly, as if he was ordering soup. He looked over at Sam, considering her. 'We took a flyer on Sam as director.'

'I wouldn't have let you have her if you hadn't, Ron. So what is your concern? Replacing Sean with Forrest?'

Radnor looked away from Sam and over to me. He made a face. 'Guy has never been in anything, never had any training, knows fuck all about making a movie, nobody knows him, and you want an extra point and a half out of the gross for him. Other than that I love him; he's perfect.'

'Well, thank you, Ronnie,' I said, 'for your support.' I didn't like being discussed as if I wasn't there. It gave me some insight into why actors suffer from permanent insecurity. You are your image and your image could disappear like a face from a mirror.

But I wasn't an actor, I was just a driver who is used to rushing into blind corners. 'Are you always this unpleasant or is this just for me?'

'Hey, I don't mean anything personal, Evers. You got to appreciate what is happening to you here. There's at least a couple of hundred old folks' homes in this town full of old crocks teetering on the edge of their grave and they are all still saying, "I'm gonna make it big in movies."

'Plus you got several thousand good-looking guys down in that valley' – he waved over his shoulder toward the smog – 'trained, qualified, and dying to play a part like yours. OK, Garner was a truck driver. And David Niven's claim to fame was he was Errol Flynn's room-mate. Now you gotta have a Kirk Douglas or a Donald Sutherland for a daddy and ten years of drama school for a start in this town. So yeah, I want a professional, can you blame me? I've got my ass on the line.'

'Not a pretty sight,' Sam said, giving him her nice little girl smile.

David watched a tall frosty glass of water descending down from overhead and placed carefully in front of him by a manicured cinnamon hand. He moved the glass a half an inch to his left. 'Thank you, Marie,' he said, not looking up. 'You saw the tape.'

'So what's a tape tell me?' Ron said putting his elbows on the table, leaning forward with a drop of sweat hanging from the end of his nose. 'I'm a businessman. What's he been in? Who's heard of him? Gimme some facts, something I can go on. You haven't got enough problems with *Juice*, you gotta throw this turkey into the middle of it?'

'Ron,' Sam started, leaning forward.

Before she could say another word, David's hand, resting on the table top, raised two fingertips a half an inch and she stopped.

'The tape from this morning's test,' David said, turning back to Ron, 'if you knew anything about the cinema, and you don't, is sensational. But I don't expect you to see that, Ron. All I want you to do is remember the one word that sold you on *Juice* when I pitched it to you ten months ago.'

'I remember two words, Sam Miles and Sean Finlay. Now you got half of that.'

'The word that sold you on *Juice*, Ron was "guaranteed". Olympic are guaranteed any and all their losses if the picture doesn't make its money back minus interest and Hozuki's expenses. Guaranteed, by Hozuki.'

'Yeah, guaranteed after expenses. So that's not even break even and break even is a loss as far as I am concerned. This is seventy-five per cent our money and I don't want to lose it on a director that never directed and an actor that never acted. And I am not all that relaxed about that Hozuki guarantee. Their stock is not doin' so good.'

'Guaranteed, Ron, is guaranteed. Your ass is guaranteed.'

'So you liked the tape,' Sam said to David, brightening up.

'It's so damn good I wish you'd shot it on film. I can't tell if the two of you hate each other or love each other but it is hot,' he said with his cool trace of a British accent. 'If you can keep that intensity we will be fine. You are a little awkward on camera, Evers. Kinda the way Jimmy Stewart and John Wayne seemed to be. A kinda, aw shucks, embarrassed to be on the screen. Great quality for a romantic lead. Makes you look genuine and vulnerable. Don't lose it.'

'Don't do this to me, David,' Sam said. 'Just because I made him look good, don't lumber me with a goddamn mechanic. Believe me, Forrest doesn't know where the camera is or what his lines are.'

Akiri said, 'Well, I didn't know he didn't know his lines. I'm not really interested in the process, just give me the bottom line. And the bottom line is Forrest looked great. And he's not a mechanic, Sam, he's a hell of a Formula One driver. And I like the way that folds into introducing a new car. Kind of an extra endorsement. My father is going to love it. There's a lot of PR potential here.'

David took a sip of ice water, considering. 'Who else would you suggest, then, Sam? You shot the thing, edited it this morning. Are you really telling me you don't think you can make *Juice* work after that slap scene? That slap scene is one of the best things you ever directed.'

'Isn't that a clever agent,' Sam said to me. 'He makes it sound as if I've been shooting for years.' She pushed her chair back and stood up. 'At that point I was *glad* to hit him, David. Of course I can make it work. I can make anything *work*. But that's not the point, is it? Evers can't carry the film. I mean if you are going to make me take him then we have to talk about his role. Right now all the emphasis is on him. What he thinks, whether he is going to be a fucking man. Which is why Sean was so perfect for the part. Sean's a twenty-five-year-old teenager. I think we have another film here, David, a much better film.'

'You aren't seriously considering changing the script?' Ron said, glaring at Sam. 'We've already costed and scheduled—'

'First of all if I have to take him, then let's not pretend he's an actor, for God's sake, because believe me he's not.'

'Never said I was,' I said. They looked at me as if I was the uninvited guest.

Sam went on after treating me to a flicker of annoyance. 'We ought to change Evers' part from a simple country boy, which he is not, to maybe a dropout all-American, more like a young Kurt Russell. Something close enough to himself so he doesn't have to reach. And we have to shift the emphasis of the story from him to Jill.'

'Wouldn't that make it into a woman's film?' Ron said.

Sam turned to face him as if she just noticed he was there. 'What's wrong with that? A woman on her own with two children; one of them is the guy she lives with. God knows, it's a common enough story.' Sam gave David a little go screw yourself smile. 'I'm not talking about a complete rewrite, just shift the emphasis.'

'Shift the emphasis to you, in other words,' Ron said.

'We have a lot of research that says more women are going to buy EVIA than men,' Akiri said, getting up and pacing with his drink in his hand. The marketing man thinking on his feet. 'They have less ego wrapped up in their cars. More likely to see the car as an appliance.'

'That's what really worries me,' Ron said.

'Making a woman's film worries you?' Sam said, lining up her arguments.

'What worries me is that damned car keeps trying to kill whoever drives the sonofabitch.'

'Well, I'm glad we agree on something, Ronnie,' I said.

# chapter eleven

It was that cold and velvet time just before dawn in the desert when the sun glowed behind the dry mountains to the east and the black highway coming down in a straight line from the mountains held puddles of red and orange light reflected from the sky.

Looking west, in the other direction, the road was less poetic. Just another black top running nonstop through a wide place in the road called Velma. I stood by the Greyhound bus, the blood red of the sunrise reflected in the mirror glass of the driver's side window. The joke goes, 'What's the difference between a working actor and a non-working actor?' And the answer is, 'A working actor only waits ninety-eight per cent of the time.'

The only action was the confident voice of the DP, William Howard Mayberry. 'If we shoot long, say like a hundred and fifty mil., we won't see the bus at all. What we'll see is a blur in the distance until it comes into focus around there.' Billy stood up and pointed to a spot twenty yards down the road behind the Greyhound Strato-cruiser. He wore a battered white hat and it made him look like Professor Bear. His voice sounded like the rasp of God. Twenty miles beyond Billy's pointing finger a winking pair of headlights was headed down the road, heading towards us with no discernible speed. Some early riser would have to wait while we shot our scene.

'And we won't see any buildings,' Sam said.

'No buildings. It'll look like the middle of nowhere.' Billy glowered towards the bus. 'I'm still getting flares on that damn thing. Tommy, can you throw some flat light through a diffuser behind the front wheel? Let me see a Mordris seventeen,' he called out, pointing with his hand.

'Then when he gets off can you pull back and show the town?' Sam asked, eyeing me suspiciously.

'We track back and pick up the town reflected in the driver's side window. Then the bus drives off and reveals Forrest standing by the side of the road. Then we pull back and see the other side of the town behind him. It's what the zoom lens was invented for, my little pigeon. But you better get a move on. We'll have fifteen, twenty minutes of magic light starting in about ten to fifteen minutes. After that we'll have to shoot it tomorrow.'

'Forrest,' Sam said, 'get back on the bus and get off again so I can see you in frame. We're going to give you a hell of an entrance. A star is born.'

I liked the idea of being a star; the adoring fans, an extensive collection of private investments, and a big ranch deep in the mountains of money that stars make. If I was going to be world famous as an ACT TOR I'd enjoy my fifteen minutes. But even overnight stars don't become stars overnight. Nobody gives the money away and if I'd had a choice I'd rather have been in bed. In dripping bloody London. With a late, long, and cosy lunch to look forward to with a sponsor who'd pay millions for his or her name on my car. And Susan in the afternoon. (Amazing how she had gone so away so far I had no idea where she was, and she could still slip in so easily between thoughts and give me a stab that made me wince. Damn I missed her.) But Susan wasn't there. Or anywhere for me. And the money wasn't there, it was here. So here, old whore for the chance to drive again, was Forrest, practising stepping out of a bus. I was supposed to be tired and beat up and I looked the part. Where the hell are the adoring fans, I thought, when you need them? I had done a couple of commercials the year before, so I knew better than to expect something to happen when you make a film. Unless you are looking through a lens, nothing happens.

Ever.

Bitch, moan, whine. I am cranky as a three-year-old if you wake me up too early. And I make about as much sense.

'Forrest,' Sam called out, 'do you have a minute?' Considering that I had been standing by the damn bus in the empty street for forty minutes in the freezing desert while they worked out their shot I guess I could spare a minute. Maybe two. Time was slipping away from me and none of it was ever going to come back. More bitch. Moan. Whine.

'What we're doing,' Sam said, 'is taking the fireball from your crash at Indy which will run under the titles for *Juice* and doing a match dissolve, a kind of blending into the sunrise with the bus coming down the highway. Almost out of the fireball of your crash. See what I mean?'

'No,' I said. Well, it was early. Why fuck around with being polite.

'OK, the opening shot of a movie if it's any good has got to establish the overall themes and maybe the character and maybe suggest the plot, like the opening bars of a symphony or the first sentence of a novel. You are Macklin, coming to Velma for a new life. Out of the flames of your crash. I mean I want to see that you have come to one end, but this could be like the dawn. A new beginning.'

'A new Disneyland.'

She ignored that. 'I want to do it in one shot, the bus coming out of the sunrise, stopping, the door opening and you getting out, the bus driving away, and then pulling back to see you looking around this remote town that will be the stage for the story. If you were an actor, Evers,' she said, warming up, 'I'd say I wanted to see that you had suffered. Suffered physically in a terrible crash and suffered defeat. You lost your job and your career. But you are not defeated. There is a toughness, a strength. You are an American Hero who has been knocked out, on the canvas, and you are coming back for another round and you know you can win. You are the spirit of America. Can you show me that?'

'Suppose I just get off the bus,' I said.

'Get off the fucking bus,' she said, 'and look around, left and right like you don't know where you are. You should be able to handle that.'

'Happy to,' I said. 'But there won't be a fireball.'

'We've got three hours of footage from ABC-TV and ESPN,' Sam said. 'Lots of fireballs to choose from.'

'Indy cars burn alcohol,' I said. 'The flames are invisible.'

'Just get off the bus,' Sam said. Over her shoulder, Billy was pointing to his watch as the first rim of the sun came over the mountains.

I got on the bus, the driver looked at me with the look of

impatience that bus drivers have, swung the big wheel, turned the bus around in a graceful arc, missing a parked car by at least an inch, and headed out of town, foot to the floor. 'Have a seat. I don't like to drive with standers,' he said with a grin. He was about twenty-six, in good shape, with long dark curly hair and the kind of sullen, intense, blue-eyed looks that made me wonder why I was going to be filmed and he was driving the bus.

'I'm not a stander, I'm a star,' I said. A little early for a joke.

'Yeah, well, we all have our moments. If you don't want to sit down be my guest. I mean I got a lot of admiration for you as a driver but I don't think you should even be here. You ask me, should be a Teamster drivin' those little tin shit-boxes. If we were drivin' em we wouldn't drive 'em, if you know what I mean. Not until they absofuckinlootly proved those fucking things are safe.'

'Forrest Evers,' I said.

'Yeah, I know. Danny Carlingo,' he said, foot to the floor, the bus continuing its lumbering acceleration. 'You should watch your ass with those things.'

'So I've heard.'

'OK, Danny. That's far enough. Turn around now and head back towards camera.' Mel's voice was on the radio.

'Hang on,' Danny said, shifting down a gear and swinging the wheel. The bus lent into a big graceful arc, roaring flat out, and there was a bang at the back and metal chewed on metal. The back end of the bus swung out and kept on swinging around, off the road, sliding for a moment across the hardpan and then caught in the sand, and as slow as a falling tree, the big aluminium Strato-cruiser fell slowly down, on its side.

As it fell, the chassis twisted, cracking the large flat pane of mirror glass on the driver's side. I watched, in a dream, as half of the broken plate-glass swung free, trailing rubber and strands of dried glue. It hung for a long moment, then fell straight down a couple of feet and gently, neatly, sliced into the soft skin of Danny's stretched neck, the weight of the heavy glass scything down to the white bone. And his blood rushed out.

I couldn't see Danny's face just below me, I could only see mine in the mirror as large as a coffee table, tilting away from me as a shawl of blood spread over the surface covering my reflection.

There was silence for a long time. Danny was suspended sideways in his seat-belt, his legs twitching once or twice, his head covered by red glass. I was stuck in slow motion. I stood up on the side of the seat below me and for a moment my head stuck out of the side of the bus where the window had been. And as I started to bend down to lift the broken sheet of glass off Danny I realized that if, by a miracle, he wasn't already dead, moving the glass might make the bleeding worse. As if it could have been worse. I looked up again and for some mad reason I was fascinated by the outline figures moving back and forth in the distance, huddling, then jumping into a car and driving out towards us; the sun, flaming red, reflected in the windshield of the white car.

# chapter twelve

I was in the air-conditioned, glassed-in enclosure outside the Star's nice motorhome with a nice lunch with a view of the desert desert and the jagged mountains.

I stared at my uneaten lunch.

Wilting lettuce leaves sticking to the sides of the glass bowl. Salad dressing long separated into its separate parts. Curling bread alongside. Pink soup room-temp under a crinkled skin. The desert looked like a grim prediction of life in the future on this polluted planet. The air conditioning droned on.

The police had been careful, respectful, The detective who interviewed me looked nineteen years old, smooth baby skin, round cheeks, a little boy mouth, and eyes around sixty years old, dead in the middle. Did I know the deceased? Could I describe in my own words what happened? Words could not describe, but I gave it a shot.

Did he think it was a set-up? I asked. He said maybe somebody messed with the bus, some kinda sabotage maybe, they were looking into that. But no way could anybody set up the glass to break that way and fall that way on a driver who just happened to stick his neck out that way. It was just bad luck, he said. Probably driver error. The guy, what's his name, Mel, said the driver was going too fast. Shit happens, he said. Five miles away a turkey buzzard was circling in for a landing. Some dead desert mouse maybe. One creature dies and another flies in for lunch.

The phone rang. 'Is this Forrest Evers? I'm Linda Carlingo. Danny's wife.' Her voice was light, girlish.

'I am very sorry, Mrs Carlingo.'

'They said you were with Danny when he was killed.'

'I was his passenger in the bus.'

'Did he say anything?'

'He was killed instantly, Mrs Carlingo. I don't think he felt any pain.'

'Call me Linda. Didn't he say anything before?'

'I don't really remember Mrs, I'm sorry, Linda,' I said, trying to think of what we'd said. 'I've got a lump on the back of my head and I'm still a little groggy.'

'I'm sorry about your lump, Mr Evers. I got two babies. How'm I gonna look after my two babies?'

There was a pause and there was nothing I could think of to answer her or even fill the silence.

'Danny never did bad to anybody, Mr Evers. He was a good driver.'

'He was a very good driver.'

'He told me this morning before he left he was gonna drive you and he was excited about it. He probably didn't let on, he likes to act like he is laid back, but he was thrilled, Mr Evers. Like a little boy. He was a fan of yours, watched you race on ESPN. He said you were maybe not the greatest driver in the world but you were up there.'

Maybe with luck, one day. The middle grid is a long way from the front row in Formula One. 'That was very kind of him, Linda.'

'It wasn't his fault, was it, Mr Evers?'

'No, Linda, it wasn't his fault. Please, call me Forrest.'

There was another long pause. I heard her crying. Then she said, 'They're saying it was. Like he was going too fast. Somebody made this happen. I know they did. Promise me.'

She was crying heavily now and I tried to think of something to say to comfort her. Something to make up for doing nothing while her husband died. The something came out, 'Sure.'

'Promise me you'll find the people who did this to Danny.'

'I don't think anybody tried to kill Danny.'

'There was an accident and he's dead. You find the people who made that accident happen. I don't know, maybe the people who made the bus. Somebody, Forrest. Find them.'

'I'm very sorry, Linda.'

'Yeah? Well do something.'

*

I said goodbye and I put the phone down. I hadn't done anything, I hadn't promised anything. Had I. I was just an innocent bystander. A Stander, Danny said. I looked over at the pretty white wrought-iron garden table where my fancy lunch lay dead. No point watching the salad.

I watched it anyway until a fly began to share my interest. I went inside the motorhome for a change of scene and I picked up the phone and dialled the number Sean had given me, his ranch up in the Santa Inez mountains.

A young female voice said, 'Hi, who is this? Just a minute. Shawwwnnnnn. Honnneeeeeee. He'll be right there, Mr Forrest.' After a few minutes wait, he was.

'Yeah, Forrest. My man. What's happening? I heard it's all fucked up.'

'You heard about Danny's death?'

'Not the details, but more than I wanted to hear. Tommy, my ex-driver, gave me a call. I gotta tell you I'm really glad to out of that shooting gallery. I wouldn't be all that relaxed if I were you. Bad luck doesn't just come in threes, you know.'

'I'm not relaxed. I just talked to his widow.'

'Jeezzzuz.'

'Anything remotely like that happen to you when you were there? Anything that looked like somebody was trying to get you?'

'Nothing I remember, but there were a lot of little hiccups. Like, you know, a remote not working, batteries going flat, and some guy starting his car every time we were recording live, but it was all little stuff. Happens all the time. OK, my accident was nasty and Jesus Christ, I knew Danny. That's a hell of thing. Poor bastard. I can't go to his funeral, my lawyer won't let me out of the house. I'm gonna have to just send some flowers. Do you think lilies would be OK? I don't want to be over the top, you know, like I don't want it to look ostentatious or anything.'

'Lilies would be fine, Sean. But the widow might appreciate a little tax-deductible contribution more.'

'Yeah, I'll have my guys look into it. But, hey, it was just a stupid accident, wasn't it? I mean it's not like there's a sniper or the cast eats potato salad for lunch and everybody dies of rat poison. It's just a nasty, terrible accident. You know, it's a little accident and then somebody is really unlucky and all of a sudden it's a big accident. It's all little piddly shit, until somebody dies. Probably it's the CIA.'

'CIA?'

'Hey, whatever. I'm just trying to lighten up the atmosphere here, eliminate the usual suspects. You know I played a CIA guy once. Remember *Free Fall* with me and Melanie? We shot part of it at Langley, Virginia, at their headquarters. Looks like the corporate headquarters for some soap company. Smells like a men's room in a bus station. Big glass buildings. I saved the President's life.'

I felt a rush of anger at him for taking Danny's death so lightly. But he hadn't been there, hadn't seen it happen, hadn't had Danny's blood on his hands and clothes. Violence from a long ways away never seems quite real. Close up it colours everything. 'Half the nation is grateful, Sean.'

'So what are you doing? You want to come up to the ranch for a couple of days? You'd like it, Evers. The air is clear, smells of pine trees, and I'm up here reading scripts and pretending to be wounded while the lawyers sort out the deal. But tomorrow's gonna be outrageous. Some ad agency, what is it, J. Walter Thompson, is coming up to shoot a TV commercial with a bunch of jet skis and sexy ladies, use the lakeside cottage as a location. I got to stay quiet for a couple more days, sit around and read scripts, but you could have a ball. You ever meet Cindy Crawford?'

'We're supposed to be making up the missing days on the weekend. Greyhound is sending another bus. Although nothing is certain. The Teamsters want the weekend off for the funeral and I think they're right. They are saying if they don't get the weekend off they walk. But Mel says we have to shoot if we are going to come anywhere near our production schedule.'

'See, it's fun to be a star. They figure what happened?'

'They, the grips, put in mirror glass in place of the regular bus windows for special effects. They wanted to reflect the town in the drive by.'

'Yeah, so?'

'Well, the glass wasn't put in right and it wasn't safety glass. They say Danny was going too fast, over-revved the engine, and threw a rod through the block. The back wheels locked up and the bus skidded on its own oil. I was there. I don't know how high those big diesels rev but they have a computer cut-out so you can't over-rev those things. And he was going fast for a bus, but he was in control.'

'You sure? Why would they tell such a dumb story?'

'Because they don't know what happened. The engine did go, but nobody knows why. Delilah says hello.'

'Are you in my fucking motorhome? What the fuck is she still doing there?' I looked behind me at Delilah on the couch. She mimed a kiss to the telephone.

'She says she misses you.'

'Tell her to do Cousin Sean a favour and forget him. Hey you're not fooling around with her, are you? She's just a kid.'

'You don't want to talk to Delilah?'

'What for? You know she's under-age.'

'Evidently she's old enough to give you the finger. Somebody's at the door. I'll talk to you later.'

I hung up the phone and there was another rap on the door. 'Forrest, are you there? Can I see you for a minute?'

'Come on in, Sam,' I said.

There were dirt stains on Sam's faded red-checked shirt and her hair was tied up with a scarf. All working woman. She gave me her pretty smile and I was glad to see her.

Then she saw Delilah. 'What are you doing here?' she said. Delilah was curled up barefoot, T-shirt and cutoffs, reading *Sassy*, a bag of potato chips and a can of Coke alongside.

'I'm trying to finish this stupid report for school and everybody keeps interrupting me. I mean Sean's not using this place and I thought it would be a nice quiet kind of retreat. Until you all came barging in.'

Sam turned to me, 'You're not . . .'

I didn't let her finish the sentence. 'I'm staying in the motel.'

'Hey, don't worry about it,' Delilah said, folding her towel. 'You guys want to talk, no problem. Doesn't float my boat to listen in. I'm outta here.' As Delilah slammed the door of the motorhome the back of her T-shirt said FUCK OFF. Which explained the front, which said, FUCK ON.

Sam was moving around the motorhome, ran her hand along the sofa, picked up a picture of Sean's twenty-five-room mountain cabin, and put it down facing in a slightly different direction. 'I think we should leave everything just the way he left it,' I said.

'Please don't make fun of me. This isn't easy.'

'I'm not making fun of you, Sam. Just trying to change the subject. We're all thinking of Danny. I am just trying to make you feel at home. Even though it isn't my home.'

'I'm never at home. I grew up in Hollywood,' she said, settling into the big leather couch, obviously at home. 'My dad was a producer and when I was a little girl, before he died, all I wanted to do was be in one of his movies.'

'Can I get you something to drink?' I thought she might be settling in.

'No, really, this isn't exactly a social call. I'm telling you I know how it works. It is so damn hard to get a movie funded and into production that once it starts production, the movie will get made. I can count the movies that didn't get made after they started production on one hand.'

'Water, beer, glass of wine? I think there's still some of Sean's Chardonnay in the 'fridge.'

'Please stop playing host. I've just talked to David. Akiri wants to pull the plug.'

I flopped down in the armchair. The armchair of a star, I thought. Or former star if Akiri was 'pulling the plug'.

'But he can't, he really can't.' Sam rubbed her eyes, weary. 'They've signed guarantees, we have a contract, the money is committed. They'd have to pay as much, maybe more, to walk as it would cost them to finish the film.'

'When is the funeral?'

'Tomorrow noon,' she said closing her eyes for a moment. 'Mel's insisting we shoot all weekend. I told him to forget it. The Teamsters will walk if we try to force them and they're right. We should all go to Danny's funeral and I've told Mel to give the crew the weekend off. I want to see if there is something we can do for his poor wife. I mean I feel responsible. Like this is my ship. On the other hand it's not the first time there have been accidents on location. OK, we have had more than our share with two men in the hospital. But what scares me is I feel so bad about Danny. If I stop and think about him this whole thing will come to a stop because I won't be able to do anything for days. And I can't do that. I can't let down the whole cast and the crew. OK, there have been some delays and some of the equip—' She stopped talking. And looked at me as if she was seeing me for the first time.

'What is it, Sam?'

'David is getting iffy,' she said. 'And that is a very bad sign. If David doesn't back us, nobody will. I can't think that he won't, he's got too much at stake. But if he pulls out, there isn't a dollar in Hollywood that wouldn't run right out from under this film and hide. He says he wants to see me.'

'He may just want to hear the director tell him what happened.'

'He knows what happened, I told him. Shit, I hate asking this. It sounds so weak. But I don't want to face him alone. Will you go with me, Forrest?'

'Sure,' I said.

'Joe's at seven thirty,' she said, getting up to go. 'Wear a tie if you have one. David like ties. The chopper will be here at six fifteen.'

Helicopters are noisy, dirty, uncomfortable, and, compared to all other ways of flying, with the possible exception of bungee jumping, dangerous. I have to tell you that given the choice, it is now my preferred method of transport to the dinner table. The sun was just setting as we rose up off the desert floor in a whirl of grit, dust, screaming turbines, and chopper blades. We skimmed along the desert floor in the dark blue shadow of the mountains, rose up over the tree tops and the lakes, and flew towards the peaks outlined with gold light.

As we rose over the mountains it was one of those rare clear evenings when the whole of LA was glittering on the rim of the dark blue Pacific and the sun was poised on the edge of the ocean, sinking. The first stars of the evening were just overhead. A few hundred feet higher, I thought, and we would have been whop-whop-whopping along in the Big Dipper and the Milky Way.

The limousine was waiting at the helicopter pad at the Santa Monica airport. The engine was running and the chauffeur was standing outside in the warm evening air holding open the door, ready to take the two stars to meet their agent for dinner. You know, the stars of the movie about electric cars. The movie they couldn't get off the ground.

# chapter thirteen

The limo crept through the fuming LA traffic, which we ignored behind one-way glass. Classic Rock on the stereo quietly sang: 'Touch me, hooooney.'

Sam looked at her face in the mirror with the cold roving scrutiny that women give their reflections. She licked a fingertip to brush some flaw I couldn't see. Her hairdresser had given her a wild, wind-blown look as if she had just come in from the edge of a cliff high in the Rockies. Underneath a midnight-blue jacket she wore a simple black shift with a high neckline. It looked businesslike, what the young and rising executive might wear to Lutece in New York, or Spago in LA. Except that she had nothing on underneath so the slightest gesture sent a wave of movement under the innocent cloth. She closed her eyes, breathing deeply. 'Confidence,' she said. 'Confidence.'

She sat, eyes shut, perfectly still while the light changed, we went down Santa Monica two blocks past the Beverly Hills Hilton, and stopped again for another red light.

'Come on, Honeeee, touch me, touch me, touch meeee. Like you used to do.'

When the light changed and the car inched forward again Sam opened her eyes and said, 'Joe's is more of a club than a restaurant. It's not like Spago, where you go to be seen. You go to Joe's to hide.'

She held my hands and squeezed, as if this was the really important bit. 'Joe's is a bad sign because it probably means that David doesn't want to be seen with me, like he's going to pull the plug. He's got Akiri and Radnor, you met Radnor at his house, remember, from Olympic. And David says he just wants to talk and let me do that.'

'I don't see how I could stop you.'

'How do I look?'

'You look fine.'

'Shit,' she said, pulling out her mirror again and searching her face.

'You are the most beautiful woman I have ever seen in my life and I have never seen you look more beautiful.'

'That's what everybody always says,' Sam said, not looking up. 'Is that your best jacket?'

I liked my jacket. It came from Paul Smith in London. Dusty-black silk. Not the price of a sports car. More the price of a family car. Not flash but hip. Mondo cool in the age of retreat. I had no idea if it was my 'best'. 'Absolutely,' I said, thinking it might help relax Sam a bit.

'David's necktie will cost more than that jacket,' she said, studying a corner of her mouth.

'Does anything count around here besides money?'

'Sure. Length.' A two-beat pause. 'As in swimming-pools and contracts.' Sam sighed and smiled her weary but brave smile as she put her mirror down. 'Look, I'm sorry, Forrest. I know you mean well, but if he's made his mind up to put us in turnaround I have to make him feel that is a bad mistake. I have to look better than Michelle, or Melanie, or Kim, or whoever the hell he's thinking of now. I have to make him fall in love with me all over again.'

'If he's made up his mind, Sam, it won't matter if you look like a frog.'

'I do look like a frog,' she said. 'Reep, reep.'

The doorman held open the door, and we stepped out of the limo and under an unmarked canopy on Wilshire. The doorman, who looked like his day job was VP Investment Securities, held open a heavy oak door and we stepped into a cool dark room with a fountain. The *maître d'* led us into a large open room with a stone floor and a waterfall in the middle. The waterfall, which flowed down on all sides, was surrounded by semi-circular booths in champagne leather. The booths were hidden from one another and the waterfall made overhearing your neighbour's conversation impossible. Looking into the booths, you could see the portable phones lying next to the water glasses, but unless someone was sitting right in the middle, you couldn't see who was at the table.

'It's the new Hollywood,' Sam whispered in my ear. 'In the old days the biggies wanted everybody to see and hear them because they wanted the credit. Now they don't want anybody to see or hear them because they're afraid they'll take the blame.'

Every racing driver knows fear like an old friend. Something starts to come loose, you wait a millisecond too long to get on the brakes or you feel your front wheel begin to slip on a patch of oil you didn't see and a jolt of fear goes coursing through your system; it's what keeps you alive. But this room of quiet voices murmuring under the sound of falling water, of manicured hands and sleek faces talking over dinner, looked safe enough. As opposed to, say, the first corner of a Formula One race or the exercise yard at your friendly local detention centre. 'What is there to be afraid of?' I said.

'What they can do to the rest of my life,' Sam said.

'Worry about that later,' I said, as three men rose from their hiding place to greet us. We slid in alongside.

'Nice flight in? Yes, lovely sunset. So clear for this time of year. Did you see that new little Australian film, *Murmurs*? The sunset there? Yes, wonderful. So beautiful, the desert. Reynolds says he wants to direct and nobody will give him a script. And have you seen Mary Alice Wintersteen in *Racquets*? The editing just cut her to pieces,' we all more or less said.

'I'm pulling out,' Akiri said. Which stopped the chit-chat.

'You are free to do whatever you like, Akiri,' David said, putting his menu down slowly. 'But you are tied by contract to several obligations. I'm sure you are aware it will cost you far more to pull out than to complete the film.'

'We, Hozuki, are in *Juice* for the PR, David. And *Juice* is not good PR, it sucks. The papers were full of Danny's death today. And now the evening TV news programmes are picking up the story of Sean's crash. They say his face is so cut up the only parts he'll get are . . .'

'His face is fine,' I said. 'I talked to him this afternoon.'

'We are in this for what the media says,' Akiri said.

'If you are just in this for what the media says,' David said, looking up at the waiter, 'then I think you had better jump ship. Good evening, Clark.'

A waiter had appeared at the opening of our circular booth,

looking as if he had stepped out of a men's cologne ad. Dark hair, green eyes, and excellent teeth arranged in a polite smile. 'Good evening, Mr Allen. We have some lobster from the Gulf this evening that Jo-Ann has smoked over Chardonnay oak barrel chips. Gives it a lovely silky texture. And shall I have Petrea bring you the wine list? Incidentally we have a new still water this evening that is not on the list, a very small spring from the Carpathian Mountains. Very fresh, high chalybeates.'

'Dracula Springs,' Ron Radnor said from deep behind his menu.

Water all around, waiter, we all decided, thank you very much. Whatever happened to W. C. Fields?

'And what would you like this evening Miss Miles?'

'Frog.'

We ordered. The smoked lobster for Sam and Akiri, Radnor had the grilled trout, and when Clark turned to take my order he said, 'Mr Evers?' Which I thought was impressive since he'd never seen me before. I ordered the wild salmon and chèvres salad and for the first time in months didn't feel at all hungry. The guillotine bus window had shut down my appetite. David had grilled veg and porcini mushrooms with a sun-dried tomato pesto sauce; a dish, Clark pointed out to the rest of us, that Jo-Ann herself prepared only for David. Radnor leaned across the table, towards Akiri. Akiri who looked back with the boredom of a man waiting for a plane. 'You guaranteed this project,' Radnor began.

David put a hand on Radnor's sleeve and Radnor went quiet. At the same time, Sam laid her hand on Akiri's silk sleeve and looked at Akiri as if he had run over her cocker spaniel. As if she understood how the little boy in Akiri felt.

Akiri gave Sam a sad smile and tore himself away to face David.

'I was saying by all means pull out, Akiri, if you are going to be interested in everything the media says. The only thing I am interested in,' David said, 'is being first. And that is what *Juice* is about. For the past few years the warm word around this town' – David included the rest of the restaurant with a wave of his hand – 'has been sequels. *Rocky 26*.' He raised his eyebrows in mild amusement. 'I don't have anything against sequels, they are the poles that hold up the tent in this circus.

But I'm not interested in them. What we have in *Juice* is a first, Akiri, a real first. You have a first in EVIA, the first electric car to give the internal combustion engine a run for the money. Firsts don't come along very often, but when a real first comes along it scares the hell out of a lot of people. What we have in *Juice* for the first time is a film that crosses the line between marketing and entertainment. Between movies and advertising. It's not easy. The public won't tolerate not being entertained, but believe me *Juice* will be a monument in marketing history.'

He paused to take a sip of the water Clark was pouring for him. 'And if you walk away from *Juice*, just because we are having some delay at the top, you will be walking away from being one of the visionaries. One of the very few men who had the perception and the guts to create a first. Shall we have some wine? Think you, Petrea,' he said taking the wine list, glancing inside and putting it down. The tall, gaunt blonde woman wore a silver medallion around her neck engraved CHEVALIER DE TASIEVIN. She held her head tilted to one side as if she was trying to guess what David was about to order.

'What about that stuff you keep for Mondavi? That 1974 Chardonnay he thinks is a secret. Comes from a little DuBlois vineyard at the top of the Alexander Valley. Do you have any of that old rotgut left?' She nodded and glided away.

'What I was going to suggest, Ron,' he said turning to Radnor, 'was that we put a little more snap into our production. If we are going to make next summer's record breaker at the box office then I think we can afford to go the extra mile, don't you?'

'What for?' Radnor said, heavily suspicious.

'Julie Phillips, who did the special effects for *Private Beach*, showed me some sketches she did on spec for *Juice*. Very interesting. I'd like you to take a look at them. I think we could do with some more 'copter shots for the driving sequences. I'm sure Sam won't object if we hire a special effects director.'

'It's a little late in the day,' Sam said, waving her hand in surrender.

'You see, with a little more effort, an all-out effort, financially and creatively, we can make *Juice* the movie, not just of the year, but of the decade.'

I was thinking he was pouring it on a little thick for a nice little soap opera when Akiri said, 'My father would like to know what you think, Mr Evers. Why have we been having all this bad luck?'

'I don't think it's just luck. I think somebody is playing dirty tricks on *Juice*.'

'You are sure?' Akiri said, leaning towards me.

'No, I'm not "sure". It's a gut feeling that I have that somebody is sabotaging the film.'

'Forrest,' Sam said, 'I know we've had rotten luck, but don't you think you are being a little paranoid?'

'I'm a lot paranoid,' I said. 'You've tried to shoot three driving shots and you've had three out of three crash. I can't wait to hop into that car and drive.'

'Who is it, then?'

'I don't know. Sean said something about the CIA, almost as a joke. And I realized with the government cutbacks they have turned a lot of agents loose in the last two years. Somebody might have hired one. Maybe somebody doesn't want Sam to be a director. Maybe somebody just doesn't like the idea of a Japanese car.'

'Or the Japanese. Will you excuse me for a moment?' Akiri said, getting up and pulling a small phone out of his pocket.

Radnor's face had turned pink to match his inflamed eyelids. He leaned forward and whispered while Akiri was busy with his call. 'What the fuck is this about more production, David? We're over budget now, the schedule is screwed up, and the major backer is saying he's gonna walk. I don't need this shit.'

'I'm perfectly serious,' David said, loud enough for Akiri to hear. 'I think the project needs some very special effects. *Juice* needs the look of a big picture. If I don't see you committing to a ten per cent increase in the budget by the end of the week, I'm pulling Sam.'

'Good. Pull her. I'll sue the ass off you both. After Kim Basinger lost that suit over walking on *Boxing Helena* I could make some money on this after all.'

'If Akiri walks, and he will unless you get more behind *Juice*, Sam has every reason to quit. She's not making her directorial début on an underfunded project.'

Radnor said, 'Cut the bullshit, David. You know as well as I do, the size of the budget has nothing to do with how good a movie is.'

'I'm not talking about how good it is, Ron. I'm talking about getting it made.'

Akiri came back to the table. 'Dad wants to talk to you,' he said, handing me the phone.

# chapter fourteen

'I hope I am not interrupting your dinner,' the old man said, sounding as if he were in the next booth.

'You couldn't care less about our dinner, George.' His real name is Hashishimitu or something like that. But rather than hear the round-eyes mispronounce his name (or be called 'Hash' as he was at the University of Oregon School of Business in the 1950s) he preferred to be called George. George Hozuki San. He was a small man with wide shoulders and a lion's mane of grey hair. He had built Hozuki Motors from rubble, starting as a simple machine shop making piston rings and the motorbikes, and it was now the world's fourth largest producer of automobiles. Hozuki engines had powered my Formula One cars for the past two seasons. They were down fifty to seventy-five horsepower on the new Fords and Renault's eight-hundred-horsepower engines and the running joke between us was that I just wasn't fast enough. Like many of the really successful men I have met George made you believe that you were the only concern he had in the world. 'What time is it in Nagoya?'

'About ten thirty tomorrow morning, Forrest. I like to think we are a little ahead of you. Akiri tells me you are having dinner with David and Ron Radnor from Olympic. And Samantha Miles. Whom I hope to meet some day.'

'Akiri tells me you are pulling out of *Juice*.'

'Tell me what you think is going on. When we were negotiating for Olympic, I had the impression I was dealing with very rich and very bright spoiled children. They have an attention span of two minutes. Except for David. Please do give him my regards. And please, tell me.'

'I don't know what's going on. I don't think it's bad luck.'

'*Juice* is our first project with Olympic. Olympic is very important to us.'

'I thought you just wanted to play in the movies.'

He laughed. 'Of course. But I wouldn't buy a studio to do that. A studio these days isn't much more than a bank. But I was interested in what they have in their vaults.'

'I don't know what you mean.'

'Film studios never sell their films. They rent them, Forrest. So they always own the originals. Olympic owns over six thousand films from Harold Lloyd and Mack Sennett through all those Gary Cooper and Clark Gable films right up to *Waterfall*, which they are releasing this week. That's a great treasure, Forrest, and it never runs out. An especially great treasure now that there are all these satellite networks gobbling up programming at an accelerating rate. That's why Hozuki bought Olympic. It certainly wasn't for the bankers. Now tell me about *Juice*. This man getting killed. *Juice* is an excellent chance for us to promote our new car and our new Hozuki fuel-cell technology. But I don't want more bad publicity. Akiri may have told you that we are preparing a world-wide film here in Japan for the launch of EVIA. Not a feature film, a promotional film. So we could use that for TV commercials. Many of my colleagues on the board feel the film should be Japanese. But I don't think we want to over-extend our welcome in America by being too Japanese. We are a global company. And I like the idea of introducing the car in a feature film. I have always found you direct, Forrest. Although I wish you had won more races for us. If it is not bad luck do you think you could find out what is the cause of our difficulties on *Juice* and fix it?'

I looked around the table. They were watching me hold Akiri's portable phone to my ear like dogs watching another dog eat their dinner. 'I could try.'

'Try, Forrest, and call me in a week.'

'I'm not the only person you are asking.'

'Of course not, Forrest. I am asking everybody. I am asking you because I know how competitive you are. And I imagine you are still capable of being quick.'

We said goodbye and I gave the phone back to Akiri.

'How is he?' David said.

'He sends his regards to you, David. He wants me to find

out what is causing our problems and call him in a week.'

'In a week,' Radnor said. A glob of celeriac purée drooled off the prongs of his fork. His fork held position in mid-aid.

'The implication is he has given *Juice* another week. He says they have another film they are shooting in Japan. From what he said, I think it's a strictly promotional film, you know, shots of cars in the sunset, models standing around looking like models. But they are thinking of using the footage for TV advertising if they pull out of *Juice*.'

'You better get started right now, Sherlock,' Sam said, smiling warmly at me as if the week was my personal gift to her.

'Well, for a start, I'd like my own mechanic.'

'Holy shit,' Radnor said. 'I've heard of stars asking for their own hairdresser, their own masseuse, their own chef, but . . .'

David laid his perfectly manicured hand on Radnor's fork arm and gently brought it down to the table. 'Your own mechanic, Forrest. Fine. Anything else?' he said.

# chapter fifteen

Sam stared out the side of the chopper at the lines of streetlights in the desert, marking off half-mile, mile, and ten-mile squares, the gameboards of developers. I tapped her shoulder to get her attention, and pointed to her pocket book, mouthing the word phone.

She mouthed 'What?'

I mouthed 'Tel-e-phone' and she didn't get it. There was no point screaming the word. I mimed flipping the gizmo open and punching in the numbers and she fished out her portable phone from her handbag. I flipped it open and punched in Bash's number. Somewhere in the hills north of LA, surrounded by racing cars, movie monsters, and road-going P-51 Mustangs, he was there. In my ear he said, 'Hello?'

I said, 'Hello, Bash. Forrest. Evers.'

He said, 'What?'

'Forrest Evers. I'm down in Velma, about twenty miles from Barstow. We're filming a movie called *Juice*, Bash, and I wonder if you have a couple of weeks to make some serious money sorting out the cars.'

'What? I can't hear you. Turn off the fucking blender.'

If the person with her thigh pressed against mine can't hear me, what makes me think somebody could hear me on the phone? Oh well, I thought, flipping the thing shut and passing it back to Sam, you can't think of everything.

Sam's limo was waiting by the copter pad, her driver, Marty, was holding open the door for us. 'So, you coming to the funeral tomorrow?' he said.

'Of course we are,' Sam said.

'Sam,' I said when we were in the back seat, 'I am going to

the funeral so it doesn't really matter. But do me a favour and don't tell somebody else what I'm going to do.'

'Are we a little touchy this evening? I didn't mean to wound your male pride.'

'My pride's fine. It's just I keep seeing glass hanging over Danny and then falling. It almost cut his head off and I just stood there and watched. I don't know if I could have deflected it if I'd moved, but I just stood there, watching. So yes, I am a lot touchy. His wife says they had, have two babies. Where are we going?'

'I thought maybe we could have a drink. Do you mind?' She, of the beautiful face and the sad green eyes and her hand on my knee, was probably up to something. She had that extra gear that movies stars have, the thousand-watt charm she could turn on. And she had turned it on in the limo from the restaurant, saying that she was coming back with me to the location tonight. That she needed to put some space between herself and LA. That she wanted, just for tonight, to sleep under the stars. All this with her hand on my knee as if she was talking about something else.

I, the tower of willpower, said, 'Fine.'

'Do you mind taking your shoes off,' Sam said at the door to her big blue motorhome.

'As long as your floor isn't covered with broken beer bottles,' I said in what I thought was about the right jaunty tone. Sam looked at me with sympathy for the culturally deprived.

When Sam opened the door to her motorhome, I was impressed. Not by the size of it as much as by the amount of money that had been flung through the front door. It wasn't to my taste, but then I've never wanted to be Queen for a day. Snowy white carpet sets my teeth on edge. As if we were not meant to walk but float above the virgin surface. There was enough space to hold a party for the cast and crew of *Gone With the Wind* and I wondered if the director and star of *Juice* got double motorhome allowance.

But of course Sam got whatever she wanted. Her little rolling abode had a second storey, a hot tub in the bedroom, she happily pointed out, and mirrors everywhere, lest a star spend a moment unreminded of the power and beauty of her face. It made Sean's leather-lined extravaganza look like an outhouse behind Versailles. All of the rooms were spectacularly neat. No doubt a team of cleaners tracked down every dust mote and lined up the silverware in the drawers. I wondered if this obsession with cleanliness signalled a dirty mind.

'Relax, Forrest,' she said in her throaty voice. 'Sit down. I'll pour you a drink.'

I aimed for the blue silk over-stuffed couch. 'I'm not sure I can relax in here,' I said. 'I might make a mark.'

'Isn't it hilarious?' Sam said. 'It was built fifteen years ago for Joan Collins. She never even set foot in it and it was just sitting in Olympic's warehouse. The insurance only covers storage and damage comes out of my production budget. So don't spill anything.'

'I don't have anything to spill.'

'Gin and tonic?'

'No thanks.'

'Oh, come on. I saw your eyes drool when Akiri ordered a G&T by David's pool. Go ahead, it's been an awful day. Tomorrow's a day of mourning for Danny so you can sleep late. In fact it will probably help you sleep.' Sam was moving under that black dress taking down bottles and glasses and filling the ice bucket.

I had an unkind thought. That she'd got herself up to perform for David, and then never really got on stage. So now I was the audience for the performance called world's most desirable woman. She clanged ice into two glasses and poured hefty doses of gin. 'How do you know Big Hose?'

'Big Hose?'

'Akiri's father. When they were putting together the deal with Hozuki the Olympic people called Hozuki Senior "Big Hose". Little Hose just does what Daddy says.'

'I wouldn't bet on Akiri being a pussy cat. It's just that their tradition is a little different; obedience counts. Anyway his father is all right. Hozuki build the engines for my Formula One car. Did you know George was a Kamikaze pilot?'

Sam handed me a tall gin and tonic, shaking her head no.

'It's one of the great stories about George,' I said as Sam sat down a demure two feet away sinking into the blue silk cushion and crossing her legs. I hadn't realized her skirt was so short. 'He was eleven in 1945 and sent up into the hills to Kamikaze camp, you know, the Divine Wind. They were loading literally a ton of dynamite into these beat-up old Zeros and sending up little boys who barely knew how to get off the ground to die and win the war for the Emperor. George had three flying lessons, one more and he could take off and dive into an aircraft carrier. The night before his last flying lesson the Allies fire-bombed Tokyo and more people died than in Hiroshima and Nagasaki combined. They could see the fire from the Kamikaze camp, but they had no idea how big it was. And in the morning it was snowing. Only it wasn't snow, it was the ashes of Tokyo that were falling. The Emperor came on the public address system and said he was laying down his sword. Surrendering. Which George knew was impossible, couldn't happen because the Emperor was divine. And in the afternoon they started loading these kids on trains to take them back to Tokyo. He said he had no idea where to look for his house. All the streets and all the street signs were burned.'

'Did he?'

'Find his house? He's not sure. There was an ivory comb, badly burned, that he thought was probably his mother's but he was never sure.'

'So what does our Hero Hozuki want, revenge?'

'His revenge is selling cars. Although if you ask him he'd probably say he wants to do something for humanity. What do you want?'

Sam set down her glass, uncrossed her legs, and leaned over to me. 'What I want, Evers, is to make a movie that actually does something, that says something. I know it's been awkward with David being such a pain in the ass checking every damn detail. But it's the only way I could direct. And I know it has been a horror story up to now. But I want to put it all past us.' She stood up and turned towards me, those green eyes looking down with absolute intensity and need, a little wobble under the black dress. 'I want to start all over again. Rewrite the script. Make the relationship between Mac and Jill work for real.' She put her hands on my shoulders. 'What do you want?'

I took a sip of my gin and tonic, savouring the cool, fresh, and bitter taste, set the glass down, and stood up. Sam moved against me, her arms sliding around my neck, pulling me down to kiss her.

'Hey what the hell are you guys doing?' Delilah was on the balcony, looking down, panties and a T-shirt. 'Mom. You're not going to bonk the mechanic, are you?'

'Delilah. Sweetheart. I thought you were asleep.'

'It's Friday. Like school is over. Like the weekend is supposed to start here,' Delilah said, coming down the stairs with an elaborate sideways vamp-descending-the-staircase stroll. When she got to the bottom of the stairs she said, 'You guys getting an early start, huh?'

'We're not,' Sam said. 'Honey, I'm sorry. I, its been uh, a terrible day and somebody died this morning and I just forgot.'

'Not what,' Delilah said, coming up to me, staring.

'Bonking, as you put it, Di. Definitely not bonking,' I said.

'Isn't it a bitch?' she said, sweetly, coming very close. 'The most powerful star in Hollywood and she can't even control her own daughter. I mean he's passably attractive, Mummy. But usually you do so much better than this.' Delilah flung her hand at me and swirled away, head thrown back.

Her mother shrugged, arching her eyebrows as in 'what can you do?'

'Bette Davis,' I said.

'Joan Crawford,' Di said. 'Much stronger character. You got any diet Coke in the 'fridge?'

'God, I thought you were serious,' Sam said. 'You can be a real pain, Di.'

'I am serious. A serious pain in the ass. You spending the night, Spike?'

'Well, shucks, Ma'am, I'd like to stay 'cause you two women-folk sure are purty. But, I, uh, reckon it's time I put the lid on the boys down at the mo-tell.'

'Jimmy Stewart?' Di said.

'Gary Cooper,' I said.

'Much stronger character,' Di said. 'But not as good an actor. Actually,' she said, coming back up to me with a little knowing, come-on smile she wanted her mother to see, 'I think you're a lot sexier than any of those guys.' She lowered her voice. 'And I'll do my Bette Davis for you one day just for you, Forrest. You know, the one where she sticks an ice pick in the guy's ear?'

# chapter sixteen

The air was still and heavy with the perfume of trumpet lilies, roses, and freeway exhaust. High overhead a happy sun in a perfect blue southern California sky beat straight down through the smog. At our feet, a gleaming oak casket with ornate bronze handles was suspended over a fresh hole in the ground. Astroturf mats ended at the edge of the grave and the smell of the earth rose up and mixed with the funeral flowers. Look down, under the coffin, see if you can see if graves like yours are really six feet deep.

The priest bent his balding head in prayer. Behind him, at shoulder height, an endless line of cars, campers, buses, trucks, and eighteen-wheelers roared non-stop on the Ventura Freeway.

'Dear God,' the priest said, raising his voice against the vague roar you get used to in LA, 'it is Saturday morning and it is a lovely day and none of us wants to be here on the edge of Danny's grave. Least of all Danny himself, although he, at least, I am sure is being well looked after.

'Here on earth, we are, all of us, busy. We have things to do. Things that must be done. And even if you add up all of the time all of us have left on earth, it wouldn't add up to much on your watch. We all have so little time. And you have an endless supply. You remind us with Danny's death that any one of us may have no time left on earth at all. That any of us could die this morning, this next breath. Is that why have you brought us here with your terrible theft of a father for Jessica and Clarissa? To make us aware of how precious our time is here on earth? To make us understand how precious Danny was to each of us? Is that the reason for this slaughter of Linda's husband, Charles and Aurelia's son, and my brother, Danny?' He looked up and I could see the resemblance, Danny's crisp good looks softened by a few extra years. The same bright blue eyes, streaming with tears, although his voice was strong.

'Why do you need to take him now? You know this terrible accident was not Danny's fault. Danny was a good man. And a careful and a skilful man. He had work to do here, a family to protect, and friends.'

He paused for a moment, looking down into the grave as if there might be an answer there. Then looked up again at the mourners ringed around the grave. 'Well, I know you,' the priest said, looking intently from face to face, 'well enough to know you won't answer except in the beauty of the day which seems to me to mock the ugliness of Danny's death. And in the beauty of Clarissa and Jessica and the promise of their lives. And in the courage of Linda who will be as strong as she and Danny together. And in the comfort of our family and in our friends. And in the kindnesses that we shall be glad to do for Linda and Jessica and Clarissa. In the mean time, Dear God, look after them all. And look after Daniel. You know he was a good man, a fine father, a good son, and our loving brother and you have him now, in your endless mansion. I just want to remind you, if you are in a rush, and you need a lift, Danny is a hell of a driver. Keep him safe for all of us. *In nomine patris . . .*'

As the coffin sank into the ground, the priest bent down and took a handful of earth and let it fall on the polished lid. Across from me, Linda Carlingo, small and slim in a black dress, dark eyes behind a black wide-rimmed hat and veil that must have been her mother's, knelt down carefully, and, hand shaking, picked up a handful of dirt and threw it in with a helpless gesture into the hole. On either side of her, her two-year-old girls in their best Sunday dresses watched their father's casket sink into the ground. They leaned forward, curious to see how far it would go.

Sam's hand squeezed mine, tears rolling down her cheeks from behind her big black sunglasses. She was dressed in a black gauzy and shapeless pants suit, her blonde hair tucked under a black scarf, and no make-up. Sam had that washed-out, ghostly look that stars sometimes have when they have no role to play. I was wearing my dusty black jacket and a black tie one of the teamsters had lent me.

When we arrived, ducking under the blades of the helicopter

on the edge of the cemetery lawn, the men and women were huddled together, dressed in black. We wear black to a funeral, I thought, because we know that when we die, black is the colour that will rise around us like water until we disappear. We wear black to a funeral because we are going to a dress-rehearsal for our own show one day.

If I had been a good boy and sat down and fastened my seat-belt, it might have easily been me sinking into the ground. Clods of earth bouncing off my expensive oak box. Believe me, I believe in seat-belts. I wouldn't drive twenty yards without one. The worst place you can be in a crash is bouncing around loose inside a car, or worse, diving skull-first through the wind-shield, or worse, out there on your own, soft flesh and easily splintered bone floating through the air at, say, five times the speed of an NFL running back, with no pads and no helmet, waiting for something solid, like a telephone pole or a concrete wall, to bring you to a stop. But if I had sat down and buckled up behind Danny, the glass guillotine might have sliced me first. I picked up a handful of dirt and threw it on his coffin, or mine, or yours. Go to a funeral and you are reminded that the line between the newly dead and you is always fine and near.

I caught up with Linda Carlingo as she was walking back across the cemetery lawn to the limousine. She pushed back her veil, a small face with dark eyebrows over dark eyes, her nose a little large, her mouth a little wide. Thick black hair leaked out of her black hat and stuck to her freckled forehead. 'Stupid goddamn veils,' she said. 'You comin' back to the house?'

'My ride back to the desert leaves in a few minutes,' I said, 'but thank you, Linda. It wasn't Danny's fault. Something broke, they'll find it.'

'You believe that broke story?' she said hoisting up one of her daughters and giving her a kiss. 'I heard a lot of things were breaking on that movie. You said you were gonna find somebody.'

'If there is somebody to find.'

'No. Don't tell me "if". There was somebody. Is somebody. That was a new bus. The best. Danny said it was like a ship, like a luxury liner, built to go a million miles and it didn't even have a thousand. That was a new bus, Mr Evers, so don't give me no goddamn "if". Give me the somebody.' She looked at me, hard and unforgiving, as if she were thinking maybe the somebody was me, and turned away, holding one daughter, the other trailing behind, holding on to her mother's skirt, running as fast as her little legs would go.

I walked across the lawn, towards the helicopter where my old friend waited, his big form casting almost no shadow at all in the high sun.

'How are you, Forrest? Mary-Ellen gave me your message and here I am.' Bash, larger than life, curly hair, faded dark sport jacket, sleeves too short, no way to button it, thrown over a fresh T-shirt for the occasion, held out a beefy hand, calloused and scarred. A welder's forearms. 'What are you doing in California?'

'Playing the part of a movie star,' I said. 'And you?'

'You heard I won the Carrera Pan-America.'

I nodded. I'd read about it in *Road & Track*. Bash had won the crazed free-for-all annual recreation of the 1950s road race across Mexico all in a Kurtis 500S (a road-going version of the 1950s Indy car) he'd built from the original plans. The other Kurtis he'd built came in second and the 175 mph 1949 Olds he'd built for last year's Carrera had finished seventh.

'The race car business has kinda tapered off. Like fallen off a cliff,' he said, 'so I've been building earthquake beds.'

'You mean like those Magic Fingers things they used to have in motels only with big fingers?'

'I mean I build them like a NASCAR stocker, triangulated space frame, kinda like a canopy bed. I built a house in the back yard and blew it up to fall on the thing. Drop a whole office building on one of my earthquake beds and you'd be fine. I'll send you the video. I think it's gonna be big in Japan. You knew him?' Bash nodded towards the grave where they were shovelling dirt into the hole.

'I'd just met him,' I said, 'and I was next to him when he died.'

'You look OK. A little stressed maybe, but OK.'

'I am OK. You have time to take on a project?'

'I have sixteen earthquake beds behind my house. Suckers don't stack and I don't really have a lot of room left for any more. So I guess I have a little time before a buyer shows up and takes one or two away. What do you have in mind?'

'The police have impounded the bus he was driving when we had our accident so I don't think you could look at that.'

'You think somebody set it up to kill him?'

'I think somebody set it up to have an accident and they didn't care whether they killed anybody or not. What I want you to do is go over the cars we're using in the film, check them out and make sure they are safe to run, and build me another one.'

'If it rolls, I can build it. What kinda cars we talking about?'

''65 Mustang skins on NASCAR stocker frames. Come down to Velma tomorrow and I'll show you.' I felt a hand take my arm. Sam took off her sunglasses and smiled up at me through the sadness of a mourner.

'Bash, I'd like you to meet Samantha Miles.'

'Call me Sam. Samantha sounds like a little pussy cat.'

'And you are not a pussy cat,' Bash said, smiling, taking Beauty's hand in his great paw.

'I'm not anybody,' Sam said. 'Not today.'

# chapter seventeen

We reshot the opening bus scene with a brand new Americruiser from Greyhound early Monday morning and it went off without a hitch. Unless you want to count the first three takes of Macklin getting off the bus when Sam said (*take 1*): 'Don't turn your whole body, Forrest. Just your head. You are a racing driver, not Charlie Chaplin'; (*take 2*): 'Don't squint. It makes your face look like a train wreck'; and (*take 3*) 'For God's sake don't rub your chin.' This last was a gesture I threw in for a little improvisational character development. A manly hesitation before the hero plunges into the unknown. 'Please don't act, Evers,' Sam said, 'just look left. Then, if you can remember, look right.'

The fourth time I got off the bus and went eyes left. Then I went eyes right and Sam said, 'Cut, print it. Let's get set up for the next shot, the bus disappearing down the road while Evers crosses the street. Is it still dark enough? I want the bus to just be tail-lights in black at the end of the shot.'

'If Spike can cross the street without rubbing his chin, we've got time for one take,' William Howard Mayberry said to Sam with a grin at me, no offence, white teeth showing in the middle of his God the Father beard. Delilah must be spreading around her nickname for me. I didn't like being called Spike, it reminded me I stuck out like a sore thumb. But smile and ignore the mild insult. Be nice to the DP. As everybody said, if the DP doesn't like you he can make you look like a collapsed football. No point in mentioning the DP looks like a hair pie with teeth. Save your petulant star tantrums for later, Evers, when they can do you some good. Oh, I am unfun to deal with first thing in the morning. Especially after an exhausting session of eyes left, eyes right.

'I can stop down,' Mayberry said to Sam, 'but we'll have *beaucoup* light in ten minutes.'

'Run,' Sam said.

We ran for two days. We reshot the drive-up scene with me taking Sean's part by the gas pumps. This time I was the dirty, hot, tired, and resentful ex-racing driver mechanic. And John Herrick, star of instant coffee commercials, played the rich racing-driver in Mel's Mercedes. It gave me a small, selfish satisfaction to see Herrick drive into the shot eleven times before he stopped on the mark. 'Here, John,' I said, grateful to do something right for a change, 'let me show you again. You get on the brake here, gradually, etc.' As an actor I was a hell of a driver.

We shot the next scene inside Macklin's garage. Jill said, 'Do you know your lines, Forrest? I'm sorry we haven't had time to rehearse but we are five days down on schedule and we need to move so we'll just do the blocking then we'll shoot if that's OK.'

My script was worn and folded. I'd gone over and over it the night before in my room at the motel, my old competitive spirit determined to get it right. It went:

**12. INT. MACKLIN'S GARAGE. 4PM.**
**(SFX. Tire machine)**
**MACKLIN is pulling worn truck tires off their rims on the tire machine, forcing the tire bar inside the rim, levering it over on to the spindle, and stepping on the foot-switch, turning the machine on and forcing the tire off the rim. It is hard, dirty work and he has his shirt off, his athlete's body sweating, streaked with tire dust. A steel splinter cuts his thumb.**

**MACKLIN**
**Damn!**

**MACKLIN goes over to the garage sink which may have originally been porcelain but is now encrusted with years of grease, dirt, paint and dried mechanic's soap. As MACKLIN washes his hands, a woman**

in a skirt appears in the open garage door, outlined against the hot white light outside.

JILL
Anybody in there?

MACKLIN considers his thumb. Now that the blood has been washed away he sees a steel splinter sticking out of the pad of his thumb. He pulls the splinter out with his teeth and the thumb bleeds freely.

MACKLIN
(Under his breath) Fuck!

JILL steps inside the garage. She looks fresh as a daisy in a light summer dress with her hair up.

JILL
Were you speaking to me?

MACKLIN turns and sees her.

MACKLIN
I was talking to my thumb.

JILL
My car is steering funny.

MACKLIN
Drive it in and I'll have a look at it.

JILL
It's just outside.

MACKLIN grimaces.

13. EXT. MACKLIN'S GARAGE. 4PM.
MACKLIN follows JILL outside where her red Mustang convertible is parked by the gas pumps. The car,

**like Jill, is pretty, neat, shiny clean. MACKLIN starts to get in the car.**

**JILL**
**Hey! Don't do that, you're filthy.**

**14. (Insert) MACKLIN'S HAND LEAVING A SMEAR ON THE CHROME HANDLE OF JILL'S CAR**
**13. CONT.**

**MACKLIN**
**Fine. You don't want to drive it in where I can put it on the rack and I can see what the problem is and you don't want me to touch it. So I'll just stand out of reach and you describe to me in your own words what you think the problem might be.**

**JILL**
**It's probably ball joints. You know what a ball joint is?**

**MACKLIN**
**If it's ball joints, Sweetie, the bushings, tie rods, track rods and shocks are probably all shot. How long have you had it?**

**JILL**
**Two years.**

**MACKLIN**
**You know if it's ever had any front end work?**

**JILL**
**I don't know, it was kind of a gift. What'll you think it will cost if I have to fix all that?**

**MACKLIN**
**Hard to say without seeing what it needs and looking up the parts. Five, eight hundred. Something like that. But there's no way of knowing without**

putting it up on the rack and putting my hands on your little pet.

JILL gets into her car.

JILL
You can keep your hands to yourself, Mister. That's way too much.

JILL starts the car. MACKLIN comes up to the car, and leans in, deliberately putting his bloodied greasy hand on the shining chrome top of the door. MACKLIN'S dirty, tired face is close to JILL's fresh and clean face.

MACKLIN
If the front end needs fixing, you better have it fixed.

JILL drives off without looking back and MACKLIN stares after the disappearing car.

MACKLIN
Before you drive into a truck.

They had offered me a stand-in for the tyre work; a man who was my size and shape and had curly chestnut hair that was just like mine until he took it off. But I didn't want a stand-in wearing a wig. I wanted to do the work myself, work up a sweat and get into the part. And I thought the scene was going well until we were setting up for the last couple of shots. Sam, sitting in the car, looked up at me standing alongside and said, 'Let's take a fifteen-minute break. Do you have a minute, Forrest?'

She slid out of the car and started walking. 'Have Marie set out some iced tea outside my motorhome, if you would please, Paul,' she said over her shoulder, striding away from the set in the little red dress and sandals she was wearing for her part. A little extra swish in her walk, I noticed, as I followed.

As we walked in the enclosed, air-conditioned veranda around Sam's motorhome, a young woman was bringing out a pitcher of iced tea. Whatever madam director wants, I thought.

'Just set it down, we'll help ourselves, Marie,' Sam said. Sam took a sip out of her tall cool glass, and I waited.

'I'm not getting any heat from you,' she said.

I waited some more. I had no idea what she meant.

'Heat. Like pride. Like sex. Like you have the hots for me. I'm talking about your character, Macklin. Sullen petulance isn't enough, Forrest. It may be enough for Sean who is twenty-four going on sixteen. But your character is thirty and you have more experience than a teenager and we expect a more complex reaction from you. When I look at you in the camera you look like you feel sorry for yourself. Are you still staying in that motel?'

'The motel is OK. It's better than driving thirty miles to that Holiday Inn where Mayberry is staying.'

'Evers, if you are going to act like a star you are going to have to start living like a star. Move out of the damn motel and into a hotel in LA. The Wilshire, the Bel Air, wherever you feel comfortable. You can take the chopper back and forth. And take Sean's motorhome.'

'Delilah's kind of adopted it for her hang-out.'

'Has she now? Well, boot her out. I'm not paying a day rate on a motorhome just so Delilah can have her little playpen. I don't know why I didn't think of this before.' Sam looked at her watch. 'I'll get Mel to tell her, if you like. Now let's play this scene as if you had some real pride. Like you had some fire in you and you couldn't wait to rip my dress off. Let me see some heat.'

'Fine, we'll shoot the scene with as much heat as you can stand, Sam. Then I'll tell Lady Di. I don't want Mel just chucking her out.'

'See, it's working already,' Sam said with her guaranteed movie star smile.

At that moment I thought Sam with her soft green eyes and that low-cut red dress looked as sexy as a bag of kitty-litter and I had a new respect for actors who could make you believe they felt passion for some selfish, manipulative, and driven actress who happened to have a pretty face.

Mel fussed about the shooting schedule and the budget but we shot the whole scene again anyway, from truck tyres to Jill driving away. I acted like I hated her and it must have given my performance an 'edge'. Sam said she loved it.

The sun was just above the Angeles mountains in the distance when we finished and I walked to Sean's motorhome, my shadow stretching out ten feet in front of me, to change and freshen up before taking the chopper into town. Sally, one of the production assistants, had made the arrangements. I was looking forward to the hotel at night and I was looking forward to moving in to the quiet comforts of the leather-lined motorhome during the day even more. My motel, with the fresh paper band around the toilet seat every day to reassure me of its sanitary protection, had a lumpy bed, fibreboard walls and a couple next door that squealed and howled from time to time throughout the night. The sound of other people grinding away is one of the least sexy sounds on earth. Especially if it reminds you that your own love-life is below zero. So I was seriously behind on my sleep and a night in the luxury of a quiet bed had real allure. But I wasn't looking forward to kicking Delilah out. She was feisty but I liked her. When I was fifty yards away, Di-Di's boyfriend, Tuna, the hippie grip with the pony-tail, bounded down the steps of Sean's motorhome, looked in my direction, and changed his, cutting behind Mayberry's motorhome. I knew I had seen Tuna creeping in and out of Sean's motorhome before when I knew Di-Di was in there and it bothered me more than it should have. For all I knew they were doing crosswords and homework together. Whatever, it wasn't my business. But maybe it was time I moved in. Took over the star's trailer as well as the starring role.

The trailer looked neater than when Sean was living in it. No empty beer bottles, the cushions on the built-in leather sofa were plumped up, and the carpet looked freshly vacuumed. Delilah wasn't in sight and when I called out she answered, 'Hi, Forrest. I'm in the bedroom, come on in.'

A backpack was on the king-size bed and Di, wearing big black clunky boots, black nylon bicycle shorts, and a red, white, and blue tank top with little hearts on it, was stuffing her socks and underwear in. 'Agghhhhh,' she screamed. 'Don't touch anything.' Her little face with the slightly bulging eyes and guppy mouth looked at me in horror.

My reflection loomed on the big mirror on the wall behind her. 'We were shooting,' I said.

'My God, it looks like they shot you. What happened to your thumb?' She moved in for a closer look, curious.

'That's just make-up,' I said. 'It's not real blood.'

'Well Jeeezuz. It probably makes real stains. You better take a shower right away. If you leave a mark on anything Sean'll kill me. You know where the shower is? I'll get a plastic bag for your trousers. Don't let them touch the carpet. Come on,' she said, holding open the shower door, 'get in there and take those filthy pants off.'

The shower was big for a motorhome with gleaming white and blue tile and chrome fixtures. I dropped my pants over the glass door and turned on the big handle and a full flood of delicious cool water washed away the sweat and prickly heat of the day. I reached for the soap, my eyes closed under the stream.

'Hey, you got a great bod for an old guy.'

'I'm thirty-two,' I said.

'Yeah, right.'

'And I like taking my showers alone,' I added as if I was thirteen uptight generations away.

'Hey, no big deal, Forrest. I'm just trying to see why Mom goes all soft when she talks about you.' Her little face stuck over the shower door, with a child's serious curiosity, like watching a fish in a fish tank.

'Get out of here.'

'Hey, that's not friendly,' she said, backing away. She was holding a white plastic garbage bag.

'Isn't it time you were back in school?'

'Don't worry about it, I'm almost packed and then I'm outta here. Laurel Canyon Incentive starts up again tomorrow . . .'

'Laurel Canyon what?'

'Incentive. My school. Karma of Capitalism in a Holistic World as they say. So I gotta go. Anyways I am outta my skull bored around here. I mean you're OK but I was only here because of it's even more boring at home. I mean I'm not on call for another week. Meantime I gotta do school.'

'Maybe you should come back for a visit. You might learn something.'

'Yeah, maybe I could watch you crash one of those dorky yellow cars face first into a cliff and learn why anybody would be dumb enough to drive one. That'd be fun to watch.'

I grabbed a towel and came out of the shower. Delilah was bent over, her long thin hair hanging over her face, scooping my dirty jeans into the plastic bag as if they were a dead animal. Her face came up again, hand sweeping aside her hair to reveal an oval face with freckles and a kid's habit of sucking in her lower lip. 'Like I mean don't you think it's weird that everybody is saying electric cars are great for the environment when if you ask me, they pollute around ten times worse. First off you're gonna need five of them because they go about as fast as golf carts. And they can't go anyplace, like twenty miles is big deal.' She tied a knot in the plastic bag.

'Sure, but this new EVIA is different. Akiri says you can cruise all day at fifty-five. And it runs on a fuel cell. Fuel goes in one end and electricity and drinking water comes out the other. Hundred per cent efficient.'

'If that's true how come they don't have any of them here? I mean not even a prototype. Yeah, I know they say they're afraid of being ripped off, but you really believe they are gonna be a big change? Like they have to run on fuel cells, right? Sooner or later, you have to dump all that lead or cadmium or whatever toxic stuff and acid they make their batteries out of. I'm just pissed off they didn't show up here with any of their real stuff. I mean what are those things you're supposed to be driving, Mustangs? You know that pre-1977 cars pollute around ninety-nine times what a new car does? Like in '97, LA says the gasoline cars gotta be ninety-nine point three per cent clean for hydrocarbon and if this so called dynamite fuel cell can match that, I'll believe it when I see it. Anyway, Tuna figured out that the average American driver, when you count parking and insurance, upkeep, gas, and all the time it takes to make the money to pay for it, like spends four hours a day and that's sixteen hundred hours a year to get seven thousand five hundred miles. You know what that works out? That works out to five miles an hour. I can walk that fast. You want me to get a pair of Sean's trousers out of the closet? They'd probably fit.'

'Just get the doorbell,' I said. 'I'll get the trousers.'

'Oh, is that what that noise is?' she said leaving the bathroom. 'I didn't know there was one.'

# chapter eighteen

'Well, hello,' I heard from the living-room. 'I heard Forrest was supposed to be in here.'

I came out of the bathroom with the towel wrapped around me and Bash, his bear shape filling the doorway, looked back and forth between me and the teenager.

'Hello, Bash,' I said. 'This is Delilah.'

'Some girls will do anything to get into movies,' Di said, putting her arm around me and leering at Bash. 'Just kidding,' she added and stuck out her hand to Bash.

'And just leaving,' I said as Delilah elaborately ignored me and settled on the couch, tucking her feet under her.

'Hey, don't leave on my account, Delilah,' Bash said unhelpfully. 'You got any cold beer in here, Forrest? I've been crawling under cars out in that desert heat and, hey don't get up, just tell me where it is.' But Di was already in the kitchen.

'You want any cheese and crackers and stuff?' she called out.

'Sure.' Bash lowered his voice and said, 'Where in hell did you get her?'

'I didn't *get her*. She's Sam's daughter and she was living here and she's moving out and I am moving in. What did you find out about the cars?'

'You want a beer too, Spike?' she called from the kitchen.

'Spike?' Bash mouthed the word, eyebrows raised over his big round eyes.

'Water,' I shouted back to the kitchen. 'She gave me the name when I was rude to her mother.'

'Makes more sense than Forrest. The cars are OK. What you said, NASCAR stockers with a fibreglass 3/4 scale Mustang skin. What do you want a replica for?'

'I want one I know hasn't been messed with. One I can lean

on without having it break. How long will it take?'

'Let's see. Find a good stocker that hasn't hit the wall more than once a week, replace all the brakes, suspension, and steering, rewire the sucker, lay a skin over it, stick in a decent motor, you care how fast it is?'

'It wouldn't hurt to be quicker than the cars you were just looking at.'

'Well, Reynolds has a couple of small block Chevy race engines on the shelf because I just sent them back to them. They're about bullet-proof and they turn five hundred and fifty horsepower on the dyno. That should keep you out front. Probably take a couple of weeks.'

'Can you do it in one?'

'If I get lucky finding a chassis and I get John Field to make me up a skin and bring in some outside help. It'll cost you twice as much, though.'

'How much?'

'Thanks,' Bash said, taking a cold bottle of Sierra Nevada from Delilah. 'Around sixty-five, seventy thousand. Plus twenty grand for the Reynolds motor. Depends on what I can find and what I have to make up.'

'Make up what?' Delilah said, handing me a glass.

I took an experimental sip. 'Thanks for the warm water, Delilah,' I said. 'Now it's time you ran home to Mommy.'

'She's not my mommy,' Delilah said. She went back into the bedroom to finish packing her backpack. On the way out she said, 'So long, Spike.' Then she said quietly to Bash, 'You know what a Spike is? It's just another name for a big prick.' Di gave me a sweet smile and slammed the door.

'Tough kid,' Bash said.

'Compared to her mother,' I said, 'she is a pussy cat.'

# chapter nineteen

Next morning's call was for seven thirty. We were going to shoot 'Our Big Scene', as Sam called it; Jill and Macklin in the bar just before they see the fire in Macklin's workshop. Mel brought in twenty one-day players for the scene. Plus there were the two principals, Sam and me, and four supporting roles; the bartender, the waitress, Harmon, a rancher, and his wife, Dolly. With the crew and the production team there were over a hundred people around the set.

I didn't take up Sam's offer of a hotel. The desert was peaceful in the evening. And the idea of sleeping late instead of rising early to catch a ride to a helicopter had a lot to be said for it. So I'd had a good night's sleep in Sean's motorhome, got up in time to see the sun rise over the mountains, made myself a cup of coffee, and walked into wardrobe and make-up to get a pair of Macklin's blue jeans, a fresh white shirt, and my crags filled in. Walking that half-mile into the empty town in the morning light I felt the excitement of being an actor; the buzz of walking in from the wings on to the bright lights of the stage. The crew and their trucks were crowded around the outside of a nice simple old wooden box of a building with VELMA in large faded red letters painted on the false front, and EAT DINE DANCING PERMITTED in smaller faded blue letters underneath. Whatever the front of the building said before the crew had painted it over, VELMA EAT DINE and DANCING PERMITTED looked as if it had been there for at least fifty years. The buzz of the generators, and the crew and the cast rushing in and out of the doors getting the first scene set up, looked like pure energy. Bright light poured from the front door and the windows, and I could hear Mayberry calling out, 'I want a Robertson twelve, for Chrissake. If you can't get me a twelve give me a sixteen with gels, but look again. I know there's a twelve out there.'

And over his voice, Sam was saying, 'Forrest, darling, you're early. Come inside and we'll rehearse the blocking for the first set-up. Pauline, can you get make-up to do something about the bartender? He looks like Clinton with a hangover.' She raised her cheek towards me to be kissed, her eyes closed and her lips puckered, kissing air. It only lasted a fraction of a second and I was struck again at how very beautiful she was, the soft curl of her upper lip, and the high cheekbones and the flawless clear skin.

Sam whirled away from me and shouted to a grip carrying in a plant. 'That's perfect, Phil, put it in the far corner by the men's room. And Mel, will you check and see if they've got the big fan rigged with a light so we can see the shadows on the dance floor? Did you sleep OK?' she said back to me, finishing the sentence with, 'Come on, let's get started.'

'Mel keeps telling me,' she was saying to me as we went into the bar, 'it would have been a lot cheaper to build a set and shoot it at the studio. But I don't want a set for our big scene. I don't think you ever get that feeling of reality I want for *Juice*. Not in a set and this place is so perfect. Like, I know it's crawling with crew and lights and cameras, but look at that stuffed bull's head. Isn't it like being in a kind of time warp?'

'A hot time warp,' I said. With the big lights blazing, it must have been 110°. But it was a nice old bar, with a 1957 League Champion softball trophy in front of the mirror behind the scarred mahogany bar. Over the last fifty years things had just settled into place like leaves on the ground. There were booths with red plastic seats and scarred and yellowed Formica tables, and in back an old pool table decorated with cigarette burns and beer stains.

'See,' Sam was saying happily, 'I want to get that feeling that some places have, like they have always been here. Look at that old Pabst Blue Ribbon beer clock and the video game in the corner. I mean a set designer would come up with a clock but he'd miss the video game. You ask them for 1957 and everything on the set is 1957. I like to see the past poking through the fabric of the present, know what I mean? I want

*Juice* to have depth. Hey! Get the air conditioners going, Julie. If it's not too much to ask,' she called out. 'We've got four ten-ton units for the heat of the lights and of course we'll turn them off while we're shooting but I don't want us playing a love scene dripping in sweat.'

'Love scene?' I repeated. I'd memorized the scene and it didn't seem like a love scene me.

'Only way to play it, Forrest,' she said, taking my hand. 'Look, OK, sure they've been living together for a year, but they haven't really understood or trusted each other. I mean on the surface they're celebrating Macklin's paying off the loan on his shop, but this is the first scene where they are really, finally relaxing with each other and with the idea of being in love. Billy, wait a minute. Can we do the cover shot in the mirror? I'll be back in a minute, Forrest,' she said. 'AND TURN ON THE GODDAMM AIR CONDITIONING!'

There was a whirr of the air conditioning turning on and the air began to cool almost instantly. I sat down to the bar and leafed through my script.

**57. EXT. NIGHT. FRONT OF THE ALMA BAR AND GRILL**
**JILL and MACKLIN, feeling good after their bottle of wine and dinner, walk down the empty moonlit main street of Alma. There is no traffic. Some cars are parked on the street, most of them in front of the bar where the music comes from.**
**(SFX: Desert presence, crickets)**
**(MUSIC: Bonnie Raitt 'Have a Heart' under)**

**58. INT. ALMA BAR & GRILL.**
**(MUSIC UP:)**
**Funky Bar & Grill in the West. There is a long bar and a few regulars on a Tuesday night. JILL comes in the door first, followed by MACKLIN. HARMON a rancher in his late thirties and his wife DOLLY are at the bar and a couple of cowboys sit a few stools down. Three young couples are scattered among the tables, with pitchers of beer, glasses, but most of the tables, like the town, are empty. JILL and MACKLIN head for the booths in the back past the**

juke box. As they walk by, HARMON nods and DOLLY turns around on her stool, glad to see them.

DOLLY

Well, our Miss Clemente. Why aren't you home marking A's on our boy's papers?

JILL

(Smiles) Soon as Billy learns what an A is, I'll give him one, Dolly. You know Mack.

They nod hello and go back to a booth in the back. As JILL and MACKLIN are sliding in a waitress in running shoes and blue jeans stands at the end of the booth.

WAITRESS

Hi, Jill. Mack. What are you all havin' tonight?

MACKLIN

(Grinning) What have you got for champagne?

WAITRESS

Beer.

MACKLIN

You got any wine?

WAITRESS

I don't know. I could look.

MACKLIN

Look for something extravagant. Expensive. Something we can brag about to our kids.

The waitress leaves and JILL leans forward to MACKLIN across the Formica table top.

JILL

What kids? Is there something you want to tell me, darling? Are you just a little pregnant?

MACKLIN

Well, one of these days we might think about it.

JILL

I recognize that shifty look, Macklin. Are you trying to tell me something?

MACKLIN

Well, I was thinking it might be easier on Candy if we, uh, one of these days, you know, got married.

JILL

That is the most backassward proposal I have ever heard of in my life. For Candy, huh?

The waitress returns with two bottles and two glasses on her tray. She sets the tray on the table.

WAITRESS

We got two kinds. You want red or white?

Macklin takes a bottle in each hand and looks at the labels.

MACKLIN

Both.

The waitress opens both bottles and puts them on the table.

JILL

You can't have it both ways.

WAITRESS

You want two more glasses?

She leaves and MACKLIN takes JILL's hands in his.

MACKLIN

Sweetheart, I want you one way or another. Or both ways or every which way.

JILL

Every which way sounds pretty good. You want to dance?

MACKLIN

I'm not much of a dancer.

JILL

That's 'cause you haven't danced with me yet.

They go out to the juke box, JILL drops a quarter in the machine and takes MACKLIN's hand and leads him out to the empty space in front of the juke box.

(MUSIC UP)

They begin slowly, in the kind of jerky and separate steps that people do at rock concerts, until they get into the rhythm of the music which is lively and sweet and they dance together. Then the music changes tempo and they dance close together, JILL's arm around MACKLIN's neck, his hand on her butt giving her a squeeze. JILL leans into him and the music stops. They kiss. And they stand still, holding each other for a moment.

JILL's face is bathed in red light. Her eyes are closed and she opens them slowly. She is feeling dreamy and sexy. That drains from her face when she realizes that the red light that is flickering on her face is a fire. And that the fire is MACKLIN's garage.

A hand was on the back of my neck, and Sam was looking over my shoulder at the script, saying, 'What do you think, Forrest. Can you play it as a love scene?'

'You're wearing perfume.'

'Don't you think Jill would?'

'I'm not thinking of Jill.'

'That's a step in the right direction. Let's rehearse this dance.'

The sparks set up a boom box with a cassette of the music and we rehearsed. Dancing awkwardly, separately, waving our hands and feet while around us the grips and the sparks moved lights and arranged the props and Billy's camera crew practised their moves with the dolly and Frank Martello, Billy's second assistant, moved around us with a hand-held camera. We moved closer together and Sam fell easily into my arms and we danced.

'You come here often?' she said.

'I thought we were sticking to the script.'

'I've always believed in writing my own script,' she said, moving against me.

'How about you are selfish, egocentric, tough as an old boot, bossy, driven . . .'

'You bet your ass,' she said softly. 'Let's try a kiss.'

We tried one. And stopped. And I looked into those deep green eyes and I kissed her again. For a long time.

'That works fine,' Sam said in my ear. 'Just fine.'

'Let's go over to my motorhome,' I said, 'and work on the script.'

'You talking to Jill or to me.'

'Both,' I said.

'You can't have it both ways.'

'Every which way sounds pretty good,' I said.

'Let's shoot the scene first,' Sam said in my ear. 'Then we'll play with the script.'

# chapter twenty

I haven't told you about her voice. At night, in the dark, Sam's voice took on a husky quality, sexy like a blues singer between the songs, telling you the secrets of her life. On the phone Sam was a young girl, sunny and innocent. Full of hope. Live, face to face, you took your chances.

Outside her bedroom in Bel Air, the long spikes of the palm trees guarded the sky. In the dark, she said, 'I love the way you smile when I look at you. As if you know me better than I do. As if you know a secret I don't.' After we had made love her voice had a contralto depth.

Of course it was more than music. Her voice was rich with what I wanted to hear. In the darkness she said, 'You are like a little boy. Such small things give you so much pleasure. You have no idea how good you are and I'm afraid to tell you because I don't know if it is some great strength you have or if it is just an accident of the light. But you have real power on the screen, Forrest. I'm afraid to shoot you next to me because I am afraid you will blow me away. You have all this light on the screen and I look terrible in the shadows.'

She said, 'You are a prince. All you have to do is describe your kingdom and it will be yours.'

She said her voice was her instrument and in the few mornings when I was in her bed in Beverly Hills, it was always the phone that woke us up and I lay back on the pillows and listened to her play. 'Yes, darling, I know. I miss you too. When? You say. I'll make time. As soon as I finish this shoot,' she said, her voice ranging from promise to businesslike efficiency dismissing some actor she had forgotten from another shoot.

'Forrest,' she said, 'you make me afraid. I have never, I

shouldn't tell you this, I have never lost myself like that. I'm afraid of this power you have over me. You look at me and I lose track of whatever it was that was going through my mind and I want to kiss you. Great sucking kisses,' she said, her voice dropping down to those low, lascivious, and delicious depths. 'I will do anything you want me to,' she said. 'Just tell me. I don't care. You strip me away clean and I feel fresh with you. Like I was sixteen.'

One night, in bed she said, 'I want to be on top now. I want to see if I can feel what it is like to give so much pleasure the way you give me. Everything with you,' she said, 'is new.'

She said, 'I am so happy when I hear your voice.'

She said, 'If you want something, Forrest, forget it. And you won't want it any more and it will be yours. I am afraid,' she said, 'that is what will happen to me. That you will forget me when you are a star. And you won't want me any more. And I will still be yours and you'll be sick of me.'

Her voice was always fresh. And I was always surprised to hear how big and wide and wonderful I was. And how she could, on the phone or in a conversation while she was shooting a scene, look at me, and make me know that she was thinking of me while she was talking about something else like lighting a door. She was everything I had ever wanted her to be. She was a wonderful actress.

We came and went by helicopter. Back and forth in the cool early morning before it was light and back in the evening long after dark. Serafina always left something out for us in the kitchen. Sam's house wasn't big. But it was exquisite, an old Spanish-style single-storey house with a tile roof, built in the thirties on Jasmine Lane in Bel Air; high-beamed ceilings, three bedrooms, a big garden, a small pool, a kitchen with all the latest equipment for a classy restaurant like a Wolf oven, a rolling butcher block.

Cataloguing these details depresses me.

She said, eating a chicken leg, 'If you are so damn fast let me see you pull a beer out of the air.'

And I went over to the vast refrigerator, opened the door, and looked into the bright cold chromium shelves with rows of sauces, a chicken neatly wrapped in clear wrap, a dozen spears of asparagus in a gold crust of butter on a blue plate, the small white bowls with the different sauces that Serafina kept handy, two bottles of Husch Chardonnay and the no-fat milk and Diet Coke and fresh squeezed orange juice in the door. I reached in and lifted a Red Hook beer from the six-pack in the back and shut the door and twisted off the cap and handed her the cold bottle and I said, 'Now you know how long a tenth of a second goes on when you are racing.'

Sam put the beer down and took a half step, her face just below me, looking up. Her hands went up to her throat holding the neck of the blue silk blouse she was wearing. She said, 'That's how I've always felt. All my life, as if everything always takes too long.' She held me with her eyes, green and clear and taking me in and she ripped her blouse wide open. Her white breasts looking wide-eyed and helpless. 'Tell me about time,' she said.

# chapter twenty-one

A faint halo outlined the jagged mountains seventy miles away. Four thousand feet below, in the slow creep of light, the desert floor was gradually rising from the darkness as if it were being born for the first time. As if nothing had changed for a million years. Either way, it was as still as a museum.

There was a short cry in the distance and another and another and the valley and the mountains around us filled with a yelping, warbling animal howling in the empty air.

Sam, her face buried in the pillow, said, 'What the hell is that supposed to be?'

'Coyotes,' I said, 'saying good morning.'

'Good morning, coyotes.' Sam rolled over and peered over my shoulder out the window, her body warm against my back. 'I'll bet they are howling because you were up before they were.' Her arm reached over me, her fingers lightly brushing across my chest. Sam's bedroom suite, complete with sunken bathtub, Jacuzzi, hot tub, and shower, covered the second floor of her motorhome. It had been designed to feel rich: thick carpet, paintings of French landscapes on the few walls that weren't all glass, and a bed wider than it was long with one of the most beautiful women in the world in it. With the dry mountains, rock, sand, and coyotes on the other side of the glass it felt like a NASA capsule on the moon.

'I'm glad we stayed overnight up here in the mountains,' Sam said. 'It's just like camping out. Think of all the $575 an hour helicopter time we're saving.'

We lay still for a while, just looking out, watching the world take shape.

After a while Sam said, 'See the blue over there in the hollows of the valleys? And the red on the ridges and the gold where the sun is on the hills below us? It's like watching a painter brushing on the mountains.' She yawned happily. 'If you have to get up at this awful hour, Evers, this is the way to do it. Where is that spike?' she said, reaching for me, finding me. 'I like an early riser.'

'You just like an early start. How old were you when you had Delilah? You couldn't have been more than fifteen.'

'I didn't. Whatever made you think of her?' she said, letting go of me and sitting up.

'You didn't what?

'Have her. Delilah is Gig's daughter from another marriage.'

'Gig?'

'Gig. My former husband. Delilah's not easy but she hasn't had it easy either. He was an even worse parent than I am, if you can believe. I mean he didn't even notice if Delilah was home or not and I don't think he cared. I couldn't leave her, not with him. So I adopted Delilah when we got divorced.'

'That's the first time I've heard you mention a husband.'

'And the last,' she said, rolling on top of me.

'What was he like?' I said, rolling on top of her.

'I forget,' Sam said, squirming against me. 'Come on, what made you think of Delilah?'

'You said Spike and that was Di's nickname for me. You remember, from when I said I'd sit on a spike for you if I had to.'

'I'm not going to touch that line. Do you think you can be nice to Di-Di this weekend?'

'I'm always nice to her. I like her. She's coming up?'

'Just for the weekend. She wants to see that Tuna person, the grip. Which I think is terrible and I've told him if he touches her I'll have his kneecaps for coasters. He says it's all innocent, and you never know, it might be. Delilah says she just loves taking long walks with him. At least I've got her to stay here, with us if you can stand it. I thought while we're setting up for your run this evening Delilah and I could rehearse the scene where Jill and her daughter have an argument about Macklin's moving in with them.'

'I thought you did that scene the first night I stayed in your house.'

'Oh come on, Forrest. We had a few words, that's all. She'll get used to you. She's just a kid. She needs a little time to adjust. She'll be all right.' We kissed, Sam rolled back on top and her voice went down into that low and warm place where Sam seemed at home. 'I saw the dailies from our love scene last night.'

'What last love scene? Last night you came in the door and nose-dived into your pillow. I never knew stars snored.'

'Megastars can do whatever the hell we like. The scene we shot last week, dummo. In the studio. Mayberry has had it processed and pushed the blue, like that light down there in the valley,' she said pointing. 'We look so good together, Forrest. You can tell we are lovers.'

'It looks authentic. Has a real feel.'

'Don't make fun of me. I'm just saying we look good together on the screen.'

'Wait a minute and I'll get the lights set up.'

'Oh, cut it out, Forrest. I'm not your lover for some damn movie. I always wanted to make love with you. Right from the first time I saw you in the screening-room at Olympic when you came in with Virgin. I said, "Get a hold on yourself, Samantha, it's just a crush. Cheap physical attraction. It'll go away." I tried to drive it away because I didn't want more complication. We hadn't even started the film and it was falling apart. That's why I was so rude to you. From the moment I saw you in the studio,' she said, kissing me. 'You have this wonderful karma, this sense of being at home with yourself, Forrest. And I always know where I am with you. In this town, that's a rare quality. And it is good for my soul, you crabby old bastard.'

We kissed again with the easy kiss of lovers who think they have all the time in the world. 'I never know when you are being Sam and when you are acting.'

'I'm not acting now,' she said, pushing down hard. 'My lovely Spike,' she breathed in my ear.

Later, the sun was up and we were in the kitchen, brewing coffee, pouring juice, toasting bread, the things that stars do in the morning when they are camping out. 'Do you ever get frightened?' she said.

'Sure. All the time.'

'I thought racing drivers were supposed to be too brave to

be frightened,' she said, pouring coffee into thick white cups on the blue counter.

'We get frightened all the time. But it's not about courage. You know that Virgin song, the one she was singing last year called "Flash of Time"?'

Sam's reflection in the window glass took a sip from her cup and shook her head, no.

'It goes,' and I sang in my croaking voice, ' "the past is as empty as a glass, and the future's just a promise full of holes. The only time we'll ever have, is the flash of time they call now." '

'That's a pretty little song, sweetie, but it's bullshit. If I didn't plan ahead I'd never get anything done.'

'Ah, the lists of Sam. "I'll be right back after I finish this list." '

'Just make sure you're on it.'

'What about now?'

'You missed it. Now's over.'

I took a piece of toast. No butter for the oversized racing driver. 'That doesn't mean it doesn't happen. Racing is finding time inside of time. You get up on that knife edge and a puff of wind, a drop of oil on the track, a slight change in the temperature can change everything. When you have that focus you make a hell of a lot of judgement calls in no time at all.'

'Focus, huh? Well in your judgement, Spike, are you focused on today's shoot or is your future full of holes?' she said, poking at my stomach with her finger.

'In my judgement, Lady Samantha, today's shoot will be a bitch for you because you are exhausted. And it will be a piece of cake for me. We're doing rehearsals and inserts this morning. Rig shots with the camera mounted on the car. This afternoon will be more interesting.'

By that time, I was an old hand, easy with the movie lingo, working the camera angles. We only had two more days of shooting before I had to fly to Portugal for a Formula One testing session and we wanted to get all the driving sequences in the can if we could before I left.

'It's all interesting,' Sam said. 'Delilah will be here around noon. You sure you don't mind if she stays here?'

'Of course not. I like her.'
'Well, try and be nice to her. She's still not relaxed about us.'
'Neither am I,' I said.
'Stop that,' Sam said, laughing happily. 'We just did all that.'

# chapter twenty-two

brAAAAAAAAAAAppp. BRAAAAAAAAAAAAAAPPPP. Whommmpittta Whammmmpitta.

Just tapping my foot. BRAAAAAAAAAAAAAAPPPP.

An old habit left over from the days before computer engine-management systems when racing engines wouldn't idle and you had to blip them to keep them running. This wasn't even a racing engine, just a hot-rod Chevy V-8 with a few bolt-on bits and its electronic brain altered to think it was a Ferrari. Still, I was as edgy and impatient as a racing driver on race day. Which in a way was what I was. The sky was dark blue now. And the whole valley between the mountain ranges was in shadow and the light was running out fast.

BRAAAAAAAAAAAAAAPPPP.

California 257 is a narrow two-lane back road running across the side of a mountain with a cliff falling off one side and another cliff rising up on the other, tricky and twisting, bumpy and crowned in the middle so the outside of the curve was banked the wrong way. I had done three practice runs and two rehearsals and I knew the road well enough to distrust it. I did not want to drive it flat out in the dark. These were 'cover' shots from the chopper and from the hillside to show the danger and the speed. Later we'd shoot close ups of Jill and Candy in the car.

BRAAAAAAAAAAAAAPPPP. BRAAAAAAAAAAAAAPPPP.

Another thing that was making me nervous was that Bash hadn't finished welding another stronger and better Puerca together so this was going to be in one of Akiri's Puerca Encantadas. Sean had crashed Puerca One in a big way and now, here was World Champion Wannabe Forrest Evers, 'veteran' Formula One driver, blipping the throttle in Puerca Two, chewing his lip, ready to pop the clutch and go. Even if Bash had finished building a replica, swapping it for Puerca Two would have been almost impossible. There was no place to hide a car on California 257. Turn left and you run into the cliff. Turn right and you run into thin air.

Whomppa Whomppaaa Brraaaapp Brraaaap.

A cage of tubes and bungee cord was bolted to the left front fender with a thirty-five millimetre camera lens staring wide-eyed back alongside the car. There was another camera mounted down in the passenger's foot well pointing up at me. Another mounted under the front grille. And of course, several cameras mounted on sandbags and hi-hats along the route. Plus, hovering nervously up above, a giant eyeball called Steady-cam sticking out the side of a Bell Jet Ranger, with Billy Mayberry aboard. They would fly along above me while I scrabbled across the face of the mountain.

Special effects were up the road four miles away, ready to roll some fake rocks into my path. We had spent six hours setting up this one shot, and as Sam said several times, we could save a lot of money and a day's shoot if we got it in one take.

Julie, Mel's production assistant, was standing next to the car, tossing her long black hair back as she put the walkie-talkie up to her ear, showing wide white teeth behind her purple lipstick in what looked like a nervous grin but could have been gas pains. On both sides of Julie, the grips waited for the shot to start, watching.

Julie leaned into the car and gave my six-point racing harness a tug to make sure it was tight. The racing harness bolted to the roll cage was my contribution to my safety. If I hit something a lap-belt wouldn't do it. It's one thing driving a vintage car and another collecting vintage injuries from vintage safety equipment. Also I didn't want the violent shocks of driving hard over a bumpy road bouncing me around. I had enough to do without worrying about sitting down.

'Turn on your lights,' Julie said, giving me a light peck on the cheek for luck. 'Day for night.'

Another twenty minutes, I thought pulling out the light switch, and we would be shooting night for night.

'Lipstick,' one of the grips said, and Julie came back to the car and dabbed a Kleenex at my cheek. The Kleenex came away with a purple smudge.

brAAAAAAAAAApp. BRAAAAAAAAAAAAAPPPP. Whammmpittta Whammmmpitta.

Under Macklin's goofy Hawaiian Surfer Saturday night shirt, I wore my Nomex racing suit to keep my body from burning up if I did crash. Another great comfort. The art director had painted the racing harness straps to match the Hawaiian shirt, world's first designer seat-belts.

If something did go wrong, I was a racing driver. I'd have plenty of time to catch it. Wouldn't I? I'd heard that Sean was suing Olympic Studios for $300 million for ruining his career and breach of contract. I suppose, I thought, my heirs could always sue. If there were any heirs.

Sam stuck her face in front of me. 'You OK?' she shouted over the noise of the helicopter hovering overhead.

'Absolutely perfect in every way,' I lied. I was worried about Sam. She had been up to one and two in the morning every night, going over shots with Mayberry and on the phone to David and to Radnor. They were pushing her hard to make up lost time and finish the film under budget and on schedule. Worried because she was also getting up at five thirty every morning to go over her shooting script with Mal and she was getting a little bruised under her eyes. Shooting outside all day was making hairline lines at the corners of her eyes and mouth. She was wound up tight, putting everything she had into making *Juice* as perfect as it could be with Radnor and David breathing down her neck and a leading actor who tended to interpret complex emotion by looking left and right. 'I've been thinking, Sam. Maybe I could do better, get deeper into the motivation of the part. Maybe I could look up sometimes. Or down. I haven't begun to explore the possibilities of the diagonal eye shift from, say two o'clock to eight.'

'Just try and keep your eyes on the road, Spike,' Sam said, giving me a worried smile. 'And keep the wheel side down. I think Billy's ready, they're just checking with the second and third units down the road.'

At least, here, I thought, blipping the throttle some more, I knew what I was doing. At least behind the wheel, I was in control.

Julie called out from the side of the road, 'Stand by, please!'

In my rear-view mirror Tuna, the hippie grip with a ponytail, salt-stained and faded red bandanna around his forehead, and the lean and weary look of a man who has already been to wherever you are headed and has come back to tell you it's not worth the effort; Tuna who liked to call himself an endangered species and wore the logos of *JAWS* and *JURASSIC PARK* from former shoots, with the hammer and pliers and roll of gaffer's tape hanging from his belt, took the radio phone from his ear and waved a green flag. Delilah, one hand in Tuna's back pocket, wearing a bright red T-shirt rolled up tight around her boobs, and cut off jeans and clunky black shoes, gave me the finger with her free hand.

Julie screamed from the side of the road, 'OK, they're rolling, Forrest. You're on.'

Sam gave me a kiss on the cheek. 'Go gettum, Spike,' she said, stepping back. 'Action.'

I let out the clutch and floored it, feeling pumped up as a kid playing fighter pilot. Well, in a way it *was* kid's stuff. I was driving for effect, not for time. I had wanted big gummy racing tyres to give the damn Puerca some grip and Mel had said no way. Racing tyres were too fat, too low, and too slick. They would look out of place with all the shots they already had. And besides, they didn't want grip. They wanted long, lurid power slides that would look exciting on film and if I was really racing be a big fat waste of time. So the crew put Puerca Two on its original narrow, old-fashioned tyres. They wouldn't corner or stop but they would slide for ever.

The back end slithered back and forth, the wheels spun, spewing smoke, and I was off, heading into the first corner fifty yards away, a tight up-hill right-hander. Hard on the throttle, first gear, second, the gear shift as sloppy as a spoon in soup, but it didn't matter, third, the tyres still spinning, I cocked the wheel right twenty yards before the turn, then left, holding it, keeping my foot down just enough so the car was arcing down towards the turn, leaning into the inside crown of the bumpy road, just touching the inside of the corner and kicking up some gravel for the camera, pedal flat to the floor and the car straightens out as I head straight up hill.

I want to pass the first camera station a quarter of a mile

away up the hill at over a hundred miles an hour so they can get a real feel for the speed. Something is loose, I thought, a bolt, in the front suspension, something is making the steering feel loose, but I can't trace it. A cluster of small flowers on the side of the road is outlined against the empty space of the thousand-foot drop over the side. The road bends to the left, and I take the corner on the inside, confident there are no cars coming from the other direction because Mel and the crew have blocked off the road for our shoot. The helicopter is just ahead of me at about two o'clock, and there is a trickle of sand coming down from an overhang of rock on the left. There is a small oil patch on the road as I come out of the easy uphill bend, accelerating hard, shifting from third to fourth. The speedometer says ninety-five. I let the car come out a little more to straddle the oil patch. Probably the oil patch is several weeks old, and completely harmless, but it reminds me to keep my eyes open for sand and oil or stones on the road. Up ahead on my left, the camera crew, three of them, are huddled over a camera pointed at me from behind a boulder, hidden from Billy's chopper overhead.

Just past them the road dips sharply down, a roller-coaster down hill, with a bend to the left at the bottom and then right with open space to my left, and I keep my foot down hard, I could take it easy here, but it is easier for me to go nearly flat out than it is to back off and go, say, seven-tenths. You probably wouldn't see much of a difference on the screen, but my concentration would be somewhere down from 100%. So I push hard as I disappear behind a pinnacle of rock, hidden from the chopper, and accelerate back up hill and the chopper is there, just up ahead, waiting for me as I continue up hill, the back wheels spinning at seventy-five, the back end of the car kicked out at an angle, kicking up dust from the side of the road. Just a Sunday drive having fun.

The second camera crew is outside a hairpin bend at the end of a short down-hill straight. They have scattered sand and gravel at the outside of the turn so I can swing wide, spin my wheels in it, and spray the camera with dirt and rocks. In my rear-view mirror, as I accelerate away, up hill towards the clear blue sky, the camera crew are sticking their heads out from behind their barrier of dirt like three baby birds in a nest.

I am steering more with the throttle than the steering-wheel. I can turn the wheel left and right and the car will change its attitude, but on these skinny tyres it doesn't want to change direction. The noise is terrific, the race-tuned Chevy V–8 wound at 6,000 rpm in second coming out of the tight up-hill hairpin turns and third on the short straights. The air is clear and cool, and before I shatter the silence of the mountains in the desert, perfectly still. When I kick up a cloud of dust it hangs in the air as still as a painting on a blue wall.

Five miles up the road, the air is thin and cool and I am sweating. Keeping the car fluid, flowing through the turns in long graceful arcs, is hard work on this choppy road. The surface changes, rough one second and smooth the next. And so does the grip. In the panorama of my windshield I can see, a quarter of a mile ahead, fifty yards up the steep side of the mountain, two men are letting go the rubber rocks. The road curves into the V-shaped gully to follow the contour of the mountain and the rocks are bounding down slowly. There are two cameras; one, closer to me and just before the gully that will funnel the rocks, is a wide-angle lens that will pan with me as I drive through the phony avalanche. The rocks aren't rubber of course, they are foam-weighted to bounce like rocks. One of them is real.

The other camera crew is just behind the gully, with a long lens pointed straight at me, hoping to shoot me coming through the rockfall. That rock can't be real.

The helicopter is coming down lower, getting close, coming up from behind and I feel the pulsing downdraught, washing the night air over the car. I softly tap the brakes to settle the car, shift the weight forward as I turn the wheel twenty yards from the gully, and twitch the wheel as the first of the rubber rocks bound on to the road, keeping my foot down on the accelerator, going about eighty-five into the tight U-bend, and the rock is real.

It is about the size of a small car but it is solid rock and heavier than the fake rocks, you can tell because it doesn't bounce like the foam rocks. It is falling with intent, I think to myself. It is about twenty feet above the road and falling down into the left shoulder and I tighten the wheel to get outside, to get to the outside edge where there is a five-hundred-foot drop before the trees.

I change my mind. I aim for it.

At racing speeds if you want to keep from hitting another racing car you aim for them because the one place they won't be is where they are now. Screw going outside, I cut back inside, the car heeling hard over on to its right side, and then the rock hits the shoulder hard, falling almost straight down and the rock rolls slowly and casually like a rock on a Sunday stroll into the middle of the road. I can almost make it inside and I will probably pile into the cliff.

But the rock doesn't keep rolling. It stops. I tighten the wheel, and there isn't enough room now to get inside it and my right front bumper hits it at seventy-five miles an hour, there is a bang tearing off the front fender and the steering-wheel almost tears out of my hands. But it is OK. I am past the boulder and I am still in one piece and I think I will keep going, try to get this run in one take for Sam.

The road curves away and I am headed for the open space of the desert valley. I am headed for the edge of the cliff now, towards the long drop into space but I am not particularly worried. I am headed for the edge of the cliff but there is plenty of time to gain control. Plenty of time, but nothing happens when I turn the wheel. The car doesn't have any grip at all. Absolutely none. It feels as if I am floating on air. If you can't steer, at least slow down. I stand on the brakes again, coming up on the cliff edge, and I have time to wonder if it makes any difference at all if you go over a four-thousand-foot cliff slowly or quickly. Maybe quicker is better.

There was a silence and the feeling of falling and the coolness of the evening air. And as the blades of the helicopter came fluttering into my dark blue sky I remember wondering if it was coming to rescue me.

# chapter twenty-three

A curtain of fog hung fifty yards offshore as an old storm was rolling in out of the mist and crashing silently against the beach. Gliding just above the backwash, a row of pelicans dipped down, one by one, scooping up breakfast.

In the foreground, thirty-five stories below, the *Queen Mary* lay nailed to the harbour bottom, its orange smokestacks canted back as if she were steaming for Tahiti. For fourteen years, from 1938 to 1952, the stately *Queen*, with the Grand Salon two stories high and a city block long, held the transatlantic speed record at just under thirty-two knots. Now they had the old lady penned in like a lion in a zoo. I remembered the story of Rob Walker, the last private entrant in Formula One and the last gentleman in England, staying there during one of the Long Beach Grand Prix. 'And do you know,' he said, 'they let me have my old room back.'

'God, it's awesome, isn't it,' Delilah said.

'Have you ever been on it?' I asked. 'There's an art deco bar on the fore deck where it looks like Fred Astaire and Ginger Rogers will be coming in for drinks with the Duke of Windsor, if you ignore the tourists from Iowa in jogging suits.'

Delilah looked at me uncomprehending for a moment. 'Oh,' she said, 'you mean that old boat. Screw that. I mean this—' She turned, waving a hand over Hozuki Industries' corporate reception room on top of Hozuki Tower. 'I mean it's not like your average VIP holding tank. What's so awesome is the lack of confidence. Like they really want to impress you so bad and they don't care what it costs.'

Well, it was flashy, but then glitz was born in southern California. The floor was wide polished ebony planks with small priceless oriental silk carpets scattered among the silk sofas and glass coffee tables. Blue watery light from the ocean flooded the room through floor to ceiling windows. The walls were hung with bright splashes of fast appreciating post-modern American paintings; a Gilburg, a LePage, and two by Horace Marsland Smith.

Ebony rafters two stories up gave the impression of vast free space until you saw the restless eyes of video cameras mounted on the beams, scanning the room.

'They musta spent zillions,' Delilah said, 'but it's nothing they can't take with them.'

'In the mean time, there's a million dollars a minute waiting to see them,' I said. Sam was in a demure little burgundy leather miniskirt and jacket with a low-cut pale yellow silk blouse, legs crossed, foot tapping, nervously shuffling through *Vogue*, and looking up at me, her face wincing with concern. David Allen and Ron Radnor sat exchanging whispers on an antique leather couch. Radnor's eyes were rimmed in pink with blue and purple bags hung under his eyes as if he hadn't slept for two days. Compared to me he looked fresh as a daisy. David had the tanned and confident look of a talk-show host; blue blazer, soft cream silk shirt, and silk tie. Shiny black and burgundy Italian shoes.

Delilah, standing next to me, wore a bulky knit sweater big enough for two of her. Her uncombed long hair and slightly buggy green eyes made her look needy, uncared for, and street smart. 'I'm sorry I gave you the finger yesterday, Forrest,' she said loudly. 'It was immature.'

'Looked grown-up to me,' I said, trying to keep it light. 'Drove me right off the road.'

'Yeah, right. Does it hurt to walk?'

'Not as long as I lean on my crutch. The doctor said I should think of walking as warm-up laps for old age.'

'Well, before you get too old, Forrest,' Delilah announced to the room, 'are you going to marry my beautiful rich megastar Mom, or are you just fucking around?'

'Di-Di, honey,' her mother called out as if she hadn't heard, 'why don't you come over and look at these stretch stirrup jodhpurs. Christy Brinkley's daughter's wearing them and I bet they'd look stunning on you.'

'Jeezzzus,' Di said, 'in a minute.' She looked at me, waiting for an answer.

'How old is Tuna?' I said.

'Tuna?'

'The grip who follows you into the bushes.'

'I know who you mean. I mean do you really think I'd be making it with somebody named Tuna? God, Tuna,' she said, staring up at me. 'He's nice to me and he really knows all the nature stuff in the mountains but he's gay, Evers.' She smiled a mock-professional smile. 'We're just good friends. And if you really think my sex life is your business, like, you know, you're jealous, I'm a virgin. For life, probably.'

'Ah, excuse me, please, Mr Allen.' A miniature Japanese woman, pale from a life under glass, was bowing in front of David and speaking to the floor. 'If you and Mrs Sam be kind enough to follow me, Mr Hozuki will be so glad to see you now.'

Akiri's office was in the corner, with floor to ceiling glass wrapped around two sides. It wasn't a large office by western standards and tiny by the *Bonanza* dimensions of Hollywood. But it had power; a spare and single-purpose look as if this was where the decisions of Hozuki US were made when they didn't come in by fax from Nagoya.

Akiri's desk was a glass slab the size of a king-sized bed, poised on a thick glass pedestal. There was a slim computer monitor on a stalk, a keyboard, and a phone with no cord. There was also a large red leather chair behind the desk. Apparently Akiri was admiring the ocean view, because the chair was turned away from us. Apart from the red leather executive chair and the glass desk there was nothing else to distract you from the grandeur of the view. No papers. No photographs, and nothing on the walls except the Pacific Ocean for a backdrop for the high and objective executive with the high and objective executive view.

There was also no place for us to sit, apart from a low, and no doubt priceless, heavily carved Japanese tea table surrounded by cushions. We stood in front of the glass desk. The tiny woman in her tiny white silk dress bowed to the back of the chair and to us and backed out.

'It is time,' Akiri's voice said, 'to stop fucking around.'

'I've been through the figures, Akiri,' Radnor said and the back of a hand appeared from the chair, stopping Radnor in mid-sentence. We listened to the ventilation system.

Akiri came around slowly in his swivel chair. He was wearing an immaculate black pinstripe suit, a new white button-down shirt, a quiet corporate necktie, and the compressed lips and lowered brow of a serious corporate man. No more just one of the boys.

The sons of the very rich often go to great lengths to show that they are really just another everyday guy. They do it because it looks safe out there in everyday guy land, almost peaceful without the high risk and anxiety that high money brings. And they do it badly because they know and everybody else knows they have money and power way beyond the trivia of platinum credit cards and mutual funds. They own the credit card companies, the mutual fund companies, and they own the bank. They know that somebody else will always pay all of their bills and their bank account will always be brimming and that all they ever have to do, if push comes to shove, is pick up the phone. So when they finally take up the mantle of their money and wrap themselves in it, they do it with surprising speed and a sigh of relief all round.

I wondered if it was the custom among the staff at Hozuki to kneel in the office of the son of Hozuki San.

'The figures, whatever they are, tell me that you have set me up, David, for unlimited liability. UNLIMITED.'

'There is insurance,' David said quietly.

'With MY INSURANCE COMPANY,' Akiri screamed. The room went quiet again. It was not a clear day behind Akiri, but I reckoned, looking out over his shoulder, that the mist would clear long before noon. Although the smog in LA, like the poor, may always be with us. 'What about you, Evers?' he said.

The doctor at the hospital had said the MR scan showed nothing was broken. A disc in the middle of my back was mildly compressed and several ligaments in my left arm were torn and the racing harness had imprinted bruises like Caribbean sunsets on my thighs and shoulders and every time I took a breath I was reminded of an especially painful bruise surrounding my belly button from the harness buckle. But apart from eye watering flashes from the crunched disc and a number of high- and low-grade dull aches, no permanent damage. My right ankle was swollen like a well-veined melon but I could shuffle along with the crutch and it would heal. And of course my face was a mess but the doctor said with rest and a couple of days in the hospital I should be up and walking. I didn't have a couple of days and I got up and with a lot of help from Sam, left the hospital. 'I'm fine, Akiri,' I lied. 'Thank you for asking.'

'I am very glad to hear you are OK, although, I have to tell you, you look terrible. What I mean is, Evers, are you going to sue?'

'I haven't thought about it.'

'Well, if you do think about it, Evers, remember this. We have the footage on film. Footage that shows you weaving long before you get to the landslide, clearly out of control. If you want to go to court we can prove that while you claimed to be an expert driver, you lost control and caused your own accident. My lawyers tell me we have an excellent case for your incompetence causing serious damage to our project not to mention writing off a $300,000 prototype if we wish to counter-sue.'

'I'll keep that in mind.' His 'prototype' hadn't cost more than $30,000, but I thought I'd let it go. 'Did you notice that one of those boulders was real?'

'They are supposed to look real. So what?'

'Was real. Somebody set it up. Somebody made me crash.'

'If you want to pursue your own action, be my guest, Forrest. You won't get anything out of *Juice* because I am winding up the production and you will have to join a long line of creditors. I'm sure David here can give you a cassette and you may view it at your leisure and identify the rock you think is real and climb down the side of the cliff to where we had to winch you out by helicopter, or, more likely, another thousand feet down to the valley floor, and find your rock, interview it, fingerprint it, do whatever the hell you want with it and then tell us what that has to do with anything.'

Akiri narrowed his eyes and leaned forward. 'We have a $300 million suit from one principal in this project and whether or not you want to fight the Hozuki Heavy Industries, Evers, there is no way we can complete *Juice* now. Not with you looking like a mugging victim. And no way can we start again with another actor. Even if we could find one, there isn't time in the production schedule let alone the budget. Have you seen your face, Evers? Do you think we could have you looking like that next to EVIA? *Juice* is dead and we are, according to my estimate, not counting the cost of defending the lawsuit but counting the cost of buying out the contracts, we are over fifty-five million dollars in the hole.' He looked at us from face to face, as if he was looking for the perp in a police station line-up.

'Naturally I assume you will share the cost of this catastrophe, David, since *Juice* was, as you kept reminding us, your baby. You only look like you died, Evers. Which is more than I can say for *Juice*. Three crashes and I am out.'

I had seen my face in the mirror. A purple, yellow, and red bruise bloomed on my forehead and a cut on my chin sprouted eleven small black spider stitches. My eyes were badly bloodshot from the impact but presumably the red blotches and veins would disappear in a few days.

The deepest cut had been delivered over the phone that morning. I'd called Barry Steele in Didcot, England, headquarters of Steele Grand Prix Development Engineering of which Barry was team manager, founder, and owner. Barry had built his Formula One team from a small garage in Surrey twelve years ago to a $200 million a year business with its own corporate jet and 245 employees. My team and my boss. Here is the entire conversation from start to finish.

FE: Good morning, Barry.

BS: It's two thirty in the afternoon. Where the hell are you?

FE: I've been in an accident. Nothing serious, Barry, but I won't be able to make the practice session in Portugal.

BS: Don't give me that shit. It's in your contract.

FS: I've sprained my ankle, Barry. I can hop around holding my right foot in the air but I can't push a brake pedal.

BS: If it wasn't for the six million dollars you are bringing with you in sponsorship from that fucking movie, Evers, you needn't come back at all. (Click of phone.)

Barry hadn't built his team on charm. On the other hand you could bank on what he said. If *Juice* wasn't going to be a movie, there wasn't going to be any *Juice* money. And with no *Juice* money, I would be out on the street, just another racing driver beating the bushes for a ride. As I said, they don't hire Formula One racing drivers to win races any more. They hire them to bring in the money to pay for the technology that wins races.

I didn't want to get back into another sham EVIA. The evil Puerca had damn near killed me. But if I didn't get back in it there would be no Formula One car to get into either. Amazing how the mind concentrates at these moments. No place to run and hide, night as well go forward. Damn the torpedoes, full bluff ahead. 'Now that you mention it, Akiri,' I said, 'maybe I will sue you. Personally. For a car that won't drive in a straight line and for a complete lack of safety precautions like crash barriers. I don't know that my acting career would be worth three hundred million dollars, but my driving career might be. Three hundred million has a nice ring to it, don't you think?'

At the moment my driving career wasn't worth ten cents. And even if my face looked like a wart hog, it wouldn't slow me down on the race track. But I wanted him off balance for the sucker punch. 'What does your father say?'

Akiri winced. 'You told my father you would find out why we were having these problems.' Just a touch of whine in his voice there. I had hit him below the belt and he knew it.

'You haven't told him about the crash?'

'I, uh, thought before I shut down the film I would ask all of you if you have any alternatives. That's uh, why I, uh, asked you here this morning.'

'I'd hate to see us walk away from this project,' David said. 'There is more involved than a seventy-five million dollar film which was our original budget.' David placed his manicured fingertips on Akiri's glass desk and leaned forward. 'It is such a common mistake, Akiri.' David's voice had taken on a fatherly note here. Concern for the wayward son. 'People climb hard to get where they are and suddenly it gets a lot steeper and a lot more dangerous. And when they look up and see the lions and the tigers up there they think, "What the hell. I've climbed far enough. I'll be comfortable here." And of course the mistake is that they won't be there long enough to get comfortable. It's one of the most fundamental laws of nature. Once you stop going up you start going down. It may be steep and painful and dangerous, but believe me up is the more promising direction.'

Father David had been staring into Akiri's eyes. The master salesman straightened up, looked at us, and walked over to the window, looking out at the fog and the shore, the man of vision now.

'Personally I'd hate to see the introduction of EVIA compromised.'

Akiri swivelled around in his chair, David's audience.'Not just here, Akiri, as you know, but *Juice* is scheduled for distribution in a hundred and twenty-seven countries. The figures you showed me some time ago indicate that EVIA and the cars that will follow in EVIA's path could reduce global pollution by thirty-five to fifty per cent. And provide millions of jobs. Moreover, I anticipate that *Juice* will make money, record amounts of money, not lose it. In any case, I don't see any reason,' David said, 'we can't use the footage of Evers' crash. It could be a plus.'

David and Sam exchanged a look, Sam arching an eyebrow, David impassive.

Akiri stared at David with narrowed eyes.

'I've always thought Sam's idea made good marketing sense,' David said quietly.

'Make it into a woman's film,' Akiri said without enthusiasm.

'Absolutely. Appeal to women. Our marketing department tells me while women buy thirty-eight per cent of new cars, they have a decisive influence on seventy-seven per cent of new car purchases. Woman are the majority of EVIA's future. Sell them EVIA as efficient and appealing appliances, Akiri, instead of a massage for male ego. Of course you can use the footage of Evers' crash,' David said as if it were Akiri's film. 'Think of it this way. Macklin is the old-fashioned macho guy, still trying to be a racing driver, all that pedal to the metal boy-racer stuff. We can use that footage, if we alter the script, to show Macklin trying out Jill's new car and testing his nerve and screwing up. He screws up because those old macho values don't work any more in a world where we are transferring from manufacturing to information. Think of Butch Cassidy and the Sundance Kid. The Macklin character is like the old West gunslinger, out of date. Let the Macklin character stand for the old world. A world that has its charm and its value but no longer works. You could use Evers in the scenes we still have to shoot looking as beat-up as he is now, because Jill would take care of him after his crash. Part of her caring and nurturing image.'

'Another burden for woman, today,' Sam chimed in smiling sweetly, 'is dragging around yesterday's man.'

'Something like that,' David said. 'We'll get Bill Shaiman to completely rewrite it. He's smart, he's house trained, and he'll know we'll want to keep what we can and shoot as little extra as possible. And he's fast. Bill's expensive and he will probably want close to a million dollars to drop whatever the hell he's working on now to rewrite *Juice*, but this is no time to pinch pennies, is it.'

Sam was glaring at David as he said this, but neither he or Akiri noticed.

David was holding his hands out as if he were shaping an image out of clay. 'And, let me see, I'm just free-wheeling now, but say when the child, Candy, is trapped in the fire, OK, Macklin rescues her but why can't it be Jill who does the driving, you know, to save her life. Right, Forrest here rescues the girl from the fire, I think that makes dramatic sense. And he can do the driving stunts but it would be a nice, unexpected touch to put the woman in the hero role for a change, in your car. Because Akiri, your car will change lives as well as save them. Yes, I like that. EVIA is more like a woman's appliance than a macho machine.'

'You'd have to re-shoot the dance scene before the fire,' Radnor said. 'That is going to be very expensive.'

'Yeah. Absolutely. But dirt cheap compared to losing fifty million. So sure, we'll have to put more money into *Juice*. A lot more money. It's a bigger, more important film. But that's just a few extra million which is a lot less expensive than losing everything we have invested, don't you agree, Akiri? Not to mention putting the most important new car launch in history at risk.'

'I'm not sure it's that important,' Akiri said.

'It is to you,' David said. 'Now. You've got all the establishing shots and the cover shots for that dance scene, Sam. With a couple of new shots, it could be a more poignant scene; Macklin dancing on his sore ankle for Jill and stumbling into the fire to save Candy. Plus you now have a spectacular crash scene you didn't have before. Audiences love crash scenes.'

'I don't like crash scenes when they involve my car,' Akiri said.

'Yeah but it's better than trashing the whole project,' Delilah said, sitting down on the edge of Akiri's glass desk.

David, too, was moving in, putting his hands on the glass slab again and leaning forward, his voice confidential as if he was concerned that he might be overheard. 'I know your father well enough to know that he will not be pleased if you have to tell him you have lost fifty-five million dollars and don't have anything to show for it. Not to mention the effect on your EVIA marketing.'

'I don't want to end up with a movie full of car crashes and actors with scarred faces,' Akiri said, looking twenty-one again.

'Yeah, well. Evers said he was going to solve that in a week, didn't you, Forrest,' Delilah said. 'So give him another week. If he crashes again, he's not going to look any worse.'

They turned to look at me. 'Fine,' I said.

'I have to say,' David said quietly, 'I've always loved the idea of making *Juice* a woman's film. But until now, I didn't think we had the balls to do it.'

# chapter twenty-four

A river of fog flowed between the spikes of the Golden Gate Bridge and buried San Francisco in wet and cold grey wool.

We banked left towards the soft green mounds of Marin County. Below us, the bay was sunny and bright. In the glittering blue water, sailboats tilted in the white-caps, freeze-framed, racing around Angel Island. In front of us the abandoned Hamilton Army Airfield rushed up to greet us with a runway big enough for a B–52. The business jet (with a small discreet torch with OLYMPIC in blue letters around it on the nose) touched down, whined across two runways, and stopped at a waiting black Jeep Grand Cherokee Limited.

'Hi, I'm Pam,' the sunny blonde driver in baggy red shorts said, reaching out a hand for a shake. She was open and friendly and apparently unimpressed by two great stars dropping out of the sky. OK, one star and one semi-maybe-gonna-be-a-real-big-star-one-day-real-soon racing driver. 'Bill told me about your crash,' she said, pausing to stare at me for a moment. 'I don't think I've ever seen so many colours in one face before. Is it very painful?'

'Every morning, a little more washes away,' I said, easing myself carefully into the leather seat.

'How's the script coming?' Sam said.

'Oh the usual. Great weeping and gnashing of teeth,' she said, driving out of the old airfield gate. 'Bill's been working on it flat out since yesterday morning so you'll just have to wait till we get there to meet the great man.'

Shaiman's house covered the top of a steep grassy hill that doubled as a pedestal for the rambling blue Victorian house. A porch ran around the house on three sides, overlooking the bay, the bay, and the bay. 'Go on in,' Pam said. 'He's in his dark and dirty cave. I'll get you some coffee and sandwiches. Third door on the left.'

We went down a hall hung with commendations and awards and a voice said, 'Don't knock, come in.'

It took a few moments for our eyes to adjust to the gloom. The monitor was the only light and it made his face green, emphasizing his pink-rimmed eyes and a three-day-old stubble. Shaiman wore jeans and a rumpled and faded work shirt, the screenwriter's dresscode. It was hard to tell, in that light, if he was a well-preserved fifty or a ruined thirty. He was saying, 'The tricky part is getting this Jill character right. It'd be easy to get her too shrill, lose sympathy for her because she is so damn uncompromising. Although, Sam,' he said, giving her a slow knowing grin, 'your face is a plus for any character. And since you are shooting yourself lemme take a wild guess here and say you are gonna use your most flattering shots. But still, I don't think the script calls for just another pretty bitch.' He turned to me, the screenwriter's bloodshot eye. 'Good God! You look like you've been chewed on by dogs. Are you the guy that drove off the cliff?' he said.

'I may have had some help.'

'Of course you had help. A great stunt like that is not a solo. Everybody helps everybody else. It's one of the most endearing things about movie people. Except when they are stomping on each other's faces with the heels of their boots, they are all helping each other.' He leaned back, into the shadows, yawning and putting his hands behind his head. 'I teach a screenwriting class in Sausalito. What's hard for beginners to take on board is it takes a lot of talent to make a movie. A lot of talent or no talent as the case may be. And for everybody else except the screenwriter, a script is a utensil. I mean you can call it a work of art if you want but mostly it's grunt work on the part of a lot of people. Starting with the writer. But if you want to write a script you have to learn to sit on your ass.' He leaned forward again to type, dismissing us.

'As long as the grunts don't show up on the screen,' Sam said.

Shaiman's face came up again. 'Hey, do me a favour. Read it through first, soon as I finish it, then we'll talk. See if maybe we can find a way to soften up this Jill.'

As my eyes adjusted to the half-light, it was obvious that

Shaiman did a lot of sitting. A pear in a chair. His broad wooden table was heaped with scripts, scrawled notes, snapshots, newspapers, coffee cups, phones, computer discs, books, magazines, CDs, and blank sheets of paper. Several layers down some food was in there liquefying, giving off heat. More books and magazines, dog eared and open, lay scattered around his feet. The one window in the room was blanked off, its shades drawn. On his left, there was a stand with a VCR and a monitor. A yellow car was headed for the edge of a cliff.

'I didn't choose you, I want you to know that,' Sam said, 'so make me fall in love with you.'

'Be my guest,' he said, coming back up from his screen like a dolphin out of the tank at Sea World. 'But do yourself a favour and talk to Pam first. She'll probably pay you good money to take me away. Hey, you don't want to fall in love with me, Sammy. You want to fall in love with the script. And the script is gonna be more loveable if you give it a little time. Live with it a little. Maybe you could even read it first.'

He turned to me as if Sam had vaporized. 'Everybody says they want to fall in love with a script. But you come in, as a script doctor, like me and everybody thinks you are gonna do a Frankenstein on their darling. Stick a lot of dead bits on it.'

He went back to the screen, stared into the white words in the blue sea and came back up again. 'Look, Sam, let me sort out a couple more things here, put a couple of bolts through its neck and I'll print you out a copy. I was up all night with this. Go out on the sun-porch. Get Pam to make you some coffee, look over the San Francisco Bay. I'll just be a few minutes. But if you keep looking over my shoulder it's gonna take a couple a two, call it three maybe more hours.'

'Can you run that crash for me?' I asked.

'You didn't see enough? Most people in a crash prefer to forget the whole thing.'

'There's a lot I didn't see. I don't remember anything after I went over the edge.'

Shaiman rolled over to the VCR, pushed a button, and the yellow car surged forward.

'What's that from?' I put my finger on a circle of dust on the pulsing image, an upside-down umbrella surrounding the car.

'Downwash from the chopper, but you won't see it on the

movie, it'll just read dust from the car. It's a hell of a shot. But then that's Mayberry. You know he earns as much as the screenwriter these days and you see a shot like that and I have to say he earns it.' Shaiman leaned over, rewound the tape on the VCR, and pressed play.

We watched the silent footage, following the yellow Mustang from around thirty feet overhead as the rocks began to slide. As the car turned first right, then raggedly left, we came in tighter, so the car filled the frame. You could see my hands working the wheel, turning left and right as the edge of the cliff approached and then the ground disappeared beneath the car as it arced out into open space with the valley four thousand feet below. The car nosed down, ploughed into the steep dirt about forty feet down from the road, sending up a spray of rocks and dust, crunching the front end and taking off a lot of the speed. The back end of the car rose up, twisted in the air like an Olympic diver, and came down on its side rolling once, twice, and three times, and stopped with a clumsy smash against a pinion oak on a promontory of rock. The windshield was smashed, the front of the car torn away, the passenger side stove in against the short tough oak and the rock, and the front and the rear of the car were at right angles to each other. I was slumped over the wheel. The shot held on the car long enough to notice there were hawks circling in the open air below. The screen went blank.

'I'd like to see it again,' I said.

'Be my guest,' Shaiman said, ejecting the cassette and handing it to me. 'But do it someplace else, if you don't mind. I've got to finish this script this morning or Sam will kill me, won't you darling. There's a video in the den across the hall.'

'He smells as bad as his scripts,' Sam said when we were in the den across the hall.

'If you ask a writer to sweat over a script all night you can't expect him to smell like a rose. I liked *Firepower*, didn't Shaiman write that one with Dicky Gere as the fighter pilot?'

'You like the worst rubbish, Evers. And don't call him Dicky, he hates that. Anyway, Shaiman got credit for it because he screwed up the story so much nobody else wanted it. Shaiman is a hack, Evers, one of the worst.'

'Then get another writer. From what I hear everybody with

a crayon in California is writing a screenplay. Why do you have to do everything David tells you? Mel would back you up.'

'Mel couldn't back a postage stamp.'

'I thought he was the producer.'

'Mel is the line production manager. He gets producer credit because he does what David tells him.'

'Like the director.'

'That's not fair.'

'OK, it's not fair. But it's true.'

'Look, I don't have a choice. How many women get to direct? If I make *Juice* work, then I'm free and on my way. I can shoot something I really believe in. Nobody gets there overnight, Evers. If you want to invent yourself, it takes time.'

'I like you fine the way you are.'

'I don't. People aren't attracted to me. They're attracted to this pretty mask, all smiling and charming and it makes me feel hollow. It's a fraud. You know I'm not a pussy cat, I'm a pushy broad who moves and shakes things and people until she gets what she wants. What happens when I'm an old prune? Look, I've already got crows' feet, and it doesn't matter how much rejuvenating cream I put on my hands, after three weeks in the desert they look like crab claws. I imagine being thirty-five and people saying, 'Can you believe, Sam used to be beautiful? She was a beautiful star.' I can understand perfectly why Marilyn Monroe committed suicide. Everyplace she looked was down. Stars go out, Evers. Well I am not going out and I am not a star. The lovely Samantha Miles is somebody else, not me. I want to do a body of work. Something more than being a dummy for a script and a camera, something substantial. You want to see what it means to be an actor, Evers, get up close to a screen. TV or movie screen, either one, doesn't matter. You get up close to it and the beautiful face disappears, you can't see anything except little dots. Being an actress is an illusion, Evers, and even if I wanted to I can't keep living on that.'

I held her because she was tired and close to crying and I wanted to tell her that I'd love her if she was a waitress in Chillicothe. I loved Sam's strength and her being a pushy broad because she had a good heart and she would never hurt anyone, but she knew what she wanted. The sweetness wasn't an act, it was part of her. But she had heard all that, not just from me but from every male she had known since she was six and she didn't believe it. 'Come on, Lady Samantha,' I said. 'Watch me playing stunt man.'

I put the cassette into the VCR and ran it forward until the car was headed for the edge of the cliff. 'Is this a telephoto shot?' I said.

'No, it's a normal lens, I think it's a fifty-millimetre. It might even be wider than that, like a thirty-eight. I wanted to get the depth of field so when the car is going along the edge of the cliff you can see the valley, how far it is down, and not just a lot of blurs.'

'So you had to get the chopper really close to the car.'

'Mayberry said he could see the hairs standing out on the back of your neck.'

I stopped the machine when the car was a foot from the edge. There was that upside-down umbrella of dust and I wondered where I'd seen it before. Then I remembered. Hovercraft crossing the English Channel; starting out on land and that big upside-down umbrella of dust rising around them as they fumbled cautiously down to the water. The big blades of the chopper were creating positive pressure, pushing up, underneath my car. Hence the big upside-down dust umbrella. Forrest couldn't steer because the car was not only going seventy miles an hour on loose dirt and gravel, it was being lifted up so it didn't matter which way I turned the wheels. It wouldn't take much, the narrow tyres and the loose surface made the car hard to control. But I hadn't even been able to swap ends, broadside the car to scrub off speed. I hadn't been able to do anything. I'd just been the crash dummy.

'Was this your idea? Getting this close?'

Sam looked at me. Not happy. 'It was David's,' she said. 'He said if we wanted to capture the danger on film, we were going to have to take some risks. But I never thought, I mean I'm sure he never meant risks to you. I think he meant to Billy and the chopper pilot. Flying that close to the ground, especially in the mountains, is very dangerous.'

I let the tape run forward a few frames and stopped it with the car just clear of the cliff edge. Blue sky above and the rocky valley almost a mile below. 'And let me ask you something else, Sam. Did you have a chopper shot of Waddell's crash, the one I saw in the studio the first day?'

'Sure we did.'

'Can I see it?'

'David didn't like it. And I agreed. It worked better from the point of view of the cops in the car, so we didn't cut it into that first footage.'

'But the chopper shot was David's idea too.'

'Not really. It was in the script. But it was David's suggestion that we come in really tight. I can have it transferred to video if you want to see it.'

'No,' I said. 'I don't need to see it. You once said that David is a fanatic about the details.'

'He used to say it was the secret of his success. God and David Allen, he said, is in the details.'

'Do you have any idea why he'd want to screw up his own movie?'

Sam looked at me and made a face.

'Well, somebody is.'

'Maybe, Forrest,' she said with no humour at all, 'you are just screwing up.'

# chapter twenty-five

'Doesn't seem weird to me,' Bash said, smiling happily, flipping his welding mask down. 'Folks go pay, what, seven maybe eight fifty a head now to sit still for that video shit they call a movie. That's weird.' His blue electric arc zapped and spat laying down a smooth lick of steel weld. He flipped his mask up. 'Sometimes, on some of the shoots I've been on, you'd swear *everybody* was trying to fuck it up. You remember *Rocky the Squirrel Comes Home*? Won best special effects about ten years ago?'

'I must have missed it.'

Bash went on, working at the steel backing plate with a hand file. 'You know how many squirrels it took for Rocky the Squirrel to cross the San Diego Freeway? Turned out the keeper's assistant had doped 'em up with a double dose of tranqs for the trip out to the location and the squirrels were stoned out of their gourd, just wandered out on the highway and circled around until some sixteen-wheeler turned 'em into Frisbees. The assistant cameraman was an animal rights activist and he's screaming at the director to stop. And the director is behind schedule and he's over budget and he wants the footage of the narrow misses, so he keeps sending another squirrel out there. The assistant cameraman can't stand it and he runs out on the freeway alongside squirrel number eleven. Big unmarked tractor-trailer goes off the road trying to keep from hitting this turkey and splits open spilling cartons of Japanese TV sets all over a corn field and six lanes of California freeway traffic stop to pick 'em up so there are thirty-five rear-enders, whiplashes, broken arms and legs, and a hundred and fifty lawsuits against the production company before the sun sets. I mean this stuff does happen. Maybe you are just getting a little paranoid, Evers. There's a lot of paranoia going around in Southern California. It's a big cash crop.'

Behind his tall bulky outline six stripped Fieros, their frames lengthened, trick fans, electronics, and hydraulics installed, waited for their long swoopy fibreglass bodies. Cars for the future of some TV pilot.

Bash carried the welded piece over to the yellow Mustang replica, eyeballed it, frowned, and brought it back to his bench. 'If you are going to keep bouncing off things, Forrest, you want to be sure the doors stay shut. Mercedes door locks,' he said, holding up the plate and the lock. 'The Krauts know how to build a door lock. Most movie prop cars are garbage. Gotta be towed around with a rope. You are going to drive this thing so it has got to be ungoddamnbreakable. A lot of it is NASCAR 'cause NASCAR stuff may not be slick, but it is strong. Like all the NASCAR front suspensions up until a couple of years ago were off a '65 Ford Galaxie 500. I've put on the new front steer, save you around seventy pounds unsprung weight up front. Then there's '82 Chevelle side rails, Fox shocks, JAZ fuel cell, full-floater rear axle, Woodward steering box and U-joints, and a Reynolds small block Chevy. Five hundred and thirty horsepower and you couldn't bust it with an atom bomb.'

'That's a lot of power for those little skinny tyres.'

'You don't have to use it if you don't want it. Just press the pedal on the right part way down.'

'You have any other driving tips?'

'Just trying to protect you from yourself, Evers. This thing you are telling me, somebody trying to screw up your movie. It just doesn't make any sense to me. You don't have to do anything to screw up a movie production. They do it all by themselves, most natural thing in the world.'

'I know it doesn't make any sense. You want a short holiday in Mexico?'

Bash's office desk was littered with bills, invoices, sketches of bat-winged cars, wiring diagrams, a melted piston, and a photograph of his wife, Shirley, smiling happily next to what looked like a grasshopper on wheels he'd built for some TV pilot. I picked up the phone and dialled.

'Hi, sweetheart. What are you up to?'

'Up to my ears in rebudgeting, rescheduling, rethinking the script, and bored with missing you. What are you doing?' said Sam's Daddy's-perfect-little-girl voice on the phone.

'I'm going down to the south of Mexico for a night. Want to come with me?'

'I'd love to but I couldn't possibly, Forrest. Shaiman's script isn't at all what I want. There's a lot that doesn't work for me. Especially Jill. I think we need to see more change in her.'

'We're leaving from Burbank tomorrow morning at eight a.m. Bring your script.'

'I can't, I'm meeting . . .'

'And your bikini. Just one night. Castleman says he's dying to meet you. Wants to know all about financing Samantha Miles feature films.'

'Tom Castleman?'

'That one. Think you can get the studio jet?'

'You rat. Can I bring Mel?'

'No.'

'OK, but I have a meeting here at six forty-five with some turkeys from Disney I have to take.'

# chapter twenty-six

The 'road' was more like a track through a tank-proving ground than a road, with steam rising off the muddy puddles. The Range Rover with Castleman's logo, a green lion's head snarling on the doors, splashed through the milk-chocolate water and yellow mud while we bounced around like Mexican jumping beans. We ploughed into one pothole, Sam said, 'I hope this car has a snorkel,' and nobody laughed.

The map said it was five miles from Castleman's airfield to his house, but the way the road twisted and turned, following the contour of the hills, it seemed like twenty. Heavy dump trucks grinding up and down the same track, drooling dirty water and churning the yellow mud into soup, pushed us off on to the shoulder or held us up until our driver worked up enough courage to pass on a blind bend. The jungle canopy arched overhead and we drove through shadow and shafts of sunlight, hearing, over the roar of the Range Rover, the ratchet and squawk of a jungle movie. Bash was up front, talking happily in Spanish to the driver.

'Tell him there is another gear beyond second,' I shouted.

'He says the noise frightens away the bad spirits,' Bash shouted back. 'His tribe lives in the hills here and he says the digging has let loose bad . . .' Bash paused as the driver added some hand waving to whatever he was saying, '*Guanaperi.* Demons. And they are really pissed off about being woken up. He says it's a good idea to stay close to the big machines.'

The driver broke out laughing, showing a lot of red-stained teeth in a wide mouth, and it was hard to tell if he was laughing at the gringos or seriously worried.

'I thought you spoke Spanish,' Sam said, jouncing against me in the back seat, her hot hand on the back of my hot neck.

'A few *palabras*. But he's speaking some coastal dialect.'

'It's Huixtalan. Indian,' Bash said turning around to look at Sam. 'He's throwing in some Spanish so I can understand him. Are you OK, Sam?'

'Terrific,' she said, slapping a bug on her arm. 'We're all set for the demons back here. Stick a few feathers in Evers' hair and he could pass for a witch doctor.'

'I thought you said you thought my face looked better. The swelling has gone down.'

'Yeah, but you'd still scare those bad spirits. Actually your face is looking Mexican this morning, Forrest. Lots of reds, blues, yellow, and purple. But you must have done something evil to make me come down to this awful place.' She put a tender hand to my cheek just as the Range Rover jolted violently.

'Zulapan,' the driver said, pointing straight ahead to a large white building in a sea of mud half a mile away. The red-tile roof was in place in the middle section, but one wing still showed rafters to the sky and another lacked windows. Castleman's Palace by the Pacific.

'Zulapan,' the driver said again.

'Zulapan,' Sam repeated.

The driver turned to stare at her, said something and grinned wildly.

'He says Zulapan means "shithouse",' Bash explained.

Ahead, a large yellow dumptruck edged out on to the road and turned towards us. The driver continued to stare at Sam.

'Bash,' Sam pleaded.

Bash touched the driver lightly on the shoulder and the man shrieked, whirled around, saw the truck a hundred yards ahead and stood on the brakes, slamming all of us out of our seats. We waited for a full two minutes while the truck, straining under a full load of dirt and rocks, approached and trundled by.

The last half-mile took ten minutes as we screamed along in first gear.

'Pleasant trip?' Castleman asked from the open doorway as we stepped out of the Range Rover and into deep mud.

His feet were brown in sandals and his stomach was flat under his white cotton trousers and shirt. He looked bronzed and a lot fitter than the last time I'd seen him. But that was in

England and the English summer makes some people sag and go grey in the cheeks. His large brown seal's eyes with the long lashes were clear now and the top of his head was suntanned with a carefully combed silver fringe. Now in his late sixties there was a slight stoop and I noticed that when he talked, he tended to look off into the distance.

When the Hunt brothers had tried to corner the silver market in the seventies, Castleman had called their bluff and bought tons of silver short. When the price dropped like a stone overnight he made billions. Which he used in the eighties for taking over large corporations, cutting them into small bits and selling them; a corporate scrap dealer. He also had an uncanny knack for getting out of the market before the roof fell in. He had a wife in Paris and ex-wives in London and New York along with houses in Maori, Melides, and Bel Air as well as London and New York. When Onassis was alive, Castleman called him a 'poor little fisherman'.

I had done Tom a couple of favours, pointed him towards Texon before anybody else knew they were broke, and last year I put him on to the coming collapse of the Emron Empire, although he might well have seen that shipwreck coming without my leading him to it. We were edgy and cautious around each other. And he trusted me about as much as I trusted him.

'Good Lord, what have you done to yourself, Evers,' he said. 'You look like you've been standing under a lightning bolt.'

'Being a movie star,' I said, 'is not all cookies and cream.'

'You should get somebody else to do your stunts. Come in, come in. It's a little steamy,' Castleman said, as we peeled off our sopping mud-caked shoes and boots and stepped barefoot through the front door on the warm tiles. 'But I loathe air-conditioning, don't you? You'll get used to it. No bugs at all inside. Electronic screens. No luggage?' he said to Sam. 'I was hoping you might stay a few days.'

'No luggage, no time,' Sam said. 'I have a production meeting at six forty-five this afternoon in LA.'

'Yes, meetings. I suppose a star does have to do dreary things. I prefer to think of you stars lounging by a swimming-pool in your bikini, reading *Variety* and fanned by tennis champions. But then I tend to think in cartoons these days. One of the many signs of senility. Come in, come in. Let's make the most of what little time we have. Small wonder you are a star,' he said looking at Sam with the smug delight of a man who has just acquired a priceless work of art. 'Follow me straight through, to the terrace. We'll have lunch and you can tell me what it would take to invest in a Samantha Miles motion picture. Come along, Forrest,' he added without much interest.

'I don't mean to be rude to him,' he said turning back to Sam. 'But you know he is here only because I wanted to see you.'

'Well, here I am,' Sam said happily, 'because Forrest wanted to see you. Did you know that stars have to pee too? I am dying for a pee.'

Castleman indicated a heavy door on his left and while we stood around in the large open space I introduced Bash. 'If you ever need anything nobody knows how to build, call Bash.'

Bash stuck out a heavy calloused hand. 'And I'll probably tell you it can't be built.'

'Pleased to meet you, Bash,' Castleman said easily. 'You might be interested in some of the things we're doing here. Most of it has never been done before, at least not on a meaningful scale.'

Sam came back and Castleman led us across the large high open room with simple leather and wood furniture and large Spanish tiles through the glass doors on the other side.

The shape of the house echoed the small peninsula it stood on: a rounded 'V' with the main room curved, pointing west, out into the Pacific, and the two wings trailing, one facing the shore to the south-west and the other to the north. Going through the glass doors and stepping out on the terrace the air was cool and fresh with the lemon and seaweed smell of the Pacific. Directly below us the waves broke against the rocks in a steady rhythmic roar. To the north, there was a crescent of white sand and the ocean turned from aquamarine to turquoise to deep blue. Castleman motioned us across the terrace to look at the south shore where an army of yellow machines were dredging, digging, and churning, turning the aquamarine water in the bay yellow brown. Bulldozers had cut a swath deep into the jungle, giant shovels were digging it up, and the trucks were hauling the muck away. Further out, cranes were dumping rocks and dirt to form a long jetty into the sea. The clank and roar of straining engines rose up with the sound of the surf and the smell of rotting vegetation and diesel exhaust.

'What do you think?' he said, waving his arm to include several square miles of jungle and ocean.

'Looks like a crime against nature,' I said, without thinking. When you scrape off the thin skin of the jungle it never grows back. There is no sustaining topsoil and all of the stored energy is in a high-speed cycle between the surface of the earth and the high green canopy overhead. Take away the canopy and the energy dissipates like steam.

'That's exactly what it's not,' Castleman said with some heat. 'I am creating an ideal lagoon for blue whales to give birth to their calves and a protected beach for the sea turtles and an inland salt marsh. In five years this will be the most perfect and protected natural habitat on the Pacific Coast. Some of the finest marine biologists, ecologists, zoologists in the world have contributed to its design. The world's leading ecologists will come here to study, Evers, although at a distance. Barring catastrophe, there will be no human access, once the construction is completed, for fifty years, beyond this terrace where you are standing. Once I die it will be owned and operated by the Castleman Preserve Foundation, underwritten and guaranteed by the Mexican government. My gift, you might say,' he smiled slightly, 'for all my good fortune. And I'll grant you it looks brutal now, but we know what we are doing and we don't have much time. Come on, let's have lunch. Nina?' he shouted.

In a moment a head appeared at the edge of the terrace. She had dark hair cut short like a boy, high cheekbones, enormous dark eyes, and as she rose up the steps, she wrapped a gauzy colourful cloth around her long, half-nude figure.

'Nina, I'd like you to meet Samantha Miles, uh, Bash, and Forrest Evers, whom I've known for far too long.' Nina smiled a cool fishmouth smile without interest at Sam and Bash. Then her face lit up when she turned to me. 'Oh, Forrest, darling,' she said rushing up to me and wrapping her long arms around me. Her body was warm from lying in the sun. 'How have you been, Forrest? It is so lovely to see you again.' In my ear she whispered, 'Shhhhhhhh.'

'Nina, tell Raoul we're ready for lunch,' Castleman said with his British boardroom drawl. Nina let go and started for the house, miming a kiss in my direction. Castleman turned to me with that mild innocent look that usually meant he was about to strike. 'I didn't realize you too have met.'

'We haven't.' Nina said over her shoulder, putting a little extra swish in her hips. 'I just wanted to piss you off.'

'The thoroughbreds are always high-spirited,' Castleman said through clenched teeth, leading us to the edge of the terrace.

'Oh, we're really all just pussy cats,' Sam said sweetly. 'And you are a little mouse, aren't you, Tom. If you can't control her,' Sam said nodding at Nina as she disappeared into the house, 'how can you expect to control mother nature?'

'Oh, I don't control anybody any more, dear girl,' Castleman said. 'I'm just along for the ride.'

# chapter twenty-seven

'The whole point, dear boy,' Castleman said, pouring Sam a glass of chilled Le Montrachet, 'is that I DON'T "mess", as you put it, with mother nature.' He mimed pouring the bottle into my glass. I shook my head no. Another glass of disgusting water would be dandy. 'Or with anybody else, come to that,' Castleman went on, setting the bottle carefully down. 'I am retired and I am going to sit on my terrace and watch my whales while the sun sets. Winston Churchill kept fish, I'm just building a bigger fish tank.'

'You're just throwing your money in the ocean,' Sam said.

'I might as well. Western currency will be worthless in a few months or a year at the outside, believe me. Beginning with the pound.'

We were on a small terrace below the main terrace and out of sight of the house. Behind us, a stream burbled out of the rocks, ran along the edge of the terrace, and disappeared in a long, thin waterfall into the foliage of the jungle below. A couple hundred yards away, just beyond the jungle, the blue waves of the Pacific rolled in on the white beach. Three small figures were running in and out of the surf.

Lunch was a fish salad and a platter of fruit. 'I apologize for its being a bit Spartan, Sam. But it's time, don't you think,' Castleman said taking a bite of a pear, 'to simplify our tastes.'

'You've always had simple tastes,' Nina said, laying a long, perfectly manicured hand on his, her smooth tan fingers hiding his age spots. 'It's just your appetite that gets out of hand.'

The sun was hot but the breeze was cool and fresh. 'I'm glad you came,' she said to us with a sudden dazzling smile. 'Gives me a chance to ruffle the old buzzard's feathers. And you get to tell your end-of-the-Western-World stories, don't you darling.'

'A toothless old tiger,' Castleman said pleasantly, 'roaring at the wind.'

A distant squeal from the beach made Nina look over her shoulder. 'Are you sure the children are all right?'

'Costanza grew up on that beach, Nina. If you are worried why don't you run down there after lunch and join them before we get into whatever tedious business we're meant to get into.' He put his half-eaten pear carefully down, took a sip of water, and folded his napkin.

'What is it you want this time, Evers?' Castleman said, leaning back in his chair. 'I have had a look at David Allen, and at Hozuki and Olympic. Frankly I don't find any of them particularly interesting. Not compared to blue whales. When the crash happens in a year or two at the most, the blue whales will be coming into my cove to give birth. While these high-priced delivery systems like electric cars and that information highway the business press has got all sexed up about will be the first to be junked.'

'What I want to know, Tom, is what is David Allen up to? On the one hand he keeps making this film bigger and bigger and on the other, he looks like he's trashing it.'

'You'll have to cut Forrest a little slack,' Sam said. 'He's new to Hollywood and he still thinks movies ought to make sense. Besides, you've been hit on the head, weren't you, darling?'

'I've never understood anything that Hollywood does,' Castleman said. 'Would anyone care for coffee?' he said, stretching his long legs under the table. 'I've had to give it up, but please help yourself.'

'Let me put it another way.' I kept on, trying to engage his attention. Castleman's eyes were ranging lazily over Sam and back to Nina. 'Why would he be messing with a movie at all? Agents like David Allen aren't interested in making movies. They're interested in building empires. So why is he messing with this movie, changing the script, putting more and more money in it?'

'He's always had an eye for detail, Forrest, as I keep telling you.' Sam said this over the rim of her wine glass, sipping slowly, watching, catching Castleman's eye and holding on.

'Well, if you want a reason,' Castleman said, leaning forward, 'I'll give you a reason. One out of seven people in North

America are employed one way or another in making cars. If it's anywhere near as good as they say it is, this Hozuki electric car will seriously damage the big oil companies and cripple the American car industry. From what I hear, you Yanks don't have the technology.'

'We've got the technology,' Bash said, 'we just don't have it in cars yet. And I don't think the friendly folks at Hozuki do either.'

'You boys play with your toys,' Sam said, pushing her chair back. 'We're off to the beach. When I come back, Tom, I want to hear more about your film career. And mine.'

Nina and Sam left and Bash took a big swig out of his bottle of Modela Negro and leaned forward, his beefy forearms on the sky-blue Mexican tiles of the table. 'OK, the new PEM fuel cells like Hozuki's using are lighter and run cooler because they use semi-permeable plastics instead of the usual liquid-transfer medium.'

'What in God's name are you talking about?' Castleman said.

'I don't understand you either, Bash. I didn't know you were into this new technology.'

'All technology is new now, Evers. And every technology in the world is going to be out of date in fifteen minutes. If you are looking for a replacement for the internal combustion engine, forget about batteries and learn about power cells. Power cells will give you around eighty miles to the gallon and they don't pollute. At all.' Bash drained his beer and twisted the top of another one.

'Power cells,' I said, keeping right up there.

'Yeah. What got me interested in power cells was I've been around the old internal combustion engine all my life. And the old banger is a moving target. Right now a Ford Indycar engine will fit in a box just under twenty-two inches wide, high, and long. And that little sucker will put out over eight hundred horsepower. OK, it needs a turbocharger to turn that much power and it fries your eardrums and wilts the trees but at around seven hundred and fifty watts for every horsepower, eight hundred horsepower will light up a small town all night long. A sled full of lead batteries will like light up a house and if you are roasting a turkey with the air-conditioning on, that's it. You can forget about running a car on batteries. They set the world land speed record for a battery car last year. A little single-seat electric racing car went a hundred and two miles an hour for about a hundred yards. After that it had to coast because it was out of power. The gasoline engine went faster than that in 1915.

'So anything coming down the pike claiming it is going to take the place of my little hot rod V–8 commands my attention because it must be a hell of a system. Fuel cells have been around a long time, Forrest. It's only since NASA started using them for power sources on their Moon shots that people began to sit up and listen. So pay attention here. You got any more of this beer?'

Castleman waved a hand in the air, spoke a few words of the local dialect to the dark, short woman who appeared by the table, disappeared, and came back with an armful of frosty bottles.

'OK, what a fuel cell does is this. You put hydrogen in from your fuel and it combines with oxygen from the air to make water and electricity. It's a chemical process, it's damn near a hundred per cent efficient; no waste, no mess. It looks like a battery but it doesn't store electricity, it makes it. And the PEM fuel cells, like Hozuki's, use a semi-permeable plastic instead of battery acid, so they weigh a lot less than your lead battery.'

'Fascinating,' Castleman said, his eyes at half mast.

'The problem is the plates inside the cell are usually made of stuff like titanium and niobium treated with platinum so figure around $10,000 a plate and you need about thirty in your fuel cell and around three or four cells if you are going to get any power.'

'So the problem is cost,' Castleman said behind closed eyes.

'Yeah. They've got a fuel cell hooked up in a bus in Vancouver and it works but it is not the swiftest bus in the fleet. And there is an outfit in West Palm Beach that has a plastic car running around with a twenty-kilowatt electric motor powered, which is what, around twenty-five horsepower, by a fuel cell. It works better than a car on batteries, but it's not what you would call a Ferrari. But think about it for a minute.'

'Think about what?' I said. My limit of listening to high-tech is around sixty seconds before my brain wanders off.

'The Japanese power companies have been building fuel cell generators for years and we've got the NASA technology that goes all the way back to Apollo. That's what the President was talking about when he announced Ford Chrysler and GM are going to develop the "US car" with NASA technology. Still, it is a hell of a leap from a heavy industrial lump putting out a steady stream of juice into the power grid to a light, flexible, and inexpensive power plant in a car. A hell of a leap.

'I mean who knows? Maybe Hozuki are almost there, but they can't get enough power out of it for the weight. Or maybe the vibration of running on a road screws it up. If Hozuki really had a fuel cell that worked and didn't cost as much as a room full of gold bars, why don't they use it in the movie? I mean think how the PR is going to look when they start promoting that movie you're doing and it gets out that you used good old American V–8s. I mean as far as Hozuki are concerned, the whole point of the movie is the PR. And if they really had those fuel cells ready to roll they could do a whole PR thing about making the movie. Get the public all worked up about the cars being driven by Sam and a Big Time Racing Driver dummy like you. If they can't put the new fuel cells and the new electric motors in the movie cars, I think maybe they haven't got them yet. Maybe they have something to hide.'

'But if they don't have the fuel cell ready why would they say they do? They can't sell EVIA without it,' I said.

'I don't know. Like I said, maybe there are last-minute problems.'

'Have you seen what's been happening to Hozuki stock in Tokyo?' Castleman said, his eyes still half closed.

Bash and I looked at each other. 'Not recently,' I said.

'Before EVIA, Hozuki stock was sinking like a stone. All the big car companies were down because people aren't buying new cars. But Hozuki was doing worse than most. They borrowed a fortune to develop a new sports car nobody wanted and a luxury car that never made it to the showroom. Now with EVIA Hozuki stock is picking up. It's not going through the roof yet, but it went up twenty-five per cent in the last two months.'

Castleman pushed his chair back and stood up. 'Maybe they don't want to sell a car,' Castleman said, his eyes glittering now. 'Maybe they want to sell a company.'

'That doesn't answer my question about David Allen,' I said.

'What do you mean, Forrest? That the man is interfering with your script?' He leaned forward and put his hand on my shoulder. 'Dear boy, you bring me tigers and you want to play with the pussy cat.'

Castleman's office was a large room with a high ceiling; blue tiles on the floor, blue sky in the large skylights overhead and blue sea in the windows. Castleman stood at a long, wide, and polished plank of wood that he used for a desk, framed by a window overlooking the Pacific behind him. Sam came into the room, her face red from the heat and the sun, her white dress showing damp patches here and there.

Castleman was on the phone to Washington, the little flip-lid phone he kept in his pocket, getting the figures of the President's directive to the Big Three (eighty miles to the gallon and zero pollution. And what's the budget? And who have they got to do the research, Lockheed?) and taking notes with a pencil on a small white note pad. He lit up when he saw Sam and he smiled and beckoned to her. Come on, come over here, he mouthed, listening and writing.

Sam said, 'Nina told me you've come here to die.'

'Charles,' Castleman said into the lid of the phone, 'get back to me in fifteen minutes.' He flipped the phone shut and he sat down behind the deeply polished plank of wood that was his desk. Sam went to him and put her arms around his head and squeezed him to her chest.

'Well,' he said after she let go. 'Nothing like a good squeeze from a hot woman to make a man feel better.'

'You,' said Nina in the doorway, the sun behind her, 'are going to have the lid of your coffin nailed shut to keep you from fondling women at your funeral.'

'And you are going to miss me,' he said.

'I am,' she said. Behind her the sky was clear blue above the whitecaps on the ocean, and the breeze blew in the room.

'Now dammit, don't cry, Nina. We've had enough crying around here. If you want to cry, cry for yourself. Or for Forrest here. We are all going to die. I've just had the good luck to be told when.'

'When,' I said.

'Not before I own a car company. I've always wanted to own a car company.'

'What the hell are you going to do with a car company?' Nina said, walking into the room and picking up one of the papers that were scattered across his desk.

'Pump up the price and sell it of course. Make you an extra hundred million for you to throw away when I'm gone. What else would I do with it?'

'We were swimming in the ocean,' Sam said, 'just bobbing in the clear water on this perfect day and Nina told me. And, please excuse me, Tom, but I have to say coming here to die is an awful idea.'

'It's what the elephants and the blue whales do. I'm afraid there's not much I can do about it.'

'Of course you can. Look, it's not my business, but, I mean, OK, I know if you can't be helped by whatever the doctors are offering these days, you can't. But you never know.'

'Sam, please,' Nina said.

Sam ignored her. 'People who don't give up just because some jerk in a white coat tells them it's hopeless. They recover all the time. Don't give up. You've got to live.' Sam was badly upset, almost crying, her voice shaking. 'Tom, why don't you live? Be alive. I think it's awful you're making another killing on the market when you could be out there on the beach with Nina and your children. They need a father, they need you and you should be there. With them.'

Castleman sighed and looked at her with the mild smile he used for telling the board of directors that they were fired. 'I suppose an actress can change her stripes any time she likes. But I am an old tiger now, Sam. And I am very good at the games I play,' he said, picking up the phone again. 'If we end up in the same place, dear lady, do remember to tell me how you spent your last months above ground. Now will you please excuse me? I've got to get some figures together from Tokyo and Washington. Thank you so much for coming down to visit.'

# chapter twenty-eight

In the roaring Range Rover lurching at five miles an hour back to the plane I said, 'What the hell did you say that for?'

'You don't understand,' Sam said, so quietly I could barely hear her.

'No, you are damn right I don't understand,' I said, loud enough to inform the monkeys in the trees. 'Forget that you are a guest in his house. Or that you have barely met him. You have to tell him your silly California way to die: "Go play on the beach." I don't understand you at all, Sam.'

'No, you don't,' she said between her teeth. 'You don't understand anything. What the hell difference would it make anyway? I mean, what do you want? You want all the facts in, get an opinion poll, and take a marketing survey before you can stand up for me? Jesus, I thought you were strong, somebody I could count on. That's so weak, 'understand'. You think you should just let him lie down and die.'

'Sam, it is not up to you or me. He is going to die.'

'I was thinking of his children. He owes them.'

'They are *his* children.'

'You can't handle it, can you? It's too much for you. "Understand",' she said again, mocking. 'Well, fuck you. You're weak, Evers. And so is that greedy, selfish old bastard. He can't even be a father. You never were, were you. You don't know what it's like,' Sam said, her face red. Then she looked away, out at the jungle. 'The other thing you don't understand,' she said in a cold, even voice, 'David will cut him to pieces. It's what he does, cuts people up into little pieces and sells them.'

'I've known Tom Castleman a long time,' I said. 'He'll buy and sell David before he knows what happened to him.'

'You don't know Gig the way I do.'

I had never really looked at the jungle before. The leaves were thick and moist. Large drops of water reflected the trees and patches of sky around them like small crystal globes. Insects were crawling everywhere in lines and at random. In the distance a green flash of a gliding bird. Somewhere in there, gliding, there were snakes as big around as your arm. In the foreground, a salamander, dull muddy green on his back with golden eyes and a bright blue under his wide chin, stared back at the face in the window of the furious machine. When you are going quickly in a racing car and the world is fluid, small details become sharp and three-dimensional against a streaming background. Things move at dream speed until something breaks, or you feel a tyre begin to slip. Then the quiet centre of your moving cocoon explodes and the blades of time whirl. I hadn't even known we'd been moving quickly. I'd had the worst, most deceptive dream; I'd thought I was in control. Sam had mentioned Gig just once before, on the first night we stayed in her motorhome in the mountains. She never mentioned him again. Although I'd thought of him often enough. He was David and Sam never told me. A wall of mud and water was arching up from the front wheel of the Range Rover, headed like a tidal wave toward the salamander, and the dummy just sat there in the pond of his choice, watching his blue sky turn to mud.

'Gig,' I said.

'Gig. David. Gig is David.'

'I didn't know.'

'Of course you know. Everybody knows.'

'Bash,' I said, 'did you know Sam was married to David Allen?'

'Sure. Like saying did you know Lili Zanuck is married to Richard. Sam and David were in every paper and magazine in America around once a week for five years. Everybody knows.'

Except me. Monks in the mountains of Bulgaria know more about the world than I do. Travelling around the world to sixteen races in sixteen countries you know everything that happens inside the circus tent and nothing outside it. 'Gig,' I said again without meaning to. Sometimes when you get a blow to the stomach the brain pauses for a while.

Sam took a deep breath. 'He was in the mail-room at Creative Arts, and when he saw the young starlets coming in he'd wait at the door for them to come out. The starlets would come in and try to get the biggest agency in LA to take them on. And when they were on their way out without getting to see anybody, he'd say, "Hey, I can get you a gig." '

'So you married him.'

'I was nineteen and he had his own agency and he was the smartest man for miles. And Di-Di was five and she needed somebody to look after her.'

'And he cuts people to pieces.'

'Before they know it. Look, this isn't good for me. I don't want to talk about it.'

'And you are still working for him.'

'There you go again. I'm not going to be judged by a stunt driver.' Then she added quietly, looking away. 'I don't have a choice. He is the best agent in Hollywood and he got me this job.'

'And Candy is his daughter.'

'Yes, his daughter.'

'And you are still baby sitting.'

'Fuck you. Fuck you, Evers. I have been through a lot of pain with Gig and with Di-Di and most of it has been for her. I love that girl and I will not have you or anybody else judge me. Go fuck yourself.'

I wanted to put my arm around Sam and comfort her, make her pain less. I wanted to get out of the goddamn screaming Range Rover and walk into the jungle. I wanted to strap on my helmet, get in my racing car, and put my foot down, scream into the first corner and not lift. I wanted to say something and all the way to the plane I could not think of a word that made any sense or would change a thing. I had crashed and as you instantly learn if you crash because you were going too fast, or you weren't paying enough attention, or something broke or somebody came out of the blue and hit you, if you crash for any reason under the sun or none at all you cannot go back and do it over.

We rode in silence until what seemed like an hour later we crawled on to the landing strip on top of a long ridge where we'd left the plane. When the Range Rover stopped alongside the wing, the driver kept the engine roaring and reached behind him to open our door. 'Guanaperi,' he said to me, showing a lot of grinning red-stained teeth.

# chapter twenty-nine

The plane bounded down the lumpy landing strip, rose up over the jungle, and banked north like a cocaine tanker. The white-caps faded in the distance and in a couple of minutes Castleman's complex had shrunk to a small brown dot on the shore of a blue ocean that stretched all the way to the blue sky.

Apart from the whine of the engines, and Sam leaning over from the seat and to say – 'Just so this isn't a completely wasted trip, here's the new script' – it was a quiet trip.

Bizarre, isn't it? After all the words there aren't any. None at all to leap into the smoking hole that opens up with no warning. Nothing sounds right because it has all gone wrong. Pass the salt, darling. Go fuck yourself, sweetheart. The look of contempt and distaste on Sam's face said it all. The old female outrage in the face of the still uncomprehending male. I'll send you your things if you want them. Your underwear and your socks. Your hunting knife you kept in the drawer by the sink. And your worn-out stories, lies, and goofy grins; I'll wrap them up with string, stick them in the mail, and say good riddance. The sheets and the bed, the pictures on the walls, the furniture, the friends, and the house are mine. You can have the dog. Go forth and sing no more. Lie down in some other empty bed.

The rain forest from thirty thousand feet is green. Very green. Steam rises from it. And it looks flat. Very flat. Every leaf angled to catch the sun. Little green fuel cells. The trees in the rain forest grow several feet a year and after a few years they look permanent. But a strong wind will blow them down like sticks because their roots are all on the surfacc. I looked across at Sam. She looked at the wall behind me, her pretty green eyes thinking of something else. It takes time, Susan said, to put down enough roots to stand up in the high winds. I need time. She said. Away from you. No roots. No nothing. The slightest wind.

The script in my lap had a new pink cover. No doubt to distinguish the new feminine version from the old version with the blue cover. David Allen liked to describe *Juice* as '*Tender Mercies* meets *Northern Exposure*'. I leafed through it, mildly curious what Shaiman had changed to make it into a 'woman's film'.

Not a lot. At least not at first glance. Maybe the major change would be in Sam's pointing the camera more at her than at me. And leaving more of my face on the cutting-room floor. Or maybe it would be a matter of emphasis, a shift from action to sensitivity. A question of pace, slowing right down from the bang bang bang of action. Or maybe a concern for PMT, menopause, and the agony of childbirth for all I knew. What the hell did I know about women's issues? I couldn't even talk to the woman sitting across the aisle making notes in her script.

I too could look like I was making notes in my script. Just like a real actor. Take out my pen. Give it a flourish here. Make a note there. There are times when your heart has been shot away that the simplest gesture can make you feel like a complete asshole. Well, it never did take that much.

There were some new scenes. And the scene where the big-time successful racing driver pulls up to Macklin's garage, that one had been cut. But I didn't see a big difference. Here's a typical scene they added. See what you think.

**42. EXTERIOR SCHOOL. EARLY AFTERNOON.**
**It is the end of the lunch hour and the children are coming back from the playground. They are first through sixth graders, most of them Latino, and they stream around JILL who stands beside the door. JILL is primly dressed in a white shirt and fresh, pressed blue jeans. In the midst of the stream of children MACKLIN shuffles towards JILL, looming like an unruly, overgrown child. MACKLIN has come from his garage and he is out of place, too big and too dirty. As he approaches JILL, the school-children look at him with curiosity.**

MACKLIN
You doing a weapons check?

JILL
That's not funny. One of the girls had a .38 in her schoolbag last week. She said her mother gave it to her to protect herself. I'm doing a head count. With state and federal funding you get head count. What are you doing here?

MACKLIN
I thought I'd take you away from all this. Buy you a beer.

JILL
I can't. Can't you see I'm working?

The last of the children looks up at JILL, curious, and goes inside leaving JILL and MACKLIN alone outside the main entrance of the school.

MACKLIN
He stands in front of her and takes her clean small hand in his large dirty hand.
The sky is blue. You've got a half an hour of free time before your next class. We could just walk.

JILL
Checking her watch.
I don't have free time. I've got three kids I'm helping with their reading. They're waiting for me.

MACKLIN
Suddenly angry.
Goddamn it, you never have any free time. They pay you shit, you work your ass off, you are tired all the time, they don't give a shit, and you think your life ends outside the fence of this fucking school.

JILL

Patient. Explaining.

This is the only chance a lot of them have.

MACKLIN

Or they are gonna end up working in a garage like me.

JILL

I didn't say that. Look, I'm late, I've got to go inside.

MACKLIN

Grinning, remembering.

Right. Back to the scene of the crime.

JILL

(Upset) Candy told me this morning she saw us.

MACKLIN

Saw us what?

JILL

In my classroom last month. (MACKLIN wants her to say it) Making love. She's talking about running away. I think it might be better if we lived apart for a while.

MACKLIN

Everybody else's life before yours. I'll talk to her.

JILL

Don't you dare.

MACKLIN

We were making love. That's not so bad.

JILL

You are not her father.

**MACKLIN**
**And you are not her mother. It's time you got a life.**

**JILL**
**Is that it? The message? What you've come from your garage to tell me? Let me tell you, Macklin, I am saving lives here. Saving lives. This is my life and if they pay me badly and nobody else gives a shit it still beats the hell out of drinking beer and welding front ends. Fuck you.**

**JILL goes inside the school, slamming the door.**

**MACKLIN**
**Staring at the door.**
**I wish you would.**

I thought it was OK, but it was just standing round talking. I don't know if people would pay money to see it. *Juice* now had more camera on Jill, and less on Macklin. At the end of the script, Jill was going to do the big drive through the mountains because Macklin was going to burn his hands saving Candy from the fire. So Jill would be a life saver too. Fine with me. Take the wheel, leave my face on the cutting-room floor. As long as they finished the movie and put their promotional money on my Formula One car, they could do what they liked with the script.

As long as they didn't push me over the cliff.

When the plane landed at Burbank we got out and stood on the tarmac for a moment. Sam said, the wind blowing her short blonde curly hair, 'We're shooting again next Monday, Forrest; first call at nine a.m. See you then.'

'See you then.'

Sam walked off, swishy white dress and sandals, the dazed sunlight of late afternoon LA framing her body with light. The driver of the waiting limo held open the door for her and she disappeared.

We watched the limo go and Bash said, 'Why don't you dump the bitch?'

'Too late,' I said. 'She dumped me.'

'All the more reason,' he said. 'You want a lift?'

'Sure.'
'Where?'
'To my hotel.'
'Where's that at?'
'I don't know yet.'

Naturally Bash offered to put me up at his place for a few days. And naturally I said thank you, no. People mean to be kind when they offer you a place to stay when you have broken something in your life. But you are not good company and you are shoved into the middle of their private conversations and all their carefully hidden secrets come crawling out from under the carpet and you stick out at the dinner table like a man without a shirt.

Besides, the studio would pick up my tab and I didn't want anybody giving a damn or even noticing when the door to my bedroom opened and when it shut.

'Beverly Hills Hotel, driver,' I said, 'and make it snappy.'

Bash had the kindness to laugh at my dumb joke. Good old Beverly Hills Hotel. Bathtub Mercedes and stretch Lincoln limos still pulled up in front and bald men still smoked cigars in the polo lounge while they talked to agents and ex-wives on the phone. The world's greatest living mausoleum to the old Hollywood suited me just fine. I felt like a ghost myself and they were accustomed to taking my money. We could all pretend that we were all just good friends.

'The Beverly Hills Hotel is closed,' Bash said. 'The Sultan of Brunei bought it and he is bringing it back up to scratch.'

'OK, driver. Make it the Beverly Wilshire.' With its lobby full of imitation Nancy Reagans pretending not to notice Al Pacino, Liz Taylor, and Michael Caine. $16.50 will buy you a cup of tea and a sandwich in the lobby lounge and if you sit there long enough you might see a faded Formula One driver with lurid face signing in for a $300 a night single room at the front desk.

So I had five days to wonder why it was that I loved her and why it had turned out so bad and I began by walking down Wilshire and Rodeo Drive where the big money comes down out of the hills to shop. I thought it might cheer me up to watch the rich spend in public. I walked a few blocks towards the setting sun, the noise of the traffic building up to rush hour, nobody else walking along this slo-mo, stop and go, urban freeway.

Sam was awkward, spoiled, wilful, and selfish. She could turn on you in an instant and forget you the next. She had thousand-watt intensity and I loved the heat. Loved to flap my wings and cuddle right up to the light. Maybe it wasn't the brightest analysis of all time, and it certainly wasn't a satisfying one. But then I haven't had much practice at analysis. Maybe I was just a star-fucker, a grown-up groupie, I thought at one bad point while I was waiting the half-hour you wait in LA for the lights to change. But I didn't miss the star at all. I missed Sam. I missed her oyster fresh sea scent when she was hot, standing in the sun, trace of lemon. And the feel of her warm in bed with me and waking up together. The great surprise of finding her there and her face happy to see me. I missed the funny, sweet, and pretty sweetheart girl she wore up front and I missed the tough, driven, swinging with both hands woman underneath. I missed her struggle to do everything on her list, and do it absolutely right away right now and perfect or it wasn't good enough. I missed her like a bear misses the sun in winter. Might as well crawl into my vast and empty hotel bed, pull the covers over my head, and let the dark take the pain away.

Walking the streets of LA doesn't take you very far wherever you are in that hollow city. The only place people walk in LA is to and from the parking lot. I walked a few more long blocks before I came to the deep, wide, and slow-running concrete river called the San Diego Freeway where I bumped into Evers LA Law Number One. If you are walking in LA, you are nowhere.

I turned around, walked back to my hotel, hired a Ford, and drove to David Allen's office. In the David Allen building. On what no doubt will one day be David Allen Avenue in downtown David Allen.

# chapter thirty

Evil is so amorphous it looks just the same as everywhere else. So easy to aim; so hard to hit the middle.

The David Allen building rises up out of a little knoll called Century City. It is thirty-five stories high, black paint on steel with bronzed mirror-glass, and it looks like its expensive neighbours; the tall faceless movie-business buildings built in the early 1970s to house the growing bureaucracy of media suits and game show experts that keep the sponsors up to date and happy. Where are you, Daffy Duck, when we need you?

Something about the polished concrete floors of LA underground garages makes a car's tyres squeal like pigs and I flat out enjoyed sliding the big Ford Taurus I'd nicknamed Borus for its stunning, enough-power-to-froth-an-egg performance, screeching sideways at thirty-five around the concrete pillars like a herd of stuck pigs and into a parking slot with the wheels locked up and smoke pouring out of the wheel wells. Yoo-hoo, David. Your star is here.

Since my last visit had been through an unmarked side entrance which led straight to the non-stop executive express, the David-and-friends-only CEO elevator, I didn't realize that the garage elevator only went to the ground-floor lobby.

The lobby of your modern entertainment corporation is not there to welcome you and even less to entertain you. It is a moat.

I knew David's office was on the top floor. So I strode across the black polished marble floor like I knew what I was doing to the bank of elevators aimed at the top floor. From behind their ocean-liner sized console with the fifteen video screens the palace guard slow-tracked my less than fresh T-shirt, sandals, and cut-off baggy jeans that made a lot of sense for an all-day flight back and forth to hot-house Southern Mexico. On the shores of corporate America, I looked like a beach bum. I was pushing the elevator button when a guard came over and said can I help you sir.

I said no thanks and he stood in front of me, a big, nice-looking man. Maybe an off-duty linebacker. Unlike me, he was freshly shaven and very proud of his aftershave. He just stood there.

'David Allen,' I said.

'Do you have an appointment, sir?'

'He's expecting me.'

I don't know why I dislike private security guards. It must be dull work and it can't do wonders for your self-esteem knowing that dogs do it better. But sympathy was not in my nature that afternoon and I said, 'Forrest Evers, Bob, reading his name from his badge. 'You ever been in the movies before, Bob?'

He shook his head a short impatient 'no' like he had heard the line a few times.

'Well get your ass over to your desk over there and tell David's team Forrest Evers is on his way up or I will have you patrolling Paramount's prop warehouse in Pasadena starting tomorrow . . . night,' I added just to be cruel.

'Yes, sir, Mr Evers,' he said, looking doubtful.

One good thing about Hollywood, unless you are a player you never know who the real players are. And even then. The short brown gentleman in the Filipino shirt open at the collar and the chino trousers could be the Sultan of Brunei. You never know. The doors opened and I stepped in, wondering if Paramount has a prop warehouse in Pasadena. The back wall of the elevator was glass for a good view of LA. A rumour of sun behind the afternoon smog gave the sky a burnt orange tinge. It's a pleasant feeling rising effortlessly to the top of the heap, watching the folks on the ground disappear. But after the thirty-five-floor flight, the ride comes to an end and the doors open to remind you, you are just a passenger, facing another moat.

I walked across the soft blue carpet to the glass and aluminium receptionist's desk. A stunning woman with a sharp nose and emerging cheekbones, about forty, an Hermès scarf at her neck, and a fresh tousled hair-do smiled corporately at me. She wore a minimal headset and the nameplate on her desk said Janice. Janice looked as slim, confident, and suntanned as if she had just stepped off her polo pony. Then, as I approached, her face fell. 'Oh dear, Mr Evers,' she said. 'Would you like to sit down? What happened to you?'

I'd forgotten I looked like a Mexican death mask.

'I'd like to see David.'

'Oh dear, Mr Evers,' she said again. 'You don't have an appointment, do you.' Not a question, statement of fact.

'I'm sure he'd be delighted to see me.'

'He's in New York.'

'All day?'

She laughed. 'Let me get Vangella, his office exec. Maybe she can fix something.' She pushed a couple of buttons, said into her headset, 'Hi, Janice. Can you tell Vangie Mr Evers is in reception? No, for David. An actor from location. What project would that be?' she asked me.

'*Juice*,' I said.

'*Juice*,' she said into her headset. 'You know, the Samantha Miles film?' She flipped the headset down, smiling welcome and confidence. 'Vangella will be right out. Can I get you anything? Coffee, tea, Excedrin?'

I had time to admire the DeKooning and the Jasper Johns on the wall, also the view of LA that went from the floor to the ceiling and the softly lighted and elaborately framed oil paintings of the stars David represented; among them, in a green gauzy thing, Samantha Miles. It was the pretty, happy, adorable, and darling girl that Sam did so well. The sweetheart with the dewy lip and the longing in her eyes. All sugar and no spice.

'She's much more beautiful in person, but David likes that picture. I think it makes her look kinda sappy, like Goldie Hawn, but Sam'd kill me if she heard me say that.' This was said at maximum speed as if it was one word.

The buzz of energy behind me looked as if she were fifteen minutes out of college, wearing a tiny black miniskirt, black tights, and clunky black shoes pointing out at right angles from each other. She had a curly mop of black hair with a lot of it on top to boost her total height. Which, with the clunky heels on the clunky shoes, was just under five feet. She had bright brown eyes, with lines of fatigue lying in wait underneath, and she was making an effort to make what she must have thought was a smile as she held out her hand. A worker bee in a land of butterflies. 'It's been a hell of a week, Mr Evers. Hi, I'm Vangella. What do you want?'

'I'd like to see David.'

'Me too,' she said with real feeling. 'He's got a breakfast meeting with IBM's board tomorrow, and they want a summary of our net US video licence franchise plus audience psychographics for the last five years and I'm not sure I should let them see our figures. He's in London in the evening with Rupert Murdoch and his group to see if we can sew up the Cable Europ franchise, he's then off to Japan where he's meeting with George Hozuki, and he should be back here on Monday to take a meeting with Intel and Pac-Telesis to link up with Disney and Tri-Star. It's our first mile down the Information Highway and we are all very excited about it. Jack wants to renegotiate the points and co-production on *Long Island Sound*, Cher's rung four times from the recording studio, and if David doesn't give me an answer on *Powerhouse* before tomorrow morning we'll have been on a nine-month dead-end detour with Columbia screwing us on the TV money and Bill will walk, I know he will.' She stopped for a moment to draw breath, looking at me as if I had spilled lunch on my T-shirt.

'I appreciate you are in *Juice*, Mr Evers, and I understand there have been some problems in production, but strictly speaking David doesn't represent you. What was it you wanted to see him about?'

'George Hozuki is an old friend of mine,' I said. 'I think it would help David if I spoke with him for a few minutes before they meet.' It was a small opening, but the only one I was likely to get.

'Write me a précis and I'll see that he gets it.'

'No.'

'OK, don't and he won't get it.'

I looked at her for a beat and she said, 'I'm up to my ears in alligators and David pays me to be the dragon at his gate. Right now you are around ninety-three on the B list. You want to move up to his top ten you have to push something large off the table. What have you got?'

There was another pause while I tried to think of something.

'You got a lump on your forehead, that's what you got,' she said. 'Does it hurt?' She reached up with a tentative finger to touch. I don't know why, but her fingernail touching my bruised skin made me think of a nasty idea. It was a cheap, and as I say, nasty shot. But I had a limited selection and I liked it. If somebody tries to push you off a cliff it's only natural to try to push back. I told myself.

'Well, if I have to go through you, tell David I'm concerned about the sex scenes with his daughter.'

She looked at me.

'Just tell him.'

'I'm sure he's read the script. If they are shooting it, David has okayed it.'

'There are two scripts.'

She thought about that for a few beats. 'Where are you staying?'

'The Beverly Wilshire.'

'I'll be in touch.'

# chapter thirty-one

Yes, the sky is blue in Beverly Hills, as long as you look straight up. I was looking to find some ideas. Plenty of blue, very few ideas in the sky in LA in the morning.

The *LA Times* sprawled at my feet. Headlines rumoured fresh riots in South LA. Inside, American troops were coming home again, but Jordan and the whole Middle East was getting ready to pop. A short piece in the business section said Hozuki's stock was pole-vaulting in Tokyo on the strength of their new electric car due out in eighteen months. Or on Castleman's strapping rockets on the stock's backside, I thought. Weather for today in the Ellay basin: more sun, heavy smog.

A pale, tired, and slender woman in a faded one-piece swimsuit told me she was from Lincoln. Lincoln, Nebraska, she said, where her husband Arnold, Arnold Rogers, was a successful Ford dealer here in town for a Ford Dealer Conference. After she was disappointed to learn that no, she hadn't seen me starring in a movie, she went back to the end of the pool and watched her twin daughters splashing in the shallow end of the pool while she angled her chaise-longue for maximum sun on a body that had been wrapped up tight against the Nebraska winter for months. She lay there for a while, squinting her eyes against the sun, then she sat up for a minute looking at me and came over again. Helen, she said. Helen Rogers. Wanted to know what I was writing.

I wasn't writing anything. So far. Crumpled balls of false starts joined the *LA Times* on the pool deck. My fourth cup of espresso was empty and my brain was buzzing in small zinging caffeine circles.

She went back to basking with an eye on the kids.

I'd told David there was a second script, so there had better be a second script. Getting it typed and bound into the new script was the easy part. AAAAH SCRIPTS to ZZZZYY REZZUMES in the yellow pages who would do it overnight on Sunday. Or anytime if you liked with ez credit card payment plans.

Screenwriters were not so easy to find. Screenwriters may be out there on the streets waving their scripts at passing Mercedes hoping there might be a producer inside. But however desperate they are, screenwriters do not hang out in the yellow pages. But even if Shaiman was hanging out in the bar of the Beverly Hills Hotel, could I trust him to blind-side the most powerful man in Hollywood? David, I could hear him saying on the phone, I just got this crazy call from this guy. Forget trust in this town. And there wasn't time to explain it all. And what the hell, if every waitress and nightclub comedian in LA had written a screenplay, why not your local friendly Formula One driver? I knew the script for *Juice* inside out and I could use it as a guide for the form. And my spelling is above average.

There wasn't much to write, just one scene.

If, say, I wrote a scene to take the place of the one in front of the school house where Jill tells Macklin to fuck off, that would do it. I mean what was the point of the scene; to show how far apart Jill and Macklin are. And to show how they are both trapped in their own way. And that Candy is not relaxed about their being lovers. I usually like nude love scenes and I wondered if I might be able to do that with a nude love scene. Uh huh. Although the dialogue would be a problem. I doubted I could write dialogue. What do people say when they speak to each other, let alone when they make love? OK, maybe I could do it without dialogue. One scene without dialogue would be fine. Stallone can go a whole movie with six one-syllable words so what was stopping me?

Try again.

And again.

& etc.

'Do you want me to get you more paper?' the nice bright red woman from Lincoln, Nebraska, asked before lunch.

'Phone for Mr Evers.'

I opened my eyes and the pool attendant, who no doubt

modelled swimsuits on the side, held out a sleek white telephone for me and I realized in a flash that having your name called for a phone call pool-side at the Beverly Wilshire Hotel is not a mark of power and prestige. It is a sharp stab of anxiety.

Who is it? I almost said. But I knew who it was.

'What's all this shit about Delilah in a sex scene?' he said.

'Good morning, David, where are you?'

'It's seven fifteen in London and we are going to land in twenty-five minutes and answer my question.'

'Fine,' I said.

'Evers, don't jerk me around. If you are jerking me around, I can promise you that you will not ever be in any movie ever again or ever drive a car again.' He said this quietly and confidentially. A little shared piece of inside information.

Nothing like a threat to get the creative juices flowing. 'It's a hell of a scene,' I said. 'Great box office.'

'I rarely swear, Evers, but what the fuck are you talking about? I have seen the scripts. Sam says you are full of shit.'

'Well, nobody tells you everything, do they?' I was counting on this. The higher you go, the bigger the paranoia. Of course people don't tell you everything, they can't. There isn't enough time in the universe to tell you everything. 'We're shooting it next week. Sam wants it to be a surprise for you. She thinks you'll like it, because it's very tasteful.'

'Evers, there is a great deal more involved here than you know.'

'You mean I am out of my league.'

'It's a different game, Evers. With some very big players.'

'Are you talking about Gig, Texon, and the United Auto Workers, or Sam, or the future of the electric car? It's hard to know where your loyalties lie here, David.'

'I don't have any problem with loyalty, Evers. And I don't have the time to explain it to you. Just do your job and keep the hell out of it. Now tell me, what's the scene?'

'Well, it's Jill and Macklin. Sam felt, and I agree with her, that we should establish their physical relationship. To show that there is at least that bond between them. So there is a nude scene of them making love. Nothing over an R rating, tasteful, but you know, sexy. And then Candy gets involved.'

'What do you mean, involved?'

There was a long pause.

'I think Sam sees it as representing the feminist's point of view that the male/female sexual act is an attack on women. Candy hears them – you know what bonking is?'

'I invented it. Get to the point.'

'It's a good scene. Just controversial enough to raise some protest. And Candy gets out of bed and goes into their bedroom, and she attacks Macklin.'

'What do you mean, attacks him? Shoots him?'

'She hits him, and they roll on the floor together. She's hitting him, he's trying to get away.'

'I can't believe Sam would shoot that. Is Di in the, ah, does she appear without uh, clothing?'

'Total nudity. To show her innocence. But they're talking about very low light.'

'Well, if Sam thinks she is going to shoot that, that is not going to happen. Not. I can tell you that. I won't allow that. Hozuki would never allow it either. Even if they shoot it I can promise you it will never reach the screen. For God's sake, Evers, she's only fourteen. What the hell are they thinking of?'

'It will be a pivotal scene.'

'Pivotal? Jesus Christ, if you are jerking me around . . .'

'Something weird is going on.'

'It certainly is.'

'I mean with the cars. Somebody is fooling with them to make them crash,.'

'I appreciate you've had quite a knock on the head.'

'And I want you to stop it.'

'I'll ignore that implication.'

'You call your dogs off me, David, and I will show you the script.'

'I don't work with dogs, Evers. Apart from you. But please do be more careful in your driving. I hear those cars can blow up any time.'

'Thanks for the tip, Dave,' I said, but he'd hung up.

I paced the pool for the rest of the afternoon, had dinner sent into my room, and by midnight I had a room full of crumpled paper and frustration. I'll spare you the false starts, revisions, and the pounding of my forehead against the wall.

Which is what I did for the next two days. I went from my room to the pool and back to my room, trying to write one scene. Except, of course, for the six times I called Sam. I left five messages on her answering machine and on the sixth try, Delilah answered. 'What's up?' she said.

'I want to talk to Sam. See how she is.'

'She's right here, Spike,' Delilah said. 'And she looks kinda tired. But she's shaking her head like no way she wants to talk to you.'

'Tell her I just don't understand what happened. One minute she was there and the next she won't talk to me. Can you ask her what happened?'

'This is weird, Spike. I'm gonna hang up.'

'Can you tell me?'

'Mom,' she said off the phone, 'should I tell him?' There was a pause and Sam's muffled voice in the background. Delilah came on the phone again. 'She said sure tell you. OK. Mom says she still has a lot of anger against men because her father died when she was a kid.'

'So she's mad at me.'

'Dr Conklin says Mom and I both have this big fear of being abandoned.'

'Dr Conklin?'

'Mom's shrink. Sometimes we go out together. He says it was the last straw seeing that old guy who was dying. And you didn't support her. Like ran out on her. But hey, don't worry about it, Spike. Mom is big on short-term relationships. I think she just has a short attention span. Like she gets bored real easy. Hey, do you know that Sylvia Plath poem goes like Daddy you bastard?'

'Never heard of it.'

'You should read it. My daddy is a bastard too.'

There was the sound of fumbling on the other end. 'Forrest,' Sam said into the phone, 'why the hell did you tell David I was rewriting the script? I mean how did you know? I certainly never told you about it.'

'I didn't know you were.'

'Well, of course I am rewriting it. The only thing that piece of rubbish that Shaiman did is good for is keeping Radnor and the wolves off my back. If that's what they want to think I'm shooting, great. But I've got the chance to do something really wonderful with this script, Forrest, and I am going to do it.'

'You're rewriting the whole script?'

'No, no. I can't do that. I mean I have to be practical and use what we've shot. I'm just redrafting a few key scenes. I feel this is really Jill's film now and I want to do it right now for her. She is a very important person for America now.'

'Jill is a character. She's not a real person.'

'Jill is the most real thing I've ever done. Look, Forrest, I'm sorry about what happened. It's not your fault, but I can't help what I feel. I'm sorry. Something just broke and I can't fix it. But why the hell did you have to tell David? He thinks I'm writing some kind of sex movie with Di-Di in it.'

'That's what I'm writing,' I said. 'As long as you are rewriting the film you should take a look at my new scene. You'll love it.'

'Right,' she said with some disgust. After a pause she said in her soft, young girl voice, 'You're not angry with me?'

'Angry? No, I'm not angry,' I said.

'Good, I'll see you Monday morning.'

Sunday evening finally came stumbling into my room and I took my scene to TYPOS (Free psychiatric advice with five copies or more) on Fairfax, proud as a new daddy.

**41. EXT. MOVING DOWN THE SILENT MAIN STREET IN VELMA. 3 AM.**

**A woman moans.**

**THE CAMERA TRACKS DOWN A SIDE STREET.**

**She moans again.**

**JILL'S HOUSE. A LIGHT GOES ON IN A BACK ROOM. WE TRACK THROUGH THE OPEN WINDOW.**

**42. INT. CANDY'S BEDROOM. A LAMP ON HER BEDSIDE TABLE PARTIALLY LIGHTS THE ROOM.**

**Another moan as CANDY props herself up in bed. The moaning is her mother in another room. Joined by MACKLIN'S moans. CANDY grabs her old teddy bear from the foot of the bed, clamps the teddy bear to the side of her head to blot out the noise and falls back down on her side and lies crouched on her side.**

CANDY lies still for a moment as the rhythmic moaning goes on. CANDY sits up suddenly and flings her teddy bear hard against the wall at the foot of the bed. She kicks off her sheet, gets out of bed, nude in the semidarkness, opens her bedroom door and goes out in the hall, walks down the hall and stands for a moment in the half light outside her mother's bedroom door.

43. INT. JILL'S BEDROOM.
JILL'S old brass bed creaks as she and MACKLIN are making love in the semidarkness. JILL's head is on the pillow, turned to the side, and her eyes are closed and her face appears to be in pain as she moans. When the light from the hallway crosses her face (as CANDY opens the bedroom door), JILL opens her eyes.

43. (CONT.) CANDY'S point of view from the doorway: MACKLIN is moving harshly on top of JILL, his hand squeezing JILL's breast. He is making a lot of noise. CANDY runs at the forms on the bed and hits MACKLIN hard with her shoulder. The three of them tangle on the bed.

MACKLIN, not knowing what is happening, flings CANDY off his back and on to the floor. JILL screams and scrambles down to the floor next to CANDY who is crying, silently, tears streaming down her face.

JILL
(Drawing a sheet around herself and CANDY and looking up at MACKLIN who is kneeling naked on the bed)
You get out. Get out of my house. JUST GET. OUT.

It might not fit Sam's definition of a 'woman's film'. But David was going to love it.

# chapter thirty-two

'It's perfect,' I said. 'But the Transportation Coordinator, Gene what's his name, can count to five.'

'Gene Govoni, right,' Bash said, fiddling with the combination lock. 'Gene can count to five. But he is not going to say anything because he and I go all the way back to Sprint cars on the dirt track at Ascot and I am renting this truck from him. We better swap these suckers soon, Evers, first available opportunity. He tells me there's some bad-ass shit going down. Someone has been fucking with your car.' In the semidarkness of dawn, his face looked pale white, like a balloon with eyes.

Bash was unlocking the back of a fifteen-foot-long straight truck. The panels were painted green and said ALL-PRO-PROPS just like the real props trucks, complete with address, phone, and fax numbers. The paint was faded, as if it had been right there, number five in a line of the five props trucks for five years.

'This is a fact?' I said.

'Probably. Gene said Frank took away your car yesterday morning and brought it back this afternoon. He said the word came down not to ask about it.'

'I thought Frank was a big fan of mine.'

'He is. But hey, don't look that way, you're not gonna get anything out of Frank. If you ask him about it he's going to say he's just a driver and he is just doing his job. He probably drove the car some place, got out, walked away. And after a while somebody else came walking by, got in, and drove it to an unmarked garage in some back alley of some industrial park.'

The doors swung open, and in the dark interior I could see the outlines of another Mustang replica, just like the other prop cars. Bash was saying, 'Four bolt Reynolds 283 running at 9.0

to 1, around five hundred and fifty horsepower, Woodward steering box, seven-inch triple disc Quartermaster clutch, and all that other good shit I told you about. I shifted the block back a bit but it's still kinda nose heavy. Same tyres as those other tin shit-boxes so it looks just the same. Treat it gently, 'cause it bites.'

'When can you swap it?' I said.

'Anytime you say, as long as it's dark and everybody is asleep. It's too late now. Half the crew is up and having coffee. But we could do it first thing tomorrow.'

'I'll let you know,' I said. I stepped back from the truck, looking at it in the line of identical trucks. 'That's the great thing about Hollywood,' I said. 'They can do anything you want.'

'Anything you can pay for, Forrest. That may look like a truck to you but it's bread and butter to me. The truck was a big extra and we are up to ninety-five grand. Where do I send the bill?'

'Send it to David Allen. By the end of today he'll be happy to pay it.'

I was wearing a cute blonde wig in the hot sun. No lipstick and make-up, just the wig. I did not look adorable.

Sam said, 'I just want to finish off these driving sequences. We'll do them over the next two days then we can release you.'

I looked at her cute turned-up lip, her pretty face with the sad, wide green eyes. Sam was looking back at me with mild interest as if we had never had our arms and legs around each other and never felt the pulse of life boom with the same beat. So long old buddy, shut up and drive. For a while there you were up among the stars and you got burned. Why should that surprise you?

The desert buzzed with silence. In Sam's latest version of the script, Macklin would be left behind in Velma, while Jill drove Candy (lying down in the back seat) over the mountains. So I would do the hot driving sequences wearing a little curly blonde Jill wig. I was trying to remind myself why I was doing this; for the six-million-dollar sponsorship the movie would bring, trying to picture myself in my Formula One car instead of this silly Mustang replica wearing a silly wig. And the buzz of the desert was louder. Not a buzzing. Helicopters.

Three helicopters dotted the hot blue sky over the mountains, loomed large overhead and landed WHOPPA WHOPPA WHOPPA, one by one.

The first helicopter was a big sleek new black Sikorsky with a thin gold stripe and DAVID ALLEN COMMUNICATIONS in small and tasteful script near the tail. Its door opened and a ramp unfolded. After a few moments David stepped out, soft powder-blue polo shirt, chinos, loafers, and the luggage of international business travel under his eyes. Radnor stepped out from his plain-jane red and white Olympic Studios chopper looking as if he was about to lose his breakfast. Then Akiri stepped from a small bright green machine that looked like a flying preying mantis with HOZUKI on the nose. Akiri was wearing a Hozuki Formula One white jacket and white slacks with TEAM HOZUKI in red script running up his leg. The generals touching down in the DMZ. No smiles anywhere.

I looked around for Sam and she was gone. David was coming towards me, telling Akiri '. . . new Sikorsky S–76 C. Max is around a hundred and seventy-eight with a range of over nine hundred miles. Normally it'll take twelve to fourteen aboard but we've shifted . . .' and walked by me as if I wasn't there. In Formula One you can disappear after a couple of races. Evidently all it takes in the movie business is a long weekend. 'Cute wig,' Radnor said over his shoulder.

Bash was waiting for me alongside 'my' car, the Puerca One that had 'disappeared' for a few hours. 'It took me a while to find it,' he said, 'it's only a little couple two maybe three ounces of plastic wired to a squib and a timer. And it's wedged up on top of the gas tank where I can't really get to it without pulling the tank. It's big enough to turn this thing to fudge. Make a hell of a bang. And the gas tank is full.'

'What's a squib?' I said.

'Just a little incendiary device. Kinda like a fat little black firecracker with wires sticking out. It's what we use to set off stuff in the movies. You see a little flash and a bang from a bullet, that's a squib. See a big whoosh of flame, that's a squib igniting a buried fifty-five gallon drum of gasoline like we did in *Apocalypse*. Give me a half-hour maybe forty-five minutes and I can get the whole thing out of there, no problem.'

'Leave it,' I said, getting into the car. The key was clipped behind the visor and I took it out and stuck it in the ignition. As I was about to turn it on I saw Bash backing away and I felt a sudden drop in confidence. 'Definitely a timer,' I said.

'Get the hell out of there,' he said in a strange kind of croaking voice. 'What the hell do you care about any of this shit?'

'I was wondering if it is going to explode when I turn the key.'

'Probably not. I don't know. It might go before you turn the key. It depends on when it's set to go off.'

'But it won't make any difference if I turn the key on.'

'Hey. I don't know. Probably not.'

'Can you tell when the timer's set to go off?'

'No way.' He kept backing away. 'Get the hell out of there, Evers.'

'Screw it,' I said, turning the key.

# chapter thirty-three

'Can you all hear me?' Sam said. She was standing in front of Puerca Two, wearing her Jill wardrobe, a yellow skirt with red birds, loose bright blue shiny sleeveless blouse with the collar turned up, and little white canvas sneakers. Matching her ensemble she also wore her adorable darling look for the cast and crew. David, Akiri, and Radnor were standing just behind her.

From where I was at the back, looking over the heads of the grips, sparks, stunt riggers, extras, she looked small and frail. I felt some friendly scratching between my shoulder blades.

'Hi, Spike. What's up?' Di dragged her fingers along my back and on to my arm. She was in today's Candy outfit for her scene with Jill; baggy cut-off jeans and a hot pink tank-top. She'd tied her long stringy blonde hair up in a knot, and her slanted green eyes were looking up at me as if I should know.

'I'm the last one they'd tell,' I said.

'They'd tell you before me.' Di turned her little pointy face towards Sam at the front of the crowd for a couple of beats and then looked down at her untied basketball sneakers and the desert dirt. 'When I saw him get off the chopper' – Delilah's voice had dropped down just short of a whisper and I had to bend down to hear her – 'I thought, "Hey, great. It's about time. Daddy's coming to see me." And he walked right by me. He looked right at me, Forrest, and he acted like he didn't see me. Screw him.'

'Yeah,' I said quietly, 'screw him.'

'Please can I have it quiet,' Sam was raising her arms and hushing the crew with her hands. 'David has just come back from Japan and he has an important announcement to make.'

'Can we get a mike?' David said, stepping in front of Sam.

'There are almost a hundred of you and I want to be sure you can all hear me.' There was a pause and the busy scuffling of assistant producers.

Di held my arm with both hands, and whispered in my ear. 'Hey, Spike. I didn't know you're such a dirty old man. Mom said you've been telling everyone I'm gonna do a nude sex scene.'

'Just something I wrote to piss off your daddy, Di.'

'Sounds cool.'

'OK,' David called out, scanning his audience, making that eye contact that corporate communicators learn to make. 'Plenty of mikes but no speakers so I'll keep it short. If you read the financial sections of the newspapers this morning, you already know Hozuki is delaying the introduction of EVIA. Indefinitely. They are having a technical problem with the car and Akiri can fill you in on the details. Normally, that would mean that the release of *Juice* will also be delayed indefinitely.' David paused for a moment letting that sink in.

'Unfortunately there is another problem. Hawker, the Australian shopping channel, with the backing of a major international financial group, has made a bid early today for Hozuki and it is, to put it mildly, a hostile take-over bid.

'In the circumstances, the management of Hozuki feels that it can no longer continue to support *Juice*. Now I don't want you to panic, this doesn't mean that we are in turnaround. We are going to complete this project. *Juice* is the property of Olympic Studios and let me repeat so there is no mistake, we will complete this film.'

'But it will be a very different film,' Sam said, stepping up alongside David Allen. 'A much more important film.'

'Every film Olympic makes is important,' Radnor complained from behind David. He seemed to be standing on his tiptoes to make himself heard. 'And I gotta tell you we are cutting the budget and we are revising the production schedule. This is coming out of our pockets.'

David continued as if he hadn't been interrupted. 'I know you have put your heart and your soul into *Juice* and I want you to know how much we value your work. Obviously, now that EVIA is dropping out of the limelight for a while, we are shifting the focus away from the car and over to America's favourite star, Samantha Miles. We still have a full production day ahead of us and I know Ron Radnor is going to shoot me if I don't let you all get back to work. So we'll take some questions but let's keep it short.'

A voice in the front wanted to know what happened to EVIA.

'Yeah, right,' Akiri said. 'Hey, I want to thank you. All of you on behalf of Hozuki of America. Because you all have done a great job and I don't want anybody here thinking that anything was their fault. OK, we've had some bad luck here. But we would have overcome that. Hozuki likes to start what we finish.' There was a hushed pause. 'I mean finish what we start. You know what I mean. We've been experiencing a problem with the polymer we're using inside the fuel cell as the ion exchanger. At the high output end of the scale, under acceleration for example, the heat melts the plastic. Twelve months ago, our engineers told us they were five days away from solving the problem. Last Friday they told us we are still five days away from solving the problem. So I don't know. We could go to a liquid, like battery acid, but the weight is prohibitive. Maybe we will be back on schedule in five days. Maybe it'll take another six months. We shall return,' he said raising his arms. The cast and crew responded with a numb silence.

After the questions, David marched through the crowd, people stepping back, parting for him like the Red Sea, to me. Right up close. About an inch away. Di gave him a short twitch of a smile, and said 'Hi, Daddy.'

'I'll catch you later, Delilah. Right now I have some personal business with Mr Evers. Will you excuse us for a few moments, sweetheart,' he said, not looking at her.

Di gave him a wry little wave and walked away.

David watched her go and turned back to me. 'You are full of shit, Evers. There is no second script, never was, and no scene with Di-Di that I couldn't show to the Harper Valley PTA,' he said. 'I don't want you talking to Di-Di or to anyone on this set. I want you off it now. We'll complete with another driver.'

'I think it's a pretty good scene.'

'Sam says it's a complete lie. My daughter is not, never was, never will be nude in *Juice*. Sam hates the idea.'

'She's afraid you'll stop her from shooting it. She thinks you'll change your mind once you see it on film. But you know Sam better than I do. Maybe she has something else up her sleeve. You want to see the scene?'

'You have a copy?'

'It's in the car.'

The pink script was on the console between the driver and passenger seat in Puerca One where I'd left it. David stood by the car looking at it. I got in the car and started it up. Big old V–8 rumble all wuffle-wuffle. Speak softly, swing big stick. David flinched, but he didn't step back.

'Just hand me the script,' he said.

'It is not a gift, David.'

'You're not in a position to bargain, Evers. If you are not off this set in five minutes I'll have you arrested for trespassing. And if that isn't good enough I'll get a couple of actresses to testify that you sexually molested them.'

'Some people may think the scene's a little risqué, but it's all in the lighting. It could make your Di-Di a star.'

He hung back, looking at the script lying on the console for a few beats. And he couldn't help himself. He leaned in and reached for the script. A fast move. He thought.

I thought, Plenty of time.'

Because he had to reach. He had to lean on the door and bend way over. A little more extra stretch with his hand and I grabbed his wrist, yanked him forward head first into the car, popped the clutch, and accelerated hard, spinning the wheel and heading out the dirt road.

Nice desert dirt road. Could have been a donkey track. Down hard on it, through the gears and we were moving through a quickee half-mile of bounce, bounce, bounce, and turning right out on to California Highway 257 heading west. David was crammed into the foot-well. Busy down there trying to get up, get some air. He grabbed my leg and I smacked him hard on the back of his head. 'Sit up, David,' I said, 'or I will hurt you.'

That got his attention and he relaxed enough to get himself turned around and sitting up in his seat. He had scratched his face and it was bleeding down his chin and on to his powder-blue polo shirt.

I handed him a clean handkerchief from my pocket and told him to hold it against his cheek. 'And put your seat-belt on,' I said. 'It's the law.'

He looked at me and at the speedometer with the needle at ninety-five and put his seat belt on, the wind blowing his hair furiously. 'This is kidnapping, Evers,' he said through clenched teeth.

'Where would you like to go?' I said. 'I thought we could drive up into the mountains. Take another run up the road where you had me blown off. We've got a full tank of gas, so, what the hell, we could drive all the way to the Pacific.'

David looked at his watch.

'You got your swimsuit, Dave? Nice day for the beach. We could run down to San Diego. How long do we have before this thing blows up?'

David turned to look at me, blood drying on his polo shirt, wind ruining his careful hairdo. He was windblown and sick and he still looked good, confident. 'Some states have brought back to the death penalty for kidnapping,' he said. 'Kidnapping should be punished by death, don't you think?' He turned away, looking out at the desert as the two-lane black-top road began to climb.

We went into the first curve, and I set the car up early, cocking the wheel, getting the back end to come around before we got to the corner and holding it there, tapping the brakes to get the front end to slide, getting back on the throttle and holding the slide all the way through the corner, coming all the way to the edge of the road on the exit. The drop off was on David's side and I wanted his attention. 'Hey, Dave,' I said.

'You are dead, Evers, you are fucking dead,' he said, looking back at me, not so good now. His face, puffy from jet lag, and his deranged hair, matted and tangled in the furious wind, reminded me of Richard Nixon, drunk, roaming the halls of the White House after midnight and raging at Kissinger.

'David Allen is in the details,' I said keeping my foot down as the black top went sharply up the hill. The air was hot and still. It was just before noon and you could smell sage in the dry desert air. In front of us the mountains were hot red, brown, and black rock rising almost straight up. 'You knew the helicopter would make my car unstable. Very impressive.

So let me take a wild guess. You know exactly when the bomb on the gas tank is going to explode.'

He tried not to. He looked out at the valley below us and he looked straight ahead at the turn coming up. But he had to look at his watch again. He looked. 'Stop the car.'

'Talk to me, David.'

'Just stop the fucking car.'

He sat back in his seat and braced himself as we entered the 'slow' 35 mph turn at eighty-five. We, of course, were barely moving at all. It was the side of the mountain that was out of control, rock face swinging around to hit us head-on at eighty-five. Long lurid slides are slow and clumsy but I wasn't interested in speed. I wanted David to believe, in his bones, that I was on the edge of losing control. The screeching tyres made it very noisy, and I think, from David's perspective, deeply frightening. I worked the wheel back and forth and blipped the throttle keeping the car up on the edge of its little skinny tyres, giving him the feeling that we could lose it either way, into the rocks or over the edge at any moment. Flying past a big tractor-trailer crawling down hill. Eat Meat For Action.

We came out of the turn, I shifted down into third for the sound effects, making the engine scream and getting back the speed we'd lost in the corner.

Suddenly David smiled and I saw him relax and sit back in his seat. 'No shit,' he said. 'I have to give you that. You really had me going, Evers. I was just thinking I am being kidnapped by this stupid homicidal moron, who can't even act even when Sam is doing everything but moving his lips for him, and the light went on. There isn't any bomb in this car, Evers. Couldn't be. Or if there is you don't know about it. If there were a bomb you'd be scared shitless. And you are not even the least little bit worried. I mean, all credit Evers, to your driving . . .' He paused as we came out to the edge of the road again, the road dropping off for half a mile on his side. 'Your driving truly scares the shit out of me. But let's face it. You can't even act enough to make me think you are a racing driver, let alone make me think you are afraid of being blown up. You can't act your way out of a paper bag and if you knew anything about a bomb within five miles it would be all over your face.'

'Shit,' I said looking at him as another curve came up.

We went around two more curves and I looked at him. 'You're right. I swapped cars.'

He laughed. 'Come on now, Forrest. Game's over. You might as well turn round.'

'There really was a bomb?'

'Turn around, it doesn't make any difference.'

'Maybe we should,' I said, sounding like the idea was just beginning to take shape. 'This is the back-up car. They're using my car for the pass bys this morning. You know, in that scene where Candy takes Jill's car out for a joy-ride?'

I kept my foot down, kept us heading steeply up hill into the mountains at ninety-five while he thought about that for a moment. Thought about what he would have to give up to turn around. Turning around meant that there was a bomb. And that he knew about it. The international banks asked his advice and paid him millions for it. Because they trusted him. His word was better than any contract in Hollywood. The biggest stars in Hollywood would kiss toads for a minute's conversation with David Allen. His company, his building, his new negotiations to integrate the world's entertainment into one huge, protected, and connected series of companies from the script to the stars to the satellite to the new telephone network into your living-room, all of that would not fall apart, but it would move on without David Allen. He would have to give up everything.

'Di-Di,' he said quietly. 'Di-Di. For God's sake, Evers, stop! Now, GOD DAMMIT STOP!! We've got seven minutes. They said it was a digital timer. Eleven thirty-five.'

I spun the wheel and the mountains and the road whirled around us. The car came screaming and squealing to a stop, smoke pouring off the tyres. The landscape stopped and the air was still and the sky above us still. And blue. Hawks circled overhead.

The car exploded into life under my right foot mashed down. No prisoners. Back wheels spinning, fishtailing, we were heading back down hill.

Going up hill you can corner harder, the car leaning into the uphill grade. Every turn is banked in your favour. Going down, every turn is banked the wrong way because the car is falling. By the second turn the brakes were overheating and starting to fade.

The thought we could be a few seconds away from turning incandescent made my driving ragged. Would I hear the boom first or feel the concussion first? Keep your mind on the road, Evers. I was driving completely differently, not like you see in the movies but smoother, faster, the seconds ticking off inside my head too, easing into the corners getting all the way to the outside of the road, oh shit, too fast, keeping my foot in it anyway, right up to the guard rail, and turning in late, and clipping the inside late to hold to the inside as long as possible so we didn't exit in the oncoming lane. We were deep inside a corner leaning all the weight of the car on the outside, accelerating hard and coming around the face of rock on the inside of the turn and the dirty backside of an Amour Star semi-tractor trailer loomed up in front of us.

Passing him going the other way on the way out and I hadn't given him a second thought. Now there was plenty to think about; twenty-six tons of swinging beef in a thirty-five-foot long truck plus the cab-over tractor.

He was not in a hurry. We were fifty feet away, going close to a hundred miles an hour, and he was going maybe thirty.

No way around him.

If we hit him straight on from the rear it looked like the car would squeeze underneath but we would leave our heads behind. No way inside.

I kept my foot down hard on the accelerator, and we swung out to pass on the outside, just grazing the front headlight against the big black mud-flap of the rear wheel, thinking, What the hell, La Puerca One doesn't have any brakes anyway so we might as well go forward. Out on to the road alongside the truck.

Facing the cop car.

One of those big wide white Chevy Caprice Classic gumball machines, red and blue lights blazing. Siren going. Two cops staring at us intently in the front seat. Oh fuck. There is no way we can get past the truck before they shut the door. There isn't any room on the outside. Where the road drops away.

A scenic vista.

A scenic vista is just past the cop car. A pull-off area to admire the view. Go all the way to the outside. The outside wheels scrabbling for grip on the loose gravel where there is no grip and the road drops away. The cop car is going to have to get over more, right next to the damn meat truck, snuggle right alongside.

BANG.

The door mirror on David's side hits the cop's door mirror and explodes with the impact. I hear it at a distance because my wheels are going over the edge and I tap the brakes thinking the inside wheels on the road might get a little grip, maybe hold us in for five more feet and they do as we get on to the wide gravel patch of the scenic vista parking lot and my foot is down to the floor again, keeping the car moving straight ahead, and it spins anyway.

And I have to admit I am not in control. The mountains go by once, twice with the blue sky in between as I stomp on the brakes and turn into the spin hoping to slow things down somewhat before we go off the edge or bang into something. The mountains go by one more time and we have slowed down enough to catch sight of the road as a stripe in the whizzing movie. Four times and as the road comes around on the dial again I get off the brake and back on the accelerator turning left and we are headed down the road at fifty-five miles an hour, the spin has slowed us down that much, and I shift down to second accelerating full whack.

David leaned over the side of the car and was heavily sick. When he looked up his eyes were streaming and he looked at his watch. 'Four minutes,' he screamed. 'You dumb stupid son of a bitch. You know that is why I put you in *Juice*? Because you are so fucking awful.'

There were three more curves on the way down. We took them as hard and as fast as a hopped-up old NASCAR stocker with a Mustang replica body will go down hill in an arc. Not difficult turns but fast. I thought I'd seen the cop car in my rear-view mirror squeezing past the truck in one piece, but I couldn't be sure. If the cops got past they would not be relaxed. They would be on the radio, saying the fucking maniac kidnapper is heading back in your direction.

A rock, something, had ripped out the muffler when we had spun through the scenic vista parking lot and the car was making a hell of a roar. David was screaming over the noise. 'Sam doesn't know shit about directing, you couldn't act the part of a window dummy, and *Juice* was going down. I would have had Olympic for thirty per cent of book, Hozuki would have taken such a bath they'd have begged me to take it off their hands.'

'Great,' I yelled back. 'They pulled out. You would have had it anyway.'

'You're damn right. I wanted her.'

'What?'

We were coming into the last turn. A long sweeping right-hander.

'What the hell do you think I did it for?' he said, his eyes wild, out of control. 'Just goddamn get us there. Four minutes.'

'Her?' I said bringing the car into the inside, lifting the inside wheels at ninety, foot to the floor.

'Goddamn her. Jesus, you know her.'

I looked back at him for a moment. 'I don't know her at all.'

'Christ, you should. You got the short course, but you know.' David put his arm across the back of the seat and leaned toward me. 'You know how she made you feel, like you had this power. Like you could spin the world . . .' He paused while we drifted out across the road, out on to the outside edge. His eyes came back to me. 'It's what she does. How long were you with her, two weeks? We were married five years. I was amazing, she was amazing. We were the *best*. Then she was gone. No note, no phone number. Nothing. No warning, no nothing. I didn't hear from her, I heard from her lawyers. Sam took Delilah. She took half of David Allen the company. My company. Half of every thing I do goes to her. She blew me up like a party balloon. Jesus, I want to get her. Like a toy balloon.'

'I know the feeling,' I said.

We came out of the turn and the desert opened up in front of us, the road a long black ramp straight down.

'I'll tell you what I wanted,' he said, quieter now, staring straight ahead, wiping his mouth with the back of his hand. 'I wanted Sam to make a mess. Little Miss Tidy, she always has to do it all herself and I thought great, let her shit in her pants in public. They said they'd screw up the production, no big deal. Not a lot of money. They were glad to. Just little things nobody would notice and I thought, Terrific. Nobody was supposed to get hurt, but I couldn't control them. It got out of hand. They said other people were involved.' He looked at me, pleading. 'I just wanted Sam to fuck up on her own. No help from anybody. Blow the whole budget. Like Cimino in *Heaven's Gate*.'

Two more police cars were in the far distance, fat white bugs crawling towards us, their flashing lights shimmering through the heat waves three or four miles away. We were getting close to a hundred and thirty-five creeping up to one forty. They were probably going about say a hundred and ten, hundred and twenty-five. Say conservatively two miles a minute so we were closing at around two fifty to two seventy-five miles an hour.

One cop car pulled out alongside the other cop car. In our lane. Somewhere between thirty and forty-five seconds, I thought, with the clarity you get when you are facing a collision. My mind wandered back to the little lump of plastic sitting on top of the gas tank with black firecracker and the wires sticking out.

The heat waves were making the white bugs shimmy, dancing with their reflection on the oily surface of the road, their red eyes flashing.

Going left, getting off the road and on to the shoulder, would be nasty. At that speed, who knows? But the least likely scenario was that we would continue right-side up. More likely we would be balled foil. Still coming. Not close yet.

Then white bug on our side thought better of a two hundred and fifty mile an hour head-on collision and pulled back in line.

More time ticked by and we roared past. WHOP-WHOP of colliding air. In the next instant in my mirror, both cops were lighting up their brake lights. Up ahead, across the valley floor, we could see the detail now, of the cranes and the silks, the heavy props and equipment trucks, the make-up and wardrobe tractor-trailers, the crowd and the motorhomes where they were shooting. Plenty of time.

# chapter thirty-four

Pounding down the dirt road; rocks, dust, and full V–8 roar flying out over the desert floor. Little rises in the road turning into take-off ramps and launching us twenty and thirty yards, the yellow Puerca flying clumsily through the blue desert sky, landing with a big crash, pounding the bump stops and wallowing, unsure of its direction. Right foot flat to the floor. The set and the film crew grew on our jumping horizon.

I leaned on the horn and turned on the lights. Every little bit helps.

I got on the brakes, easily at first, letting the car settle on to its bounding front wheels, then hard, sliding La Puerca's ass end towards the open mouths and wide open eyes of the film crew, staring at us as we slid towards them in a cloudbank of dust and roar.

Some of them began to run.

We slid to a stop a few inches from a bank of triangulated steel stands holding up silks, an acre and a half of nylon that Mayberry had put up to diffuse the harsh noon desert sunlight, and David was out and running, waving his arms, and screaming 'DI-DI. DI-DI. GET AWAY FROM THE CAR!'

Di-Di was between takes, standing alongside Puerca Two, chewing gum, her hand shielding her eyes from the sun, watching him as he ran towards her, his arms pumping.

He grabbed her, lifted her off her feet, turned and stumbled, kept going and broke into a run, carrying her clumsily. She was heavy for him. And he didn't have a good grip on her, his arms were around her waist and her feet were dragging. But he kept going, running in a zig-sag stagger away from the car until he tripped and they fell on the ground.

I was out of Puerca One, holding my script and keeping my

cool for maybe two steps and started to run. Frank, my not so faithful driver, was on the edge of the production crew and stopped me. 'Hey chill out, Forrest. Fuck is goin' on?' he said.

'Keep an eye on it for me, will you, Frank?'

He gave me a pissed-off look, scrunching up his face like it wasn't in his contract, and he looked back at Puerca One.

So, a beat later, Frank was the only one looking at Puerca One when it exploded. I felt the concussion from the blast, turned around, and an eruption of flame engulfed the silks in a balloon of flame and for a few moments the flame and smoke took over the blue sky.

Then it was quiet. The back of the car had disappeared except for one of the rear tyres, a burned and twisted shape around a wheel-rim drooling black ooze in a blackened hole in the ground. Forty yards away the front half of Puerca One was upside-down but it still looked like it had once belonged to a car. The left wheel was turning. Gradually we became aware of the distant sirens of the police cars.

David said, not loud, but loud enough for me to hear. 'You son of a bitch. You fucking son of a bitch.' He got up carefully and glared at me as Delilah picked herself up. Her lip was cut. She put her bare child's arms around herself, tears streaming down making paths in the dust on her face. Sam ran to the girl and put her arms around her. They were like that when I came up to them. David standing apart, Sam and Delilah holding each other. Survivors.

'Your word,' he said, 'against mine.'

'It's more than your word, David. There was Pierson Waddell and Danny Carlingo. I would have been the third if I hadn't been lucky. Then there's Frank.'

He looked blank. 'Frank is the Teamster who brought my car back with a bomb wedged underneath it. The bomb you just told everybody here you knew about.' David looked back at the front half of Puerca One.

'We can go either way on this, to the police or to Frank's friends. Tell you what I want, David,' I said, pointing my script at him. 'You are going to need another Puerca. There is a very good one in that truck over there.' I said, pointing my script over to the fifth prop truck. 'I want you to buy it from my friend Bash.'

He nodded.

'Next, I want you to complete this film, any damn way you please, call it *Jill*, *Juice* or *Junkyard*, I don't care, as long as you live up to your contract to spend the money to promote it on my car.'

He nodded again. No problem.

'You'll stay, won't you, Forrest?' Sam gave me her look of deep concern. 'We can't complete without you unless we go to stand-ins. It won't be the same. Can't you stay for three, four days?' Sam was the lost little girl now and she looked at me with the old longing in her eyes, as if nothing had changed and all I had to do to make her world go round was say yes. David looked down with mild curiosity at the blood on his shirt. Sam put her arm around his daughter again and quietly took David's hand, still looking at me, as if everything depended on me.

I wanted to believe her. That she needed me or what the hell, just wanted me around. That soft mouth and those pretty eyes had me seeing one more time how it had been, for a little while, in the dream where Forrest and the beautiful star were lovers. 'I'll miss you, Sam,' I said, 'but you'll manage. And now that David has guaranteed my money, I've got to get back to my day job.'

David looked up at the mention of money. 'There are no guarantees in this business.'

'Just one more thing,' I said.

'Don't push your luck, Evers,' David said, wiping his face, starting to get his presence back.

'Linda Carlingo.'

He looked at me blank, not knowing.

'The wife of the bus driver who died in one of your accidents.'

'Nobody was supposed to get hurt.'

Behind him the cops were getting out of their cars. David looked at them over his shoulder, running his hand through his hair.

'You want to suggest something before the police get here, David? Something for Linda and her two daughters.'

'It was an accident.'

'Twin girls, three years old. Ask Di-Di what it's like to grow up without a father.'

Sam gave him a little knowing smile. 'You can fix it, Gig.

You're the man who can fix anything, remember?' She touched his cheek and he closed his eyes and sighed, the fight gone out of him.

'OK, I'll set up a trust fund,' he said, nodding. 'Two hundred and fifty thousand, guaranteed.'

'Five million.'

'No fucking way.'

'Over here, officer,' I said.

'One million.'

Sam pulled his hand and he came around facing her. 'You could do it, Gig. You could set up a tax-free, fully deductible charitable trust fund out of the production budget, name Danny's brother as executor. He's a priest. You might even get Frank's friends to chip in. But maybe that's pushing it. Anyway, it doesn't have to come out of your pocket, David. It's what a good father would do.' Her voice took a hard edge. 'Do it.'

'OK, you stay, Evers, finish the scenes Sam wants.' He couldn't resist a little smile at the thought of me in Sam's movie. 'I'll go four five. No way can I go higher than that.'

'Five,' I said. 'Hello, officers.'

'Fuck you, Evers. Five.'

'I'll have my lawyers call your lawyers.'

The two cops made a show of putting their guns back in their holsters and pulled out their notebooks.

'You are a real bastard, Evers,' David said. Then he relaxed and smiled. 'But, hey, take off that wig and you'd make a hell of an agent.'

David took a step towards me, as if to shake hands, and stopped. He looked puzzled, looking down at his foot. And screamed.

His foot looked as if he had stepped in sandy mud up to his ankle. He lifted his foot up and it was covered with dirty honey, fizzing.

Not fizzing.

Sizzling.

We looked at him, amazed. His face went white and his eyes bulged. And he screamed again.

Sam reacted first. 'Water, for Christ's sake. Water somebody. Hurry. Hoses, buckets. Julie, hurry.'

David reached down to scrape the stuff off his foot and his

hands jerked away. He held them palms out to us to show us, burned scarlet, purple, and black. He fell on his back, kicking his foot as if trying to shake off the stuff and he screamed again. A deeper scream, his eyes wide, his mouth wide.

I looked up where he was looking and another drool of dirty honey the size of a basketball fell out of the sky from the bent framework that had held the silks. The hot aluminium frame was twisted and smoking; the fire had melted the nylon to a fiery ooze and the near corner of the frame was drooping and drooling molten nylon from the silks.

I grabbed David by the wrist, thinking I was yanking him out of the way of the falling stuff, and there was a stench of burn. Sand and grit clung to his back. Underneath the crust the molten nylon had burnt through his polo shirt and clung to his back and the back of his neck, sizzling as it burned through his flesh. I pulled him to me and held his arms like an awkward dancer as two grips threw buckets of water on him. He screamed again and the stuff on his back turned solid.

They threw more water on us. Then they stopped.

I started to lay David down carefully on his back, thought better of it, turned him, and laid him down on his stomach, his head to the side, and his eyes and his mouth were open wide. His mouth a round O of surprise. The nylon was a thick crust on his back, hard as a shell, a harsh and smokey smell rising up from his charred back.

I looked up when I heard an ambulance siren, and three paramedics came running, pushing their way through the crowd to kneel next to him. They turned him on to a stretcher, thumped his chest, and jolted him with two electrodes. After a long time they stood up. One of them, the woman walked over to the ambulance and came back with a blue sheet which she unfolded and draped over him.

# chapter thirty-five

'Forrest. Darling. What are you doing out there?'

'Sitting in the sun. On Sunday. Soaking up spring.'

My terrace is at the top of an old town house in Holland Park and the view of West London goes on long enough to fade into blue with the green of Kew Gardens just about halfway to scenic oblivion. Go far enough in that direction and you'd end up in Malibu. I picked up the paper again flipping through the business section (where Hozuki, now owned by an international holding company call Blue Whale, announced 'significant progress' on their electric car) and turned to *The Culture* magazine one more time.

# Jill comes tumbling down

*By Isobel Rodekill.* (Exclusive to The Sunday Times.)
As the British cinema slowly glides to oblivion, with its dim cargo of souls even more miserable than ourselves and ripped lino and gaps in blackened teeth as its farewell *leitmotif*, the cheerful irrelevance of Hollywood becomes increasingly attractive. And not just to those of us in the audience. Some of our more promising directors, Adrian Lyne, the brothers Scott, and Tony Parker to name but four, left the rigours of British TV-commercials long ago for even more gold in them thar Beverly Hills. No one embraced the genre of Hollywood irrelevance more fervently than they with such icons of our times as *Top Gun*, *Fatal Attraction*, and *Mississippi Burning*; films of such sublime silliness that one could not help but love 'em.

Alas, when that cultural exchange flows in reverse, and mainline Hollywood aims for issues of social import, Hollywood steps in deep doo-doo.

Which brings us to *Jill* (starring Samantha Miles, directed by Samantha Miles, and written by Samantha Miles) which opens this weekend in London. Women should be warned that while this flick is billed as 'one woman's story', it is more aptly described as one woman's face, treating us to some of the longest-running close-ups in the history of the cinema. Apart from Ms Miles' fine green eyes and the steep hills and declivities of her occasionally nude body the film has all the usual weaknesses of Tinseltown taking on 'serious issues'.

*Jill* looks at the hard road of the single parent, the macho delusions of the American male, and the future of our wayward children. All worthy subjects, no doubt, and Ms Miles is to be granted civic awards for attempting to tackle them head on. Alas Ms Miles suffers from the old Hollywood malaise, a slippery grip, and these themes slide by her virtually untouched.

But back to our story. Jill, the Ms of our tale, struggles to bring up her adoptive daughter, Candy, and to make sense of her life with a failed racing driver, while she teaches school in a remote American south-western desert town, named, curiously, Velma.

Macklin, the failed racer, is played by the real-life racing driver Forrest Evers who, you will appreciate in a flash, has never acted on screen before. Evers has a certain animal charm and if you like high camp, you will adore him. His portrayal of Macklin, the race driver turned mechanic, is so wooden it is solid mahogany. Or possibly oak, whichever wood is heavier. When he first steps off the bus and into the movie he turns his craggy face left and right. When Jill tells him to begone from her door, Evers turns his head left and right. No doubt endless repetition serves Evers well on the race tracks of Formula One where he has taken to winning of late with *Jill* emblazoned on his side pods. But one cannot help but wish Ms Miles had drawn Evers aside and broadened his repertoire. As in looking up or down.

In one of *Jill*'s juicier moments, Candy (played by Delilah Allen, daughter of deceased Hollywood super-agent David Allen who suffered a fatal heart attack during the shooting of *Jill*) disrupts a noisy sexual imbroglio between Jill and Evers the race driver (turning his head left and right). It's a potentially clumsy scene with nude bodies colliding on the bed and ending on the floor, but Delilah Allen carries it off with unusual intelligence and restraint. We will, I'm sure, see more of young Delilah Allen.

*Jill*'s production budget is rumoured to have run upwards of fifty million, and (despite William Howard Mayberry's lush evocation of America's small desert towns) it's hard to see where the money went, apart from the gold bars that must now line Ms Miles' bank account. What is yet more difficult to comprehend, with so many trivial issues lying about (the fate of rich children left at home alone, the return of robots from the future to cite but two evergreen surefire formulae in the Hollywood canon) is how some films ever make it to the silver screen.

I put the paper down and soft arms went around my neck.

'Any news of fresh disaster?' Susan said.

'I could have been a star,' I said.